Because of Shoe

AND OTHER DOG STORIES

EDITED BY
ANN M. MARTIN

FISH

HENRY HOLT AND COMPANY

New York

D0121949

SQUARE
FISH

An Imprint of Macmillan

BECAUSE OF SHOE. Compilation copyright © 2012 by Ann M. Martin. Illustrations © 2012 by Olga and Aleksey Ivanov (except those appearing on pages 57, 58, 60, 77, 78, 81, 85, 86, 94, 95, 106, 112–113, 241, 243, 244, 246, 251, 255, 257, 260, 261). All rights reserved.

Printed in the United States of America by R. R. Donnelley & Sons Company, Harrisonburg, Virginia. For information, address Square Fish, 175 Fifth Avenue, New York, NY 10010.

Square Fish and the Square Fish logo are trademarks of Macmillan and are used by Henry Holt and Company under license from Macmillan.

Square Fish books may be purchased for business or promotional use. For information on bulk purchases, please contact the Macmillan Corporate and Premium Sales Department at (800) 221-7945 x5442 or by e-mail at specialmarkets@macmillan.com.

Library of Congress Cataloging-in-Publication Data
  Because of Shoe and other dog stories / edited by Ann M. Martin.
      p.   cm.
  Summary: An illustrated anthology of stories about dogs and their relationships with humans, for readers of varying levels.
  Contents: Dognapper / by Wendy Orr — Because of Shoe / by Pam Muñoz Ryan — Science fair / by Mark Teague — Patty / by Thacher Hurd — Picasso / by Ann M. Martin — The God of the Pond / by Valerie Hobbs — Trail magic / by Margarita Engle — Things people can't see / by Matt de la Peña — Brancusi & me / Jon J Muth.
  ISBN 978-1-250-02728-3
  1. Dogs—Juvenile fiction.   2. Children's stories, American.   [1. Dogs—Fiction.   2. Short stories.]   I. Martin, Ann M.
  PZ5.B388 2012   [Fic]—dc23   2011033501

Originally published in the United States by Henry Holt and Company
First Square Fish Edition: May 2013
Book designed by Elynn Cohen
Square Fish logo designed by Filomena Tuosto
mackids.com

10 9 8 7 6 5 4 3 2 1

LEXILE: 810L

Contents

Editor's Note

SADIE

*B*onjour. *Je m'appelle* Sadie Martin. I am Ann Martin's dog, and I don't really speak French, but like some of the dogs you'll read about in this collection of stories, I enjoy showing off occasionally.

Also, not to brag, but if it weren't for me, you wouldn't be reading this collection at all. For most of her life, Ann Martin was a cat person.

Then, when she was forty-two years old, she adopted me, her first dog. By the time I was housebroken and had learned a few commands, Ann had fallen in love with me. Therefore, I was solely responsible for turning her from a cat person into a dog-and-cat person. And this is why, when someone at Henry Holt and Company, the publisher of this book, asked Ann if she'd like to edit a collection of stories about dogs, her answer was yes.

At this point, you're probably saying, "Thank you for all your good work, Sadie!"

You're welcome.

Between the covers of this book you'll read about a boy who turns into a dog, a dog who brings a family together, a dog who lived a long time ago and was a companion to a very great artist in Paris, and about funny dogs, adventurous dogs, brave dogs, smart dogs, and dogs who perform rescues. I'm happy to have been able to bring you this collection of stories, and I hope you enjoy reading about the superior race of canines.

—Sadie Martin

Dognapper

by Wendy Orr

illustrated by Olga and Aleksey Ivanov

Max

Tyler could hear Max howling as soon as he turned onto his street.

Max the Dax never howled, except when Tyler's mom, Officer Olson, drove up the driveway with her police siren on—she liked doing that when she finished work the same time as Tyler finished school. But school had let out early today because of the Grand Parade.

The parade that opened the county fair was the biggest event of the year. There would be brass bands, firefighters and police, jugglers, popcorn sellers, baton twirlers, fancy horses, and performing dogs. Tyler's mom would be marching with the other police officers—but the parade didn't start for two more hours. Right now she was still at work, and there was no siren to be heard.

If Max was howling, then something was wrong.

Tyler started to run.

Max was a black weiner dog with tan bits on his chest like a bikini top, twitchy tan eyebrows, and a tan nose. His legs were short and stumpy, his back was long, and his bark was as deep and strong as the bark of Officer Olson's police dog, Gus.

Gus was a German shepherd; he was very smart and very well trained. Tyler's mom said he knew more about right and wrong than most people did. Sometimes he stole bones

from Max and dropped
them over the front fence,
to remind Max that he was
bigger and stronger, but
Tyler's mom said he was
just teasing.

Gus

Lately Gus had been
much too busy to tease
Max. He was the only
police dog in town, and two weeks ago the
poodlenappings had begun.

Cassandra Caniche's silver poodle was the
first to disappear. Cassandra herself was as
elegant and graceful as any prizewinning
poodle. She ran the Poodle Parlor, and when
she'd washed and cut her poodle customers'
wool, she spun and wove it into wonderful
capes and coats.

But now every poodle that had been
groomed at Cassandra's parlor had disappeared. Tyler's mom and Gus had searched
everywhere, but they hadn't found a single
clue.

By the day of the parade, eleven poodles were missing.

Tyler grabbed the emergency key from under a rock. He was supposed to go next door to tell Mrs. Lacey he was home before he picked up Max, but he couldn't wait to find out what was wrong with his dog. His hands were sweating as he unlocked the door and tapped in the security code.

Max stopped howling when he saw Tyler, but he whined restlessly at the front door, hackles prickling and brown eyes anxious. He didn't even ask for a pat.

Something was badly wrong.

Tyler grabbed his phone. He had just pressed "Mom" when Mrs. Lacey pounded at the front door.

"Have you got Pippa?" she gasped.

Pippa the poodle was Max's very best dog friend. She had creamy curls and long dark eyelashes. If she and Max hadn't played together for a few days, Pippa would bounce up and down in her yard, her silky ears flapping high over the fence, until Max started digging. Max had short stubby legs, but his shoulders were strong, and his paws were nearly as big as Gus's. When he dug a tunnel from his yard to Pippa's, dirt sprayed so far out behind him it disappeared like magic.

Pippa

Now it was Pippa who had disappeared like magic.

Pippa had been poodlenapped.

"Tyler?" said his mom's voice.

"Max!" shouted Tyler, and tossed the phone to Mrs. Lacey as the dachshund slipped between his legs.

The little dog raced across the lawn to Mrs. Lacey's back gate. He was whining so pitifully that Tyler let him in so that he could see for himself that Pippa was gone.

Max ran straight up to the back door. A chunk of raw steak was on the top step, and the dachshund gulped it down before Tyler could stop him.

"That's strange!" thought Tyler. Mrs. Lacey always cooked Pippa's dinner and fed her in the kitchen.

Max checked the steps for more food and lolloped through the open dog door.

"Even stranger!" thought Tyler. Pippa's dog door had been locked tight since the first poodlenapping.

But the flap had been unscrewed from the outside—and a scrap of navy blue fabric was caught in the corner of the dog door.

Mrs. Lacey, when she wasn't wearing a creamy Pippa-wool coat that Cassandra had woven, wore mostly pink. She hated navy blue because, when she was six, she'd fallen out of a boat while she was wearing her brand-new sailor suit. She'd never worn that color again.

Tyler pulled the scrap out and put it in his pocket.

He called Max, and the dachshund's nose appeared through the door. His head and front legs followed, and finally his back legs and tail. He slinked down the steps and scratched at the gate to the carport.

Mrs. Lacey opened the door. "Come in," she said, sniffing sadly. "Your mom's on her way."

Tyler followed her back into her house. Mrs. Lacey plunked down at her kitchen table and burst into tears. "All the time I was out shopping, I was thinking about the fun we'd have going to the parade to watch your mom and Gus. Then I opened the door, ready for Pippa to jump up the way she does, with her front paws around my neck . . . but she wasn't here!"

Tyler didn't know what to do. Seeing Mrs. Lacey cry was almost as bad as wondering where Pippa was. He gave her a box of tissues and a hug, just like she used to do for him when he was little. Then he fixed her a cup of coffee. That made her smile, but she still couldn't stop crying.

"Mom and Gus will find Pippa," Tyler reassured her, and looked outside to see if they were coming.

The yard was empty, front and back.

Max was gone too.

A cold hand of fear closed tight around Tyler's neck, but as he jumped off the back steps, the fear burst into a fiery rage. No one was going to steal his dog!

Then he saw the tunnel. Max hadn't been stolen—he'd dug under the fence and escaped through the carport. Tyler raced down the driveway, but there was no sign of a short-legged, long black dog.

Tyler started to run.

Max was tracking.

Max had always been a pet, but his great-great-great-grandparents had been hunting dogs, and Max's nose was a sniffing, tracking, hunting nose. That nose followed the scent of Pippa and the poodlenapper out to the carport and locked on to the smell of the vehicle they'd driven away in.

Being a small dog who lives with a police dog is a bit like being a little boy with a grown-up brother—sometimes Max wished he could go to work every day doing exciting things, instead of staying home all alone, waiting for Tyler to get home from school. But right now he wasn't thinking about Gus, or Tyler, or anything at all except following that scent.

Luckily the dognapper had taken quiet back streets. Max was running along the scent trail of the tire closest to the sidewalk, but it was still a precarious place for a small dog.

Tyler ran as fast as he could to where their street met a busy road. It was a good plan, because that would have been the most dangerous way of all for Max to go.

It was a good plan, except that it wasn't the way Max had gone.

Tyler turned down the busy road and kept on running until he heard a police siren.

People on the road stared as a police car,

with a large German shepherd in the back, pulled up beside the boy. Tyler didn't notice the stares. He jumped into the back seat beside Gus.

"Max has gone too!" he gasped. "I think he's following the dognapper."

"He's not a trained tracker," said his mom. "He could be anywhere!"

She cruised slowly down the street for a mile and then turned around. "He couldn't have gotten farther than this. We'll go back to Mrs. Lacey's and let Gus start tracking properly."

Mrs. Lacey had been so shocked when Max disappeared too that she knew she had to do something. By the time Tyler and his mom returned, she was knocking on the door across the road, asking if they'd seen anyone go to her house that morning or seen Max run away half an hour ago.

She'd been to three houses already, and no one had seen anything.

"Only the parcel delivery van," said one neighbor.

"I haven't ordered anything!" Mrs. Lacey exclaimed.

"Well, that's what I thought it was," said the neighbor. "It was a white van—or maybe cream. Actually, I think it was light brown."

"That's very helpful," said Officer Olson, who had joined Mrs. Lacey and was jotting everything down in a notebook.

Mrs. Lacey and Tyler showed his mom Pippa's open dog door and Max's tunnel from the backyard to the carport.

"Seek!" Tyler's mom ordered.

Gus sniffed at the tunnel, then trotted along the driveway and down the road, away from the busy street Tyler had run to.

"I'll go on asking the neighbors," said Mrs. Lacey. She started for the next house.

Tyler jogged after Gus. He couldn't help thinking that if he'd turned that way the first time, he might have found Max already.

His mom cruised slowly behind in the

police car, following Tyler, who was jogging after Gus, who was tracking Max, who was hunting the poodlenapper who'd stolen Pippa.

Max was still running along the side of the road with his nose to the ground. He was tracking so hard, he hadn't noticed how sore his paws were or how thirsty he was, but his legs were moving more slowly and he was panting heavily.

The street had turned into a country road. The houses were big, with wide lawns and tall fences. There were exciting country smells of horses, sheep, other dogs, rabbits, and squirrels. Max would have loved to stop and sniff if he hadn't been so busy tracking Pippa.

Then the scent led Max up the driveway to a building humming with hair dryers. Chemical shampoo smells wafted out, drowning everything else, and Max had to circle for a moment before he found Pippa's own poodley, best-friend scent again. He followed it out of the driveway and on down the road.

Half a mile along was a huge old house, with the widest lawns and tallest fences of all. It had black chimneys, tiny windows, and pointy Rapunzel towers. The fence and gates were black iron with sharp spears on top; the bars were so close together that Max had to put his nose right up to them to see through.

But Max wasn't staring. He was sniffing, and even though he couldn't see them, he could smell dogs. Lots of dogs. And somewhere in that rich bouquet of dog scents, he could smell Pippa.

Max bayed his big, deep bark, and from a hidden pen behind the house, he heard Pippa's shrill yip.

Max started to dig.

Tyler was in the police car with his mom. He was getting more and more worried. If he'd become too tired to run any farther, how could Max still be tracking, on his six-inch-long legs? Even Gus was starting to look tired.

Then Gus circled in a hairdresser's driveway. Officer Olson parked the car and went inside.

Excitement and fear spidered up Tyler's throat. Any second now, his mom was going to find his dog and maybe Pippa too. But what if the dognapper was still in there?

His mother came back out just as Gus found the scent again. "No one there has seen a dog all day," she said.

Inside the dark house, a man was throwing a torn navy blue shirt into his trash can when he heard a deep bark.

He shuddered. He was sure it was the same police dog he'd heard that morning, from the house next door to the beautiful poodle. It had made him shake so badly, he'd nearly dropped her as he ran to the van.

Now the big-voiced dog was at his gates. He needed to get out of there fast, before it brought the police to his door.

The van was still backed up against the poodle pen. Two minutes later, it was tearing down the driveway.

The fence was set deep in the ground, and Max was head down, with dirt spraying out behind him. He was digging too hard to hear the electric gates swish open.

He did hear the skid of gravel as the van sped onto the road—but once Max was digging, he couldn't stop. The heavy gates clanged shut, and he dug even faster.

From inside the speeding police car, Tyler stared at the huge old house with the black iron fence and gates. A cloud of dirt was spraying out from under the fence. In the middle of the cloud of dirt, he could see the tip of a long black tail.

"Max!" Tyler screamed, and his mother slammed on the brakes.

Max slithered out of the tunnel and into the garden. He sniffed the air and knew Pippa had gone. He turned around and crawled back under the fence to Tyler.

Tyler hugged him. So did his mom. She checked that the little dog wasn't hurt and lifted him into the back seat.

"You've gotten us this far, Max!" she said as they jumped back into the car. "Now let's finish the job!" She spoke into her police radio and took off after the disappearing cloud of dust.

The siren screamed; the light flashed; houses and lawns blurred past. Tyler sat tight, holding Max. He'd never been with his mom when she was chasing a bad guy. He'd never gone anywhere so fast!

But the van was too far ahead. They were still two blocks behind when they reached the town. They could see the van turn onto Main Street.

By the time they got there, it had disappeared.

"We'll never catch him now!" exclaimed Tyler. There was so much traffic, they couldn't see ahead—and there were so many side streets and alleys that they could never guess which one the van might have turned down.

The police radio crackled. Tyler couldn't hear what the officer on the other end was saying, but it made his mom smile.

"There's something the dognapper doesn't know about Main Street today," she said as the police car inched along through the traffic and the crowds thronging both sides of the street. "All the side roads are blocked off. The road we just came in on was closed as soon as we turned off it—there's only one way the van can go."

"The parade!" exclaimed Tyler.

His mom nodded. "But I guess Gus and I won't be marching this year!"

Tyler always felt proud watching his mom and her dog lead the other police officers down the street. In fact, he loved everything about the parade: floats, fire engines, and high-stepping horses. Sometimes he even wished that he and Max belonged to a club or could do tricks so that they could march too.

But rescuing Pippa was more important than a month of parades.

The road ended at the fairground parking lot. It was full, and nearly every vehicle in it was a van: vans for cotton candy and pop-corn; changing-room vans for acrobats and clowns; vans full of toys and prizes; vans for selling arts and crafts, homemade brownies, and homegrown apples.

And one van hiding a stolen poodle.

Tyler's mom got Gus out of the car and gave his spare leash to Tyler for Max. "It's too hot for you to stay in the car," she said, "but remember, this is police business. You and Max are not to get involved!"

Tyler nodded.

Max didn't.

They started around the outside edge of the parking lot, Gus striding proudly in front, sniffing each vehicle as he passed. Tyler and Max had to jog to keep up.

The parade was about to start. Tyler paused to watch. Bands were playing, jugglers were juggling, clowns were clowning, and dogs in sparkly collars were quivering on their leashes. Crowds were streaming through the exit, racing for the best spots along the parade route.

Suddenly Max began to bark.

As the dachshund's deep voice echoed through the parking lot, a man sprinted toward the parade, knocking over a baby in a stroller and two kids on bikes. There was a flash of silver as he threw something into the ditch beside the parking lot exit . . . and then he disappeared into the crowd.

"Not good!" said Tyler's mom in a voice that meant she was so angry she was scared she'd say something really bad. "If we'd found the vehicle, I could have sent Gus after him, but I don't have anything for Gus to sniff!"

"I might," said Tyler. "I found this in Pippa's dog door." He pulled the scrap of navy blue material out of his pocket.

His mother took it and grinned. "Thanks, partner—that's exactly what we need! It'll have the dognapper's scent on it—Gus can easily track it."

She held the scrap out for the big dog to sniff. "Seek!" she commanded, and disappeared into the crowd with Gus.

"Stay here!" she called over her shoulder to Tyler. "If I'm not back in ten minutes, call Mrs. Lacey!"

But Max was already tugging Tyler forward. In the next row of vehicles was a gray van with dirty license plates and windows up against its roof. Every few seconds, the tips of two floppy, creamy ears floated into the window and down again.

As they reached the van, they could hear excited yipping.

"Pippa!" Tyler shouted. He grabbed the back door handle and pulled—but the van

was locked tight. Even the windows were sealed shut. The air inside would soon be dangerously hot. They had to get her out before that happened!

"Keys!" thought Tyler, remembering that flash of silver. He raced back to the exit with Max and jumped down into the ditch.

The keys weren't there—they had to be in the pipe under the road. Tyler threw himself onto his stomach to peer into it. He couldn't see anything except black; he couldn't reach anything except mud and slime.

He wiggled back, and Max wriggled in.

Ten minutes later, a slimy black nose appeared at the other end of the pipe. A long, muddy body slinked out. Clamped tight in a strong, muddy jaw was a key ring with one dangling silver key.

They raced back to the van. Pippa yipped once, but she'd stopped leaping.

The key worked. The door swung open.

Twelve black poodles rushed to greet them.

Tyler had been so sure he'd seen Pippa that he'd broken into a stranger's van. Where was the cream-colored poodle now?

But while Tyler was still figuring out what to do, Max had hopped into the van. Now he was bursting with joy: licking, sniffing, and dancing with one of the black poodles, exactly the way he did with Pippa.

The tips of this poodle's ears were pale and creamy.

"Pippa?" said Tyler, and the black poodle with creamy ears jumped to his shoulders, with her arms around his neck.

Tyler patted her, and his hand came away black.

"So that's why the dognapper went to the hairdresser's!" Tyler said. "But he didn't take Pippa in with him; he just bought the dye!"

The van was getting hotter and hotter. The dogs were panting, and there was no water. He had to get them out of there.

A long rope was coiled under the front seat. Tyler tied it to the handle of Max's leash and then looped a leash length through the ring on Pippa's collar and knotted it too. One by one, he took the poodles out of the van, tying the rope to each collar so that all twelve poodles were strung out in a long line behind Max. There was just enough rope left for him to hold.

He looked around the parking lot. His mom was nowhere in sight. It had been more than ten minutes since he'd seen her—time to call Mrs. Lacey.

Except that his phone was on Mrs. Lacey's kitchen table. And he couldn't even stay where he was, because thirteen thirsty dogs were pulling him to a water trough at the start of the parade.

The band was already blaring its way down the street, followed by two rows of police officers and firefighters, a row of kids twirling batons, and horses with white-shirted, red-cowboy-hatted riders.

Clowns and jugglers tumbled along, weaving in and out of the groups of marchers. One of the clowns ran right to the start of the parade, grabbing the bandleader's baton and conducting wildly.

The crowd laughed and cheered—and then gasped as an enormous German shepherd leapt into the air and knocked the clown to the ground. It held him there until Officer Olson ran up to clap handcuffs onto the clown's wrists. Two other police officers stepped out of the line to help her, and the crowd cheered again, thinking it was all part of the parade.

Tyler's mom looked up and saw Tyler being towed by Max and twelve poodles. The poodles ran even faster when they saw the handcuffed clown, passing everyone till they were nearly at the front, right behind the band.

So Tyler, Max, and the twelve black poodles followed the band and led the marching police officers and firefighters, the baton-twirling kids, and all the rest of the parade. It was a long route, right through the town, past houses and apartment buildings, past the town hall, hospital, and schools, past corner stores and shopping malls.

The band marched to the bandstand in the middle of the park to play one final song. Tyler looked around the crowd. He couldn't see his mother, he was hot and thirsty, and he had thirteen dogs at the end of a rope.

Suddenly he heard the wail of police sirens. Four police cars pulled up, and his mom and Gus ran to the bandstand.

Mrs. Lacey and eleven other people got out of the cars and followed them.

The poodles began to yip and dance on their rope, tugging Tyler toward the bandstand.

A policeman came over to help him. He winked at Tyler as Mrs. Lacey and the eleven other people climbed up onto the bandstand. Officer Olson started to speak.

"As you know, there has been a spate of dognappings in this town," she said. "We believe we have the dogs here, even though these poodles are black, and the stolen dogs were all different colors.

"Tyler," she continued, "could you please untie the first dog?"

Tyler untied the poodle closest to his end of the rope. In two bounds, the little black poodle flew up the steps to Cassandra Caniche, as if she were the only person on the bandstand.

One by one, Tyler let the other poodles off. One by one, they raced straight to someone on the bandstand, until Mrs. Lacey and the black poodle tied next to Max were the only ones left alone.

Tyler untied the last loop.

The little dog flew into Mrs. Lacey's arms, wrapping her front paws around her owner's neck and covering her face with licky kisses.

"I think you can see," Tyler's mom said finally, over the noise of licking and yipping, patting and sobbing, "that even if humans might not have been able to work it out, the dogs knew who they belonged with!"

Another policeman came up and handed her a message. Tyler's mom scanned it quickly.

"The dognapper has confessed. After last year's fair, when Cassandra Caniche won prizes for the Best-Groomed Poodle, the Best-Spun Poodle Wool, and the overall Best Item for a poodle wool coat, the dognapper asked her to marry him. When she said no, he threatened that she'd never again have the glory of winning so many prizes. So, two weeks ago, he teased Cassandra's dog with fresh, juicy steak until it followed him out into his van. He then stole all the other poodles in the same way. He dyed them black so no one would recognize them—and so he could win the Best-Matched Poodles prize tomorrow! Fortunately we arrested him first. When he heard what he thought was a police dog, he ran away, knocked down a clown, and stole his costume. But he'd left behind a scrap of his shirt when he stole the last poodle— and so the real police dog knew who he was."

"Hooray for Gus!" shouted someone who'd seen the police dog tackle the clown.

Gus lifted his head proudly, and Tyler's mom patted him. "Gus caught him," she agreed, "but the true hero is the dog who tracked him down and rescued the poodles."

Everyone was surprised, because everyone knew there was only one police dog in the town.

"Max!" called Tyler's mom.

The little dachshund had tracked a vehicle

and run for more than an hour, dug two tunnels and searched a drain, found his friend, and led a parade of lost poodles through the streets of the town. He was sound asleep.

But he woke up when Officer Olson called, and he followed Tyler up the steps on his strong stumpy legs.

The policeman who'd brought the message stepped forward and held up a small gold tag.

"In recognition of Max the Dax's outstanding service today, I'm awarding him the title of honorary police dog."

He threaded the tag onto Max's collar.

The crowd cheered; Cassandra Caniche and all the other people who'd been reunited

with their poodles hugged Tyler while their dogs licked Max. Mrs. Lacey kissed them both. Tyler's mom and the other police officer shook Tyler's hand and Max's paw.

Gus leaned down and licked Max's head. And Max licked him back.

Because of Shoe

by Pam Muñoz Ryan

illustrated by Olga and Aleksey Ivanov

Shoe

I cannot talk. And that's not like me.

I am at the beach with my family: my
mom and Theo; our little poodle, Lucky; and
my German shepherd, Shoe, who is leaping
over small waves like a jackrabbit. Shoe is
soaked to the bone. Suddenly she stops and
turns to look back at me, tilting her head to
the side. I know what she's thinking. She's

thinking it's strange that I'm not talking, because usually I never stop. But after what happened today, my heart is puffed up with emotion, like a balloon about to burst, and I'm afraid if I say anything, I'll start to cry. See, earlier, at the courthouse, everything changed. And it was all because of Shoe.

"Can you tell the court your name?" asked the judge. His black robe, long face, and dark bushy eyebrows made him look like a vulture.

"Lilianna Parker," I said from the witness stand. "But everyone calls me Lily."

The courtroom was filled with adults and other children who had come to court with their own petitions and waited to sit before the judge.

"And, Lily, how old are you?"

"Eleven years old."

The judge put on his glasses and peered at me.

"I know," I said. "I look younger. I'm the shortest in my class. That's my mom over

there." I pointed across the room to where Mom sat at a wooden table. "She's a nurse at Memorial Hospital, and she's barely over five feet. My pediatrician says that when I grow up, I will only be a tiny bit taller. But I'm *really* hoping he's wrong. Anyway, my freckles and thin hair don't help either. Plus, I'm trying to grow out my bangs because I think that *no* bangs will make me look more like a fifth-grader, which I *am*, instead of a third-grader, which I am *not*."

The judge smiled. His cheeks puffed up like peaches, his eyes twinkled, and he didn't look like a vulture anymore. He looked like someone's grandpa. "Well, Lily, let's move on. We're not going to be too formal here today. Can you tell us about the circumstances that brought you to my courtroom?"

I looked at Mom. She nodded encouragement. Mom had already coached me, but not about lying, since I wouldn't do that anyway. Instead she had given me the talk about keeping my answers brief, which is really hard for me. I always tell way too much information. Mom said, "Make the long story short." And I promised I would try, I really *would*. But my mind had a mind of its own.

"Lily?" said the judge.

I nodded, twisting a long strand of brown hair around one finger and trying to find a beginning. "It all started about a year ago, with Shoe."

The judge looked puzzled. "A shoe?"

I sat a little straighter. "No, not *a* shoe. Our *dog*, Shoe. We adopted her from the Coastal Humane Society. See, I had been wanting a dog for a long time, and finally Mom thought it would be a good idea. She said we should get one for protection since we were two girls living alone, on account of my father disappearing off the face of the planet before I was born. Besides that, I was spending more time at home by myself because I didn't go to after-school care anymore. But believe me, I wasn't a latchkey kid because our next door neighbor, Mrs. Gonzalez, was always checking on me. But Mom said that she'd feel more comfortable if there was a dog in the house. We really couldn't afford a dog from the pet shop, and even if we could pay eight hundred dollars, Mom wouldn't do it. She thinks everyone should adopt from animal shelters because of the current dog population, which is extremely high. She also has this thing about overbreeding."

I glanced at Mom. She was gently tapping the side of her cheek with one finger.

That was a signal that meant Too Much Information.

I took a deep breath, which is what I was supposed to do if she signaled me. "So we went to the Humane Society, and the minute I saw Shoe, I knew that she was the dog for me. I put my face near hers, and I just asked her, 'Do you belong to me?' And I know you're not going to believe this, but she answered. I mean, not in English, but you know, in the way she *looked* at me. Mom said that from day one, Shoe and I had this secret communication thing. So we adopted her. At first, we could not decide what to name her, but then—"

The judge held up his hand. "Lily, I need to interrupt for a moment. Does the dog's name have *anything* to do with why we're here today?"

I nodded vigorously. "Oh, yes. It has *every-thing* to do with it!"

Some of the people in the courtroom chuckled.

Mom rolled her eyes.

"Then you may continue," said the judge, leaning back in his chair.

"Okay. So we adopted her, and as soon as we brought her home, she started this thing with shoes. She would sneak into a closet, and I mean that entire skulking thing that dogs do when they don't want to be noticed. She would pick up a shoe in her mouth and then run out of the room. Then we'd have to chase her to get it back. But a few hours later, she would do the same thing. It's not that she chewed on the shoes or wrecked them or anything. And when I asked her, 'Why are you doing that?' she pulled the shoes closer to her chest, crossed her paws over them, and laid her head down and licked them. See, she thought they were *puppies*."

The judge leaned forward. "Puppies?"

A smattering of giggles traveled through the courtroom.

"Yes! It was the weirdest thing. She carried the shoes to her favorite places, like, behind the couch or the back of a closet. Then when she had a pile of them, she'd protect them and nose them and even *talk* to them. Not human talk, of course, but dog talk. You know, whining and little barks. So, Mom and I had to put all of our shoes up on the closet shelves. But then Shoe sniffed the floor, and whined, and looked at me and Mom with the saddest eyes and said, 'I'm begging you, please give me some shoes.' We couldn't resist. I gave her my soccer shoes that were too small, and Mom gave her a pair of high heels she never wore because she said they hurt her feet and when did she go dancing anymore anyway?"

Mom cleared her throat.

That was another signal. If I heard Mom clear her throat, I was supposed to pause and think about what I *needed* to say, not what I *wanted* to say.

"So Mom and I started calling her Shoe

Mama, because of her shoe puppies. But eventually we just called her Shoe. After a few months, she grew out of the whole pretending-shoes-were-puppies thing. It was like she just woke up one day and said, 'Oh, silly me. These are *shoes*, not my babies.' And just like that, she wasn't interested in shoes anymore. Until the incident."

"The incident?" asked the judge. His forehead wrinkled with concern.

I nodded. "But that came later. See, when we adopted her, the people at the Humane Society said they didn't know exactly how old Shoe was. They *thought* she was about a year old and wouldn't grow much larger. But they were so wrong. She grew a lot more. The vet said she was one of the biggest German shepherds he'd ever seen *in his whole entire life.* Everyone said she was too much dog for us. But we couldn't take her back because by then, she already loved us and we loved her. And besides, how could I give back a dog who reads my mind?"

"She reads your mind?" asked the judge.

I nodded. "Yes! I can just look at her and *think* that she needs a walk, and she will go sit next to her leash. Or one time I couldn't find my backpack and I was looking all over the house for it, but I wasn't saying, 'Where's my backpack?' I was just *thinking* it. And Shoe started whining and pawing at the door. When I opened it, my backpack was right there on the back steps. See what I mean?"

The judge nodded. "I think so. Let's get to the incident."

"Okay. So Shoe started being really protective of Mom and me. If anyone came near us, she went ballistic with her barking." I leaned closer to the judge and whispered, "For a while, Grandma wouldn't even come to our house because she was so scared of Shoe."

The judge raised his eyebrows and nodded knowingly.

Mom cleared her throat *and* tapped her cheek.

I took a deep breath and thought about what I *needed* to say. "Okay. So the Humane Society offered obedience training on Saturdays at Ocean Bay Park. We took Shoe to the first class, and there was this humongous line of people with their dogs, and it was hardly moving because once you got to the front of it, you had to fill out all these forms. The guy in front of us was thin and over six feet tall, which is *really* tall for short people like us. He had curly black hair and black glasses and was wearing workout clothes, but he wasn't sweaty or smelly or anything like that. He had on running shoes with those short socks, and a T-shirt from some marathon, the type you can only get if you actually *run* one. What was funny was that he was holding this weensy white poodle. This great big tall guy and this itty bitty dog. Mom and I were standing a little bit away from him because of personal space. And because people sometimes get nervous when Shoe is too close to them. But Shoe kept tugging on her leash, straining and whining and trying to move as close to him as possible. Finally, the man turned around and said to Mom, 'If you act like the pack leader, your dog will calm down.' Mom started laughing, and it *was* kind of funny. Because after all, we were in line for *obedience school*."

The judge nodded. He took off his glasses, pulled out a handkerchief, and began cleaning the lenses. "What happened next?"

"Well, by this time Shoe was all hyper and jumping from one side of Mom to the other. So the guy does this amazing thing. He points at Shoe and says, 'Sit!' And Shoe *sat*! Mom and I were so surprised because Shoe *never* obeyed. Mom said, 'If you're so good at making a dog obey, why are you here?' "

The judge put his glasses back on. "Why *was* he there?"

"He said he was really good with big dogs. But that he'd never had a little dog in his life. See, the poodle would have never been his *choice* for a dog. He *inherited* it from a neighbor, a little lady who lived next door. The guy was always driving her—the lady, not the poodle—to the store and to the bank and fixing stuff around her house, and so when she died, she left her dog to him *in her will*. So how could he say no? But the poodle had some . . . uh . . . problems, like taking the guy's laundry outside—even his underwear— and leaving it in the street. And being afraid of feathers. If the poodle even *saw* one on the ground or especially floating in the sky, it started trembling and crying, and it was pitiful." I put my hand on my throat.

"Are you okay?" asked the judge.

"Yes. Sometimes when I talk too much, I start to gulp air and then I have to rest."

"Anytime you're ready," said the judge.

I massaged my throat and then began again. "So, we were at the park standing in line. The little poodle was wearing a tag with its name on it. Mom reached over to pat the poodle and said, 'Lucky? Your name is Lucky? I should have adopted a little dog like you.' And at that moment, the poodle leapt into Mom's arms, nuzzled into her neck, and started licking her ears. Mom was cooing and holding the poodle like a baby and tickling his tummy. And that's when it happened."

The judge leaned forward.

"While Mom was going all crazy for Lucky, Shoe stood up and walked a little closer to the man and sniffed around his feet. Then she looked up at me. I bent down and said, 'What is it, Shoe?' She looked at the man and looked at Mom and then at me, and it was like *she knew.*"

The judge's forehead crinkled. "Knew what?"

"That we were all MTBT. Sometimes dogs just *know*. And Shoe wanted to do something about it. So she did."

"MTBT?"

"Meant to Be Together."

The judge nodded slowly. "Okay. And what did Shoe *do*, exactly?"

Everyone in the courtroom leaned forward.

I took a deep breath. "Shoe squatted and peed right on his shoes."

There was a collective gasp and then a burst of laughter.

"Oh, my," said the judge.

"I know! Mom was seriously horrified. Shoe had never done *anything* like that before. And Mom didn't know this guy or how he'd react. Or if he'd be furious or even *sue* us."

"What *did* he do?" asked the judge.

"He just stared at his shoes. The pee was streaming down the outsides *and* the insides and soaking into his socks and everything. Then he stared at mom *and laughed.* He just laughed. And then Mom began to laugh too, and she kept saying, between laughing, 'I'm so sorry.' And he kept saying, 'Really, it's okay.' And Mom said, 'No, no, it's not okay.' When they were finally taking deep breaths and calming down, he looked at me and asked, 'What's your dog's name?' When I said, 'Shoe,' he looked at Mom and they started all over again, but this time they were laughing so hard that they were all bent over and holding their stomachs. I mean, a dog named Shoe pees on his *shoes.*"

The judge smiled. "Yes, I see the irony."

"Somehow, I ended up holding the little poodle and Shoe's leash because Mom and the guy were hysterical. And all this time, Shoe was being absolutely well-behaved. She was just sitting there calmly at my side, smiling. Some people say dogs don't smile. But I promise you, Shoe was smiling."

A side door to the courtroom opened, and

a clerk walked up to the judge and handed him a paper. "Your honor, the schedule is quite full today."

"How long do we have left?"

"About ten minutes," said the man.

The judge turned to me, "Lily, can you wrap it up in ten?"

I swallowed and nodded. "So I just stood there, holding Shoe's leash and Lucky, and watching my mom and this guy laughing so hard they were crying. I was surprised at Shoe because it wasn't good dog manners to pee on someone's shoes. But the thing that was the *most* surprising was hearing my mom laugh like that."

"Why was that surprising, Lily?" asked the judge.

"Well, see, it's been really hard for her taking care of me by herself all these years. She hardly ever did anything like go out with people her own age or on a date. Not that guys didn't ask her out. They did. And sometimes she went out with them, but so far, they'd been *so* not her type. And Shoe didn't like *any* of them. There was this one guy who only talked Mondays, Wednesdays, and Fridays. And another who only ate orange food for dinner. Oh, and one who whistled through his nose when he breathed."

Mom was practically coughing from clearing her throat, and her cheek was pink from all the tapping.

I took two deep breaths and paused for a second. "She sort of gave up dating and just concentrated on me. And that was okay. I was her top priority. Sometimes, though, I wanted someone special, besides me, to concentrate on *her*. That day in the park, it was so nice. The way he was holding her arm and looking at her and laughing with her was nice . . . really nice."

"I can imagine it was," said the judge.

"You want to know a secret?" I asked.

The judge had his elbow on his desk and had his chin resting in his hand. "Yes, Lily, I actually do."

"Kids *really* like to hear their parents laugh because it means they have happiness in their hearts. See, most of the time parents' hearts are all filled up with responsibility and seriousness. When Mom was laughing out loud in the park, all I could do was just stand there and listen and smile, because . . . well . . . it was like a favorite song I hadn't heard in a really long time."

The courtroom was very quiet. I wasn't sure how many minutes I had left, but I started talking right away because there was more I *wanted* and *needed* to say. "See, it's kind of amazing how much you can learn about a complete stranger by simply standing in line with him and watching your dog pee on his shoes. We were really lucky that the line was so long, too, because by the time we got to the registration table, Mom discovered that the guy's name was Theodore Ochoa, but everyone called him Theo, and that he knew one of Mom's friends from the hospital. And what were the chances of that? He lived

practically in our neighborhood and sometimes jogged by our house. He said he used
to have a dog who ran with him, but that dog
died, and he missed having a friend at his
side. To make a long story short . . ." I looked
up at the judge to see if he got my joke.

He winked at me.

"Theo started stopping by to take Shoe for
a run. And Shoe just *loved* Theo, but not as
much as she loved me, of course. And when
he took Shoe for a run, Mom and I would
dogsit Lucky. We just made sure to put away
the feather duster. And sometimes Theo would
stay for dinner. And well, one thing led to
another."

There was a tiny smile on Mom's face.

"Lily, let me get this straight. Your mom
married Theo—"

"Yes."

"And that's why you have petitioned the
court?"

"Yes. Since Theo's last name is Ochoa,
and now Mom's last name is Ochoa, I'd really

like to be an Ochoa, too. But the rule is that you have to get permission to change your name from all the parents listed on your birth certificate, even if you've never met them in your entire life. And if you can't, you have to come to court so the judge—that's you—can decide if it's in my best interest. I hope you decide that it is, because all I ever had for a father was a name on a piece of paper. And that's not very real."

I looked at Mom and thought about how happy Theo had made her and me. "See, *real* is the father who does stuff with you, like drive you to soccer practice, and go for walks on the pier with you and your dog, and help you with your homework, and bring you a quilt when you're cold in the middle of the night. That's the one who is real."

The judge took off his glasses again—not to clean them but to blot his eyes. "And where is Theo now, Lily?"

"He's waiting right out in front of the courthouse with Shoe and Lucky so that if we need him, he can trade places with Mom at a moment's notice."

"That won't be necessary, Lily," said the judge. "You're the only one I need to talk to today."

"Afterward, no matter what your decision, we're going to Dog Beach, where you can let your dogs off leash to run around and play and jump in the waves. We can take Lucky now, even though there are a lot of bird feathers on the sand, because we did behavior therapy with him. And Shoe hasn't peed on *one other person.*"

"Well, I'm glad to hear it," said the judge.

The clerk came back into the courtroom.

The judge turned to me. "Lily, I think you've given me enough information to make my ruling. You made my job easier today. You may step down."

I slipped out of the witness stand and went to Mom's side. The judge made his decision and passed the paperwork to the clerk, who passed it to Mom, who smiled.

There was something happening inside me, something filling me up with so much emotion that my throat felt tight. I couldn't say good-bye to the judge. All I could do was hold up my hand and bend my fingers in a tiny wave. Mom stood up and put her arm around me, and we headed out of the court-room.

The clerk called the name of another child, and he and his family took our places. I hoped they would have a good outcome.

Outside, Theo was waiting on a bench. Shoe sat next to him and he held Lucky in his arms. Lucky started wiggling as soon as he saw us.

Theo drove us to Dog Beach, and Mom held Lucky in her lap. I sat in the back seat with Shoe. Each time I looked at her, she tilted her head to the side and stared at me. I stroked her chest and talked to her with my eyes. When we arrived at the beach, Shoe and Lucky jumped from the car and ran toward the water. I held back and walked hand-in-hand with Theo and Mom.

"You're awfully quiet, Lily," said Theo. "That's not like you. Everything okay? Do we need to see a doctor? Do you have a temperature? You know, your mom has connections at the hospital."

I smiled.

Shoe races toward me, wet from the waves. She stops at my side and shakes. Droplets spray over me. I bend over and put my face near hers. Wildly, her tail wags, and she licks my cheek. I want her to be the first to hear. I whisper, "Lily Ochoa."

Shoe leaps back and plants her front legs apart, then jumps forward again, egging me on. Suddenly, I don't feel like being quiet anymore. I spread out my arms. Shoe runs, and I chase her. This time, I yell into the ocean breeze. "Lily Ochoa!"

Lucky barks. Shoe barks louder.

Mom and Theo laugh.

All my happiness spills over, and as usual, my mind has a mind of its own. I yell my new name again, and again, and again.

Science Fair

Written and illustrated
by Mark Teague

Howard

Soon after Judy Nussenbaum moved in next door, Howard Eubanks became a dog. To most people in Fenwick Grove, the events were unrelated. Boys rarely became dogs, after all, and Howard's transformation was considered a sad and mystifying event. But Judy didn't think so, and neither did Howard. Every time she walked by his house, he barked.

"It's not my fault!" she called from her own front yard. "How was I supposed to know it would work?"

The question was unanswerable, especially by Howard. But even in his dim, doggy state, he blamed her.

The day they met, Howard was working in his lab, as usual. When Judy pounded on the front door, he emerged from the base-ment, blinking like a mole. "What do you want?"

"Mom says we have to go outside." She had frizzled hair and pointy elbows. Sunlight glinted on her braces.

"I don't even know you."

"I'm Judy Nussenbaum. Who're you?"

"Howard Eubanks, and I'm busy. The science fair is in two days. Now go away."

For Howard, the science fair at Arturo V. Mortensen Middle School was the year's most important event. Twice he'd entered and twice—inexplicably—he'd lost.

His first attempt came in sixth grade. He was sure he'd win. All year he'd been winning chess tournaments and debate tournaments and spelling bees. He'd programmed his clock radio to send signals in Morse code. He translated the Gettysburg Address into Egyptian hieroglyphs. Everyone knew he was a genius. The *Fenwick Times* featured him in an article titled "Ten Kids to Watch Out For."

"I'm simply better than everyone else," he confided to his diary.

And yet, somehow, Monique Moldinado won first prize at that year's fair. Her invention, a tap-dancing robot, took the event by storm. After renditions of "I've Got Rhythm" and "Mr. Bojangles," it brought down the house with a spirited performance of "Singin' in the Rain."

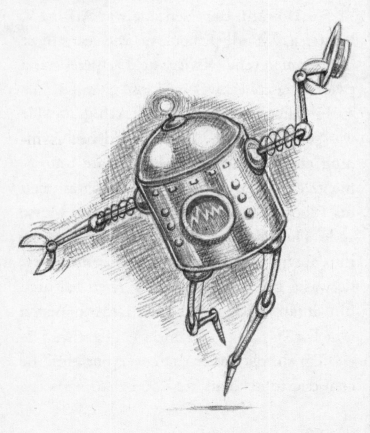

Howard had to settle for honorable mention. His solar-powered pooper-scooper was a remarkable and useful device, but it couldn't dance.

"Don't listen to them," said Mr. Von Epps, his science teacher, when Howard's classmates giggled. "Foolish people may call you names, but you must never be deterred."

"De-TURD!" gasped Wayne Funderberg, as if he'd been handed a precious gift.

"De-TURD! De-TURD!" chanted the rest of the class.

The nickname stuck. "My school is infested with morons," wrote Howard.

The worst thing about morons was that they were too dumb to know they were morons. They were even too dumb to know that he, Howard, was made of finer stuff. "I will have to show them," he wrote.

He began planning for next year's fair. As a demonstration of behavioral science, he trained a dozen chicks to play "Jingle Bells" on a piano. "Let's see Monique Moldinado top that!" he wrote. But it was Tommy Alvarez who won first prize. Flown by a crew of hamsters, his miniature zeppelin was a triumph. The crowd went wild. The hamsters danced in their tiny cockpit.

Meanwhile, Howard learned that chicks, however musical, cannot be house-trained. The mess they made on the keyboard brought a familiar chant.

"De-TURD! De-TURD!"

"Cretins!" Howard wrote. "They ridicule what they don't understand."

What he could not understand was how Monique Moldinado and Tommy Alvarez could have beaten him. He was the genius, after all. And geniuses never quit!

"My final attempt," he wrote, "will be the greatest achievement in the history of science fairs!"

So Howard brooded while the chicks grew to rangy adulthood. At night he lay awake, scheming, while roosters crowed in his backyard. He realized that training birds had been a mistake. Nobody liked poultry. If he wanted to win, he would need rodents, like Tommy Alvarez.

A plan took shape in his mind. He Googled information on genetics. He learned everything he could about DNA and RNA, chromosomes and mitochondrial extraction. He bribed the Trevinos' bulldog, Larry, with ham bones so that he could scrape skin cells from its tongue. He constructed a laboratory in his basement and disappeared for days on end. He manipulated chromosomes and spliced genes. He injected his mouse with formulas derived from mutant dog cells. He cackled. His brilliance would shock the world!

The fair approached. Howard was just one step away from dazzling his fellow students with the world's first dog-mouse. He worked harder. Dark circles appeared under his eyes.

Then Judy Nussenbaum showed up.

"Go away!" he repeated. "I'm at a critical point in my experiment."

"Snotty." She peered through the screen door. "You got a lab down there?"

"Yes, and it's quite extensive. As I said, the science fair is in two days."

"I'll probably win that," she said in an off-hand way.

Howard's face reddened. "You will not! The fair is highly competitive."

"So am I. If you're lucky, maybe I will help you."

"Like I need your help!"

She examined him closely. "Trust me, you do."

"You're the one who needs help," said Howard. "As in psychiatric help. For your information, I'm doing research that will change the whole world."

"Uh-huh." Judy yawned. "What did you do for last year's fair?"

The question surprised him. "I taught chicks to play 'Jingle Bells' on a piano."

"Well, that's sort of interesting. Where'd you get the little pianos?"

"Stupid! There weren't any little pianos! It was a dozen chicks on a regular-sized piano. Each one pecked a separate note."

"Chickens are dumb," she said. "Your roosters keep me awake all night."

"Never mind chickens. This year I'm doing something much more sophisticated. I'm going to create a dog-mouse."

"A dog-mouse, huh? Will it dance?"

"No, it won't dance!" Howard slammed the door.

Back in his lab, he was unable to concentrate. Had he said too much? What if Judy Nussenbaum really did have a plan to win the fair? Could she be another Monique Moldinado or Tommy Alvarez? "Don't let it happen again!" he wrote in his diary. That night he slept fitfully. The roosters crowed.

Judy caught up with him the next morning on the way to school. Howard put his head down and sped up. The fair was coming. He mustn't be distracted.

"Look at the way you walk," she said. "All

hunched over. You might as well tape a 'kick me' sign to your back."

"Leave me alone."

"I wish I could," she said. "But I'm interested in you, and when I take an interest in something, I'm very persistent. Know what I'm going to do?"

"No. Nor do I care."

"I'm going to fix you so you aren't such a dwid. It's my new project."

"I'm not a *dwid*, whatever that is. For your information I was voted one of the *Fenwick Times*' Ten Kids to Watch Out For."

"Ten Dwids to Watch Out For," said Judy.

Across the street, Wayne Funderberg yelled, "De-TURD!"

"If you carry yourself with confidence, people won't think you're such a doofus."

"Why should I care what these halfwits think?" A corn muffin hit him in the chest.

"You care," said Judy. "Why else would you make a zombie mouse in your basement?"

"I'm not making a zombie mouse! And don't talk so loud. My project is a secret."

Someone yelled, "De-TURD has a girlfriend!" Someone else threw a banana. Judy caught it.

"See?" said Howard. "They don't like you, either."

"Not yet," Judy said calmly, eating the banana. "But they'll come around. People admire my originality."

Howard was sure that wasn't true. Still, it stuck in his mind. In English class he wrote a short story in which superintelligent aliens from another galaxy conquer Earth and enslave its people. They regard Earthlings as a grossly inferior race and treat them with contempt. The only exception is a single, brilliant boy named Broward. Unappreciated by his own race, Broward is greatly admired by the aliens, especially their princess, the lovely Xandra.

It was a terrific story until the princess started speaking. For some reason, she sounded exactly like Judy Nussenbaum. Howard erased her dialogue but could not figure out how to rewrite it. The story limped to an unsatisfying conclusion.

When the final bell rang, the kids ran out in a screaming mob. Howard followed cautiously.

Judy caught up with him by the flagpole. "Buy me an ice cream."

"Buy yourself an ice cream!" He hurried past her.

"I've been thinking about your experiment," she said. "A zombie mouse isn't much of a crowd-pleaser. You ought to consider doing something with more pizzazz."

"Oh, really! Like what?"

"I don't know. Why not drink the dog juice yourself? You could be like Lon Chaney."

"Who?"

"Lon Chaney. He played Larry Talbot in the original *Wolf Man*. He became a werewolf after Bela Lugosi bit him. It might be interesting if you could pull off something like that."

"Don't be ridiculous," said Howard. "That's not science, that's just a stupid movie."

"It's a scary stupid movie."

"It wouldn't make sense to drink the formula, either. The material must be injected."

"So inject yourself. You can be a dog for a few hours. It'd be an improvement, if you ask me."

"I didn't ask you. And for your information, genetic changes are permanent!"

"Only if you do it wrong."

"No, not if you do it wrong! You're so dumb! The only way to reverse the process would be to develop an antidote to restore the original genetic balance. Which has never been done, by the way."

"Chicken."

"I'm not a chicken. It's just that it would be crazy to experiment with something so dangerous."

"Cluck, cluck. Now I know why you have chickens in your backyard. They're part of your flock."

"You're insane," said Howard.

"Maybe. But at least I know how to win a science fair."

"You're not going to win!" Howard ran inside his house and slammed the door.

In the basement, he tried to calm himself. It wasn't easy. Even Wayne Funderberg wasn't as annoying as Judy Nussenbaum. He fiddled with his microscope for a while, then quit in exasperation. His dog-mouse looked up at him and wagged its tail.

"Boring!" muttered Howard. Somewhere in his mind a robot tap-danced. Hamsters steered a small zeppelin around a gymnasium. What was a dog-mouse compared to that?

But a dog-*boy*? That was interesting. That was something to make the kids at Mortensen sit up and take notice. He pictured himself strolling into school half dog, half boy, with shiny fur and glistening canines. Wayne Funderberg would scream. Monique Moldinado and Tommy Alvarez would turn green with envy. And Judy Nussenbaum—well, at least maybe she'd shut up for a while.

Almost without thinking, he began to calculate the formula. He spliced genes culled from Larry the bulldog and added the mixture to a mitochondrial solution and a sample of his own tonsils that he'd been saving since their removal three years earlier. He mixed the formula in a sterilized beaker. Would it work? Why not?

No! screamed some other part of his mind. *Are you mad?* The idea was too risky. And for what? To win a school science fair? He leaned on his workbench. What was he thinking?

It was Judy Nussenbaum. She was making him crazy. Before she showed up, he had been perfectly happy with his dogmouse. More than just happy—he'd been euphoric! Whether the subhumans at Arturo V. Mortensen Middle School understood it or not, his project marked a turning point in science. He had invented a whole new species! The world would never be the same! And now here he was, nearly throwing it all away for the sake of mere showmanship!

He was about to dump his formula into the sink when his mother appeared in the doorway upstairs. "Howard, it's the girl next door! She wants to see you."

"Tell her I'm busy."

"I will not! Now, be a gentleman."

Moments later, Judy clomped down the stairs. The door closed behind her. "Hey, Frankenstein," she said. "What's cooking?"

"What do you think?" he muttered. "I'm working on my project."

She peered into the mouse cage. "It looks a little bit like a Chihuahua. I guess that's sort of interesting."

"More than I can say for you. If you even have your own project, that is."

"Mine's already done. I've got a volcano, lava, the whole shebang. Lots of razzle-dazzle. You need help with that dog juice? We could mix it with lemonade so it tastes better."

"I told you, I'm not changing myself into a dog!"

"Well, what's your dog-mouse going to

do? Fetch? Roll over? You need something that'll get the judges' attention."

"It's a genetically distinct species. That should be enough for any judge!"

"Yeah, right. Hey, let's go to the convenience store and buy some candy."

"No! I told you I'm busy!"

"Doing what? If you aren't going to win the fair, what's the point schlubbing around in this basement all day?"

Howard had an idea. "If I drink the juice, will you leave me alone?" He held up the beaker.

"What do you mean, 'alone'?"

"I mean will you go away and stop bugging me?"

"You'll drink that goop?"

"Every drop." Howard smiled to himself. Drinking the juice might not taste good, but it couldn't harm him. His body would simply digest it. It was injecting the material that could cause a problem. But dingbat Judy didn't know that.

"Deal," she said.

"Deal," said Howard, and he drank the beaker dry.

Judy watched him for a few minutes. Nothing happened. After a while Howard reminded her of their deal.

"All right, I'll go. That juice doesn't work anyway." She trudged back up the stairs. "See you at the fair."

Howard felt only a moment's relief. Then panic set in. Judy was right. His dog-mouse needed to do something! He tried training it: sit, fetch, roll over. Hours passed. He missed dinner. He went through handfuls of tiny dog treats. Without thinking, he ate some of the treats himself. The dog-mouse merely stared at him, tail wagging. "Hopeless!" he complained.

It was long past bedtime when his mother called for him to quit. "You can finish in the morning, dear."

Howard was too weary to argue. He staggered to his bedroom and turned off the light.

That night he had the oddest dreams. He chased squirrels and rode in a car with his head hanging out the window. Then he chased the car. Then the car chased him. Then he chased a bunch of squirrels inside a car. The car smelled funny. The squirrels smelled delicious! His hind leg jerked.

When he woke up, his body was covered in thin fur. A pink tongue lolled from the side of his mouth. His nose was cool and wet. "The fair!" he thought excitedly. "The fair! The fair!" Though his hands felt clumsy, he managed to get dressed and rush downstairs.

"Mouse!" he thought. "Mousemouse-mousemouse! Eat mouse!

"NO!" he corrected himself sternly. "Not eat mouse. Mouse for fair!" He grabbed the cage and bolted out the door.

"Name?" said the woman at the desk.

"Howard!" he woofed.

She wrote down "Woof" and directed him to a table where he could set up his presentation. It went badly. Trying to write a description of his project on index cards, Howard mangled the words. His paws had grown clumsy. He whined and licked his nose. He ate the pencil. "Mousemousemouse," he thought.

The other kids came in and set up their projects. Everyone was busy. Nobody noticed him. If they had, they would have witnessed a remarkable transformation. Howard's hands and feet shortened into stout paws, his ears flopped, his forehead flattened, and his coat grew thick and shiny. By the time the fair started, Howard was no longer Howard at all, but a bulldog wearing Howard's clothes. The clothes fit poorly. Even as a dog, he lacked pizzazz.

Judy was the only one who recognized him. "Howie?" she asked.

"Rowf?"

"Oh, Howie, it worked! Who knew? It really worked!" She ran to tell the judges, but they were unimpressed. Rules, they said, prohibited dogs from entering the science fair.

"But it's Howard Eubanks!" she said.

"Rules are rules," said Ms. Feldspar, the principal.

With Howard disqualified, Judy easily won first prize. Her experiment wasn't much, really, just a papier-mâché volcano that spewed steam from dry ice and melted cheese. But the sight of a village on the volcano's slope being engulfed by oozing Velveeta

delighted the judges and thrilled the crowd. "JU-DY! JU-DY!" they chanted.

Howard was inconsolable. That afternoon he lay in the backyard with his feet in the air. He refused his kibble. He ignored the chickens. He growled at the crowd of reporters who appeared, seemingly from nowhere.

For two days the "dog-boy" story dominated the local news. "Could your child be next?" asked anchorwoman Mindy Sneffins.

Fortunately, the answer appeared to be no.

When a family of Stone Age cave dwellers

was discovered living in the hills west of Mungo, the reporters departed.

Things returned to normal, except that Howard was still a dog. And he was angry. He was angry with the school and the judges and the mailman (for no clear reason). But mostly he was angry with Judy.

"What did I do?" she asked.

"Growf!"

"It was your idea. I just encouraged you."

"Rowrowrow!"

"Well, anyway, you can't stay mad forever!"

Howard thought he could.

But Judy was persistent. "I passed around a petition," she said one day from behind the fence that separated their houses. "It says we think you should have won the science fair."

"Roop?"

"Sure. I got all the kids to sign. It was a great experiment, even if you didn't think it through very clearly."

"Broo!" Howard barked.

"Okay. Maybe I'm partly to blame. The point is, we all liked it." She slid a ham bone under the fence.

After she left, Howard chewed the bone thoughtfully. His tail began to wag.

Slowly he adjusted to life as a dog. It wasn't bad, really. He ate and slept and chased the chickens. Everything smelled wonderful. He developed a passion for squeaky toys.

After school (Howard had been expelled), Judy took him for walks. At the convenience store she bought candy and chewy bones. She told him about the day's events and about books she'd read and movies she'd seen. He tried to tell her about being a dog—the smells, the sounds, the pleasure of rolling in dirt—but it was difficult to explain. "Row-rowrowrop!"

They walked home with the leash loose between them. "I'm proud of you, Howie," she said. "It's hard to change. Lots of people just stay the way they are forever. Especially the dopey ones."

"Rodope!"

"Of course you were a dope. The only thing is, you may have changed too much."

"Arp!"

"I know, I know. You drank the dog juice. But, Howie, that juice should have been injected."

"Ri-no!"

"Everyone knows that's the way to make a genetic change. What you did shouldn't have worked at all."

"Arf!" he barked.

"Why did it work? I don't know. Maybe it's psychosomatic."

"Woof?"

"Psychosomatic. It means it's all in your head."

Howard knew what it meant—he just didn't believe it. "Fruff."

"Say what you want," said Judy. "It's the only thing that makes sense. You knew you were going to lose the science fair, so you were upset. And deep down, you were tired of being a dwid. Becoming a dog offered the only solution to the fix you were in. It was brilliant, really."

"Broof?"

"Broof. I mean it. But now you can stop."

Howard shook his head. Spittle flew from his jowls.

"You can, Howie. Trust me."

"Owruf."

"Of course you can. You can do anything you put your mind to."

So he did. Becoming human wasn't easy, the way it was for Lon Chaney in *The Wolf Man*. He had to improve his attitude. He had to stop thinking he was better than everyone else. He had to shed a *lot*.

His ears shrank, his fingers stretched, his fangs receded. He stared at the mirror.

Judy stared too. "I wish they could have seen this at the science fair."

But Howard no longer cared about science fairs. Not at all. He cared about clothes! He ran to his bedroom and threw on a pair of jeans and a shirt.

The next morning Judy walked with him to school. As they drew near, Howard began to fidget. He sniffed the air for flying muffins, but couldn't smell a thing. He tried twitching his ears, listening for the chant of "De-TURD! De-TURD!" but his ears wouldn't twitch, and the chant never came.

Instead, someone shouted, "Hey, everybody! It's Howie!"

A cheer went up. For a few glorious moments, it seemed as if the whole school had come out to welcome him back. Then a food fight started. Howard and Judy hurried to class.

For Howard, things did not get better all at once, but they did get better. Monique Moldinado smiled at him in the hallway. Tommy Alvarez offered him a ride in the new zeppelin he was building. Wayne Funderberg was hit in the head with a corn muffin, and nobody ever discovered who threw it.

And one day, as they were working together in the lab, Judy declared her project a success.

"What project?" asked Howard.

"Remember? I said I'd fix you. Well, I did it. You're not a dwid anymore."

"I'm not?" He watched his dog-mouse carefully. "Singin' in the Rain" played in the background.

"Not much, anyway. I'd say you're more of an original now, like me."

Howard smiled. It was good to be an original. If he'd had a tail, he would have wagged it. In its cage, his dog-mouse began to tap-dance.

Patty

Written and illustrated
by Thacher Hurd

Patty

Me and dogs.

Let's keep it simple.

Let's just say that I used to think one way about dogs, but after that trip to Grams and Grampa's last summer, things were a little different with me and dogs. Especially Patty. Just a little different.

I mean, I still think dogs slobber too much,

and we really need to do something about dog breath. Maybe it's time for some doggie mouthwash.

People seem to think dogs are the answer to all of life's problems. If we go running with our dog through sunlit fields of wheat like we're in a dog food commercial, then all our problems will be solved? I guess I'm supposed to like dogs. I'm a kid, and kids like dogs, right? We have a nice black Lab named Patty who wags her tail and gets all slobbery when I come home. My parents really like Patty a lot. They think she can do no wrong. I just wish she wouldn't want to slobber all over me when I give her a hug.

I don't want to make too big a deal out of this, but I have to mention that Patty may be sweet, but she also tends to throw up at strange times. Like the time my parents went out for a while but then they got delayed and it got dark.

I don't like being home alone at night. At first it's okay, but then I get the feeling the bogeyman is looking in the window.

So my parents go out, and all I do is go in my room and shut the door, and I make Patty come with me, and I won't let her out. She doesn't like that, but I feel nervous, and I end up in my bed with the covers pulled up high and my palms sweating, and I am thinking that every little noise in the house is someone coming up the stairs to chop me in little pieces and make me into soup.

Patty is supposed to be the watchdog, but then she starts getting nervous too, and she's pacing around my bedroom making little noises and then scratching at the door like she needs to go pee, but I know she doesn't because I just took her out right before I made her stay in my room. So I know she's faking that, and I don't want to let her out anyway, though if you think about it, it would probably be better if she was out roaming around the house being really fierce and all and protecting me with her big growl (which she doesn't really have) and her sharp teeth and her bad breath. I mean, her bad breath would drive anybody away.

But no, I keep Patty in my room, and I get more and more nervous, and my palms get sweatier and sweatier and then I hear a terrible noise, and I look out from under the covers.

Patty has thrown up. A big pile of throw-up in the middle of my rug. Great. It smells really bad, and I don't know what to do. Just then my parents come home and open the door to my room and smell the barf and then things get complicated. They say, "David, you shouldn't have done this," and "David, you shouldn't have done that," though all I did was get scared—the dog did the throwing up. But as usual, it's me in trouble, my parents petting the dog and looking down at me, and the dog looking up at me with those I-didn't-do-anything-I'm-just-the-dog eyes.

Maybe you're thinking at this point, Who are this kid's parents that they would leave him alone at night?

But the Lyonses live next door, and they're pretty helpful, except that Mrs. Lyons drinks twenty cups of coffee a day and vacuums her house twice a day and their son Robert is always cheating me out of stuff. One night at two A.M., when my parents *were* at home, I got up in my pajamas and bare feet and sleep-walked over to Robert's house and knocked on the door, and when his mother who drinks the twenty cups of coffee a day answered the door, I said, "Can Robert come out and play?"

Robert's mother walked me home in her nightgown and woke up my parents, and they put me to bed, and maybe they thought about putting a lock on the front door so I wouldn't escape. Patty slept through the whole thing. Patty doesn't sleepwalk. Just in her dreams. You can see her paws twitching when she's dreaming. Maybe she's running through sunlit fields of wheat.

Most of the time, my parents get a baby-sitter when they go out to dinner. I like it when Julie Saylor is the babysitter. She's funny and has blond hair, and she's only a few years older than me, and she likes to play games like poker. It was especially fun when she told me that joke about the two babies named Sam and Joe, twins in the womb. I was wondering how babies get in the womb in the first place, and it all seemed especially interesting because Julie looked so nice with her hair and her smile. Then she got to the punch line, where Sam and Joe come out of the womb (how does that happen?) and they look at each other and say, "Weren't we womb-mates?"

Julie and I laughed at the joke, and I thought it would be very exciting to be in the womb and have a twin brother named Joe because I don't have a brother. Or a sister, for that matter. All I have is Patty.

Then there are the other babysitters, like Mrs. Menzer. She's okay, but really old, like maybe fifty or something, and I like her, and she plays games with me, but she always gives me my dinner with the food mushed together on the plate so the mashed potatoes get mixed up with the vegetables, and the chicken gets mixed in too.

The worst babysitter was the old lady my parents found somewhere who looked like a witch. She only came once, and she wasn't very friendly. I didn't know who she was, and she came in a scratchy wool dress and had a pinched face. Everything was okay until I went to bed and turned out the light. Then somehow I got the idea that she *was* a witch or a really bad person and maybe she had a gun and she was going to come in my room and do something terrible. I lay in bed sweating just like I did when my parents left me alone with Patty, my mind going round and round, and I couldn't go to sleep. Then my parents came home, and everything was fine. They never knew that there had been the possibility that the babysitter was an evil witch. I feel like Patty should have at least barked once at the witch babysitter.

Last summer we drove way up north to visit my grandparents in their little house in the woods. That's where the big adventure happened, which was also all about Patty and me and being alone in the dark, except that this time Patty didn't throw up, not at all.

On the way up, I sat in the back of the car, and I made my own little cave out of a blanket. At first I wouldn't let Patty in, but she kept sticking her wet nose into the fort, so finally I let her in, and everything was fine until she decided to fart a big smelly fart, and I coughed and gasped, and she looked at me with those I'm-just-a-dog-I-can't-help-it-aren't-I-cute eyes, while I rolled down the window as fast as I could. Then Patty sat on my side of the seat and stuck her head out the window for the rest of the trip. She really likes that.

Finally we got to my grandparents' house in the country, and there was Yap Yap, their dog. Her name is Lucy, but I call her Yap

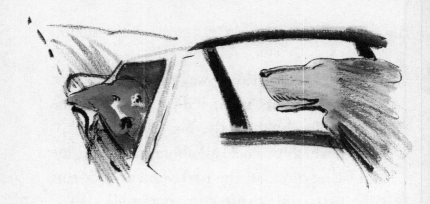

Yap, because it seems like no matter what is going on, she's barking. No matter how many times I've been to Grams's house, still Yap Yap barks at me and goes crazy as if I'm an evil intruder. She always has a pink sweater on, even in the summer. She's tiny, but she looks like she really wants to chomp on my ankle. Not to mention that last year she chewed up my copy of *A Wrinkle in Time* for no reason at all.

Grampa, who has this big mustache and always wears army boots, said to me, "The secret is, son, don't look at the dog. If you don't look at her, she won't feel threatened. Then she won't bark." He gave me a long lecture about why a dog is a man's best friend, but it was hard to concentrate on what he was saying, because Yap Yap was getting so thrilled and barky at the thought of taking a chunk out of my ankle.

One day on our visit, we went for a walk in the woods with Grams and Grampa. Their house is surrounded by a forest, and the year before, I got to make a fort in a big oak tree there, but now we were just going for a walk in the woods. I was thinking to myself, What is the point of this? Just walking? Why can't

we run, or be like woodsmen from the days of yore and hide behind trees and hunt deer and have terrifying adventures?

And then I thought, not knowing what was to come, The best would be if we got lost and there was a huge snowstorm, and everybody was about to die from the cold and snow, even Grampa, who is supposed to be such a great woodsman. But just in time I would step forward with bravery in my eye. Using our tracking skills, Patty and I would blaze a trail through the snow to the safety of a cave. We would all huddle by a fire that I would make by rubbing two sticks together. Then in the morning, everyone would pat me on the back and thank me for saving their lives. In the meantime, I would have discovered that the cave goes deep into the mountain, and I would uncover a strange native burial site with lots of artifacts in it, and the Museum of Natural History would give me a job, and I would work there and go on expeditions to Africa and Mongolia and dig up stuff. And Patty would come along, I guess. As long as she didn't throw up. That was my big brave thought.

But no, we were just going for a walk, and it didn't look like much of an adventure, so Patty and I were dawdling behind. Actually it felt kind of good to have Patty sticking close to me, her soft black fur against my leg.

We were walking through a little clearing when suddenly Patty put her nose in the air and started sniffing and then she ran straight into the woods, barking her head off. We called, "Patty! Patty!" and after a long time she stopped barking and came back. It looked like she had a white beard, and she wasn't barking—she was whimpering instead—and Grampa said, "I don't believe it. She's got into a porcupine."

Patty had all these quills in her mouth, and she looked really unhappy.

Grampa said, "We'll have to take her to the vet."

We started back toward home, but when we came to the big field behind Grams and Grampa's house, Patty took off again. We could see her chasing something black and white through the meadow. The black and white something raised its tail and then Patty came back to us, and she smelled so bad it was way, way beyond a bad smell. It was so bad it made you want to throw up, like a whole new universe of bad smell from the stinky planet. All together, we said, "Skunk!"

Now, right here you're thinking to yourself, That could never happen. A skunk and a porcupine in one day? Not one chance in a million.

But I didn't make this story up. We just hit the jackpot, the super double sweepstakes of smelly and porcupine, as my grandfather called it. Grampa drove my parents and me to the vet's with all the windows down and everyone holding their hands over their noses. Patty smelled so bad that the vet had to take the quills out in her garage. It was hard to watch, because it looked like it hurt Patty a lot. Even so, I could see Patty was really a brave dog, and she took it like a man, or a dog, I guess you would say. Afterward the vet washed Patty with something that looked like tomato juice to get rid of the skunk smell, but she still smelled crazy bad. I gave her a big hug anyway on the way back from the vet's, and Patty gave me a look like, "I'm really sorry. It's just my instincts. I'm a dog." And then I kissed Patty on her poor nose and said, "It's all right. You may be a dog, but you're a brave dog."

When we got home, everything was in an uproar. I mean, how could things get worse than they already were? But now Grampa thought he had put Yap Yap down in the field when we first saw Patty chasing the skunk, and then in the confusion had left her behind. Everyone had been so absorbed in Patty that they hadn't noticed how quiet things were. No yapping. You would think Yap Yap would bark her head off after being left behind, but . . . nothing. Maybe she was knocked out by a whiff of the skunk smell.

While we were at the vet's, Grams had been yelling and yelling for Yap Yap in the back meadow and walking around the fields calling, but no answer. She was kind of hysterical, and now it was late afternoon and we were all tired from the big day, but there was no way Grams and Grampa were going to let Yap Yap stay out all night. After all, she might get her little sweater dirty. Oh, sorry, didn't mean to say that.

So, even though it was late afternoon, it was time to organize a search party. Grams and Grampa and Dad and Mom and me and Patty. This time Grampa said we had to put Patty on a leash, so she wouldn't get into any more trouble, and I was on leash duty, bringing up the rear as we walked across the meadow to where Grampa thought he might have last seen Yap Yap. Grampa brought a couple of flashlights, in case we had to search all night or something.

We walked all the way through the field and didn't find Yap Yap, so we went on into the woods. Everyone began talking about where they thought they had seen Yap Yap earlier and what she must have been thinking, and how the poor little dog must be cold and shivering somewhere all alone. In her pink sweater, I thought. And not barking. That's a relief.

The whole time they were talking to each other, though, no one was thinking about Patty—Patty, whose ancestors were great hunters in England or somewhere, dogs who had amazing noses and could sniff anything from a mile away and find anything lost. But nobody was thinking about that; they were just trying to use their brains to find a brown dog with a pink sweater instead of using their noses, the way Patty would.

Grampa set off up a hill, saying that's where she must have gone. "We took her up that hill once, and she sat on the bench at the top of the hill, and she liked the wind in her fur. It's just a little ways up the hill, and if she's not there, we'll split up and search for her in teams. Maybe she's back in the field after all."

Grampa always likes to be the leader, the commander-in-chief.

Away we went, Patty and me following behind. I was wondering if her mouth was still hurting from all those quills, since she was holding back. She kept sniffing something off to the left, and the others started to get ahead of me. Then all of a sudden, Patty pulled hard on the leash and ran off sharp left, dragging me along behind her. I tugged on the leash to make her stop, but she just kept on and wouldn't let up.

Was it another skunk?

The branches were slapping my face as we went on, and I tripped on a log and went flying into the dirt. But Patty kept pulling. I got up, brushed myself off, and spat the dirt out of my mouth, and Patty took off again, zigzagging back and forth, her nose to the ground. At first we were running downhill, then the ground flattened out and we were in a pine forest, which was good because the trees were farther apart and I could follow Patty without getting my face whapped every two seconds.

By now I was thinking, Good dog, Patty, you'll find Yap Yap. I know you will. What else would make Patty run so fast?

I called out, "You're a real hunter, a real hunter. Nobody can find Yap Yap but you."

This seemed to get her going even faster. We kept running like this for a long time through the woods, and then I noticed that Patty was nosing back and forth in the same place, over and over, and then around in circles, and then . . .

She stopped and sat down.

I looked at her.

She looked up at me.

We listened. It was quiet in the woods. Just a little swishing in the pine trees. I looked at her again.

She'd lost the scent.

Maybe she still smelled too much like a skunk to smell anything else.

I listened some more. I couldn't hear my grandpa or my mom or dad. Patty moved a little bit. I told her to sit still, and I listened hard for a sound. But there was only the swish of wind in the trees. Nothing else. I looked around. The daylight was fading fast. I could hear an airplane high above.

A little part of my mind, a fear part, was getting bigger. I turned around in a full circle, peering into the woods. Everything looked the same. Which direction had we come from? What was Patty going after? Whatever it was, Yap Yap or something else, she had definitely lost the scent. She was just sitting there panting. My heart was pounding.

I sat down in the leaves and tried to think. Actually, I tried not to think. Not to think the one thing that my mind was already thinking: We're lost. And it's getting dark.

The trees were starting to fade into each other, turning into black angular shapes. Quiet all around. I petted Patty.

"Where are we?" I said.

She looked up at me with those big Patty eyes and shifted on her feet and then stared off into the woods. Was she afraid? Was she going to throw up like she did in my room? I started talking to her.

"It's okay, we'll get home. Patty, can you find the way home? Can you smell the way home?" Patty didn't move. She just looked off into the woods. No matter how hard I tried to get her to move, she just sat there on her haunches.

"Where is Yap Yap?" I whispered in her ear. Patty was like a statue—only her nose twitched a little.

We were lost, and Patty the wonder dog was definitely not coming through with a big batch of heroics. The dark trees looked darker, and the wind died down completely, and now it was definitely turning to night. I remembered something they taught us at camp about getting lost: Stay where you are. Don't try to find your way home. You'll just get more lost. At least that was what Counselor

Jake had said. Or I thought that was what he'd said. I wished I'd listened to what he was saying.

I sat down and leaned against the scratchy bark of a pine tree. Patty curled up next to me.

There was nothing to do but wait. I tried not to think about being in the woods all night, but in the back of my mind, the thought was looming, like a dark cloud. My palms were sweaty, and I wished I was at home curled up in bed with a good book and my dad downstairs listening to the stereo and everything right with the world.

Patty and I sat there for a long time, and then I saw the moon coming up through the trees. As it rose, the woods brightened, and light shone through the branches, and soon it seemed as bright as day. I could see anything in this light.

Anything at all.

Good, bad, or—

I heard a branch crackle, then another. Not far away. Just behind the tree I was leaning on. I peered around and saw a dark shape under a tree. Patty was up now, too, growling. Then she started barking, loud.

CRASH! The thing ran toward us, then stopped a few feet away and stood stock-still in the moonlight. Patty stopped barking. We both stared.

Then I saw its antlers.

A deer! Just as I realized what it was, it wheeled and ran gracefully away through the pines. Patty wanted to chase after it, but I grabbed her leash and held on tight, and this time she didn't get away from me.

My heart was still pounding. I stood for a long time, listening, then went back and sat down against the pine tree. Patty lay down next to me, and I put my arm around her and petted her head and felt her cold wet nose. Why do dogs have wet noses? Maybe it makes them better at smelling.

I looked up at the moon through the trees. The high branches rustled in a tiny breeze. Maybe the deer was just as afraid as I was.

I felt Patty's warm body next to mine. I rubbed her back, and she wagged her tail in the moonlight, and I remembered when my parents first brought Patty home. For a few years after our dog Trio died, we didn't have a dog, but then one night my parents went to their friends' house for dinner, and I was sleeping on the porch—and yes, don't worry, we had a babysitter—and it was really nice to be out there in the cool air in my sleeping bag. I had fallen asleep to the sound of the cars going by and, far away, a train. I woke up a little later when I heard my parents come home. The moon was shining that night, too.

Very quietly, they opened the porch door and slipped a little black ball of fur into my sleeping bag with me, and that was Patty, and she was our dog, our own little black Lab, and she had a cold wet nose and soft black fur just like now, far away and lost in the north woods.

Somehow, sitting there against that pine tree, I felt like we were going to be okay, Patty and me. I wasn't in a sleeping bag at home, but the night was beautiful and calm, and slowly I calmed down, too. After a long time, I fell asleep, even though the moon was so bright. I don't know how long I slept, but I woke to a sound in the distance.

Patty was up already, staring into the dark. I got up and turned, and though I couldn't see anything, I could hear a sound that was unmistakable and—

Irritating.

And wonderful. More wonderful than irritating at that moment.

Now it was close, cutting through the quiet of the pine forest: Yap Yap, barking that screechy, whiny bark.

Then I saw flashlights and heard my father calling, "David! David!"

I jumped up and down and called back and ran toward them and jumped some more and held Patty close and laughed, and soon they were all there, Mom and Dad and Grams and Grampa, hugging and happy and crying and everybody wanting to know what happened. I felt kind of stupid as I told the story, but no one seemed to mind that at all. When I finished, they put an old army coat of Grampa's on me and then we walked home in the moonlight.

I don't need to tell you the rest, except that Yap Yap hadn't been lost at all. She had walked home on her own and fallen asleep in the basket of clothes in Grams' laundry room, and no one thought to look there.

Ha!

I was hungry when we got back to Grams and Grampa's house, and nothing tastes better than scrambled eggs and toast at eleven-thirty at night, cooked the way Grams cooks them.

Then my mother tucked me into bed and gave me a long hug and cried a little bit but didn't say much, and I knew they had been through a lot looking for me—probably more than I had been through, actually. I lay in bed afterward, thinking, slowly unwinding my mind and getting used to the thought that everything was fine. That took a while.

I slept later than I've ever slept, and Patty did, too, and then the next day we said good-bye to Grams and Grampa, and Yap Yap barked as usual, but I did manage to get one pat in on her head before she tried to nip my finger.

Then we were headed home, Patty with her head on my lap as we drove down the inter-state, her cold nose snuffling now and then, and no more smell of skunk, but every so often a whiff of her bad breath.

I wondered what it would be like if Patty and I could talk like friends talk. Just Patty and me. She definitely wouldn't talk in front of anybody else. That way we could share each other's secrets. We could lie on the hill behind the house and talk about what's really on our minds.

I wonder what Patty would say first.

She wouldn't say, "I'm Patty," because then I would say, "I know that already."

She wouldn't say, "I'm a dog," because I know that, too.

And she wouldn't say, "How are you? Glad to meet you," because we already met long ago, and I've known her since she was just a little ball of fur in my sleeping bag on the porch when I was little.

Maybe she would say, "I've always wanted to be a hunter."

"A hunter?" I would reply.

She would say, "Yes, all my ancestors were hunters, or we helped hunters find their prey, or we fetched it when it was downed."

My eyes would grow wide imagining long ago in England or somewhere like that, hunters in furs or big overcoats with guns or spears hunting deer in the woods, and it was a big deal because they weren't hunting for sport—they were hunting because they needed to eat.

Then I thought about Patty and me, together in the far north in the winter, bounding over the wild steppes with fire in our eyes, hungry—me with my spear and big fur boots. The winter night is closing in and

we must find shelter before the storm. We will sleep in a cave in the far north after our meal of dried meat, sleep by a fire and dream of the coming spring, Patty's paws twitching in the firelight as she runs through fields of wheat. We could be cozy together, Patty and me, hunters in the far north.

Then I wonder, What were we chasing when she was pulling me through the woods like that? It wasn't Yap Yap, that was for sure. Maybe it was that deer we saw, or a wooly mammoth or another animal from days of old. I guess I'll never know.

Picasso

by Ann M. Martin

illustrated by Olga and Aleksey Ivanov

Picasso

I am in charge of things today. Completely in charge and home alone for the first time in my life. Okay, it isn't as if my parents had some big epiphany (look it up) and realized I (a) am twelve, (b) have never been in serious trouble, and (c) got straight A's on my last report card, so therefore I can finally be considered old enough and responsible enough to stay at home alone. No. Sadly, there was no epiphany. There wasn't time for one.

What happened was that my little brother fell off his dresser, which of course he wasn't supposed to be standing on, and broke his wrist. We all heard a huge crash (my brother landed on his truck collection) and went tearing into his room—Mom, Dad, Picasso (dog), and me. And there was Anthony sitting on the floor with a bath towel tied around his shoulders, rubbing his wrist and crying, "But I'm Superman!"

No one commented on this remark. My dad untied the towel (which wouldn't have been my first response in such an emergency, but whatever), and my mom examined Anthony's wrist and announced, "I think he broke it."

Picasso and I looked on in fascination—Picasso because he had just realized that the strong smell of peanut butter in the room was coming from a sandwich Anthony had been holding at the time of his experiment and which was now lying, only partially squished, on the carpet by Anthony's bottom. I was fascinated because I want to become a doctor and this was the first actual broken bone I had ever seen.

The next thing I knew, Dad had picked up Anthony, and Mom was calling to me, "You're in charge, Delilah. Take care of things until we get back." I couldn't actually hear the last three words of that sentence, since Mom said them after she had closed the back door, but I knew what she meant.

I disposed of the squished sandwich before Picasso could eat it. Then I looked at Picasso, and he looked at me, and I said, "We're on our own."

So now here we are. At any rate, here I am.

Picasso is sort of missing.

He hasn't been missing for too long, which is the good news. In fact, he's been missing for only about ten minutes, so I am not panicking. Yet.

Still, I keep gazing around our backyard, trying to catch sight of some part of him: his tail, which has very long fur and waves in the breeze like a golden flag; or his head, which is on the large side and includes a nose that is half brown and a quarter white and a quarter yellow (let's face it, he isn't the most attractive dog); or any of his feet, which also have very long fur and make him look a little like a Clydesdale horse.

I don't see any parts of him or hear any of the noises he makes: woofs, yips, howls, growls, sneezes (he has allergies), or burps. Picasso is the best burper I know. Usually he waits until he has settled himself in your lap and is looking directly into your face before he lets loose with a belch that is like a fake one you'd hear on TV, that's how loud it is.

"Picasso!" I call. Then I listen for a few moments. I actually cup my hand to my ear, as if that will help me hear better. "Picasso!"

Nothing. Just the wind in the trees and

two barn swallows chattering to each other, and from far across the field, a roar, which I'm pretty sure is our neighbors' tractor starting up, so it must be mowing day.

"Picasso!" I shout. "Picasso!"

Now panic is setting in. It's amazing how quickly it can happen.

The day is very hot, and I don't feel like trekking all around our yard and into the woods beyond. The woods are on a hill. Well, so is our yard, but the hill is steeper where the woods are, and there aren't any paths through the trees, so searching is difficult. But I have to find Picasso.

I run inside, grab my sneakers, and shove them onto my feet. I always leave my sneakers pre-tied, not for speed in getting dressed, but because Picasso chews the laces if he sees them trailing across the floor. The day is not only very hot, but also very sunny, and I think that if I'm going to be outdoors for a while, I should wear sunblock and a hat. Then I think how proud my parents would be if they could see what I'm doing. It would certainly demonstrate to them that I'm responsible enough to be home alone and in charge of things.

Except for immediately losing the dog.

I run out of the house in my sneakers, sunblock glopped on my face, still pulling my ponytail through the back of my hat.

"Picasso!" I yell. "Picasso, Picasso, PICASSO!"

I lope to the edge of our property, where the woods begin, and stand by the old pear tree, looking down at our house. The house somehow seems bigger from up here, and I wonder if Picasso likes the view, since I often see him sitting in the exact spot where I'm standing now. He sits up straight and tall, the way Ms. Dooter, my science teacher (who deserves a name like that and, by the way, was the only one to give me an A- on my report card instead of a complete A), tells us to sit if we want good posture. Although I ought to point out that she is not a very effective advertisement for good posture, what

with her neck sticking out in front of her at approximately a ninety-degree angle.

I sit on a large rock for several seconds and listen again. No Picasso sounds. Then I stand on the rock and call his name a few more times. I know I'm beginning to sound a little hysterical, and I try to calm myself. After all, Picasso has only been missing for (I check my watch) twenty-one minutes.

I wonder how long my parents will be at the hospital with Anthony. Surely Picasso will return before they do. Or maybe not. Dinner, an event Picasso would never miss, is hours away. I slump a little. Then I get to my feet. "Picasso!"

I stand in the sunshine and close my eyes, which makes the insides of my lids turn bright red. I tell myself that if I call Picasso three more times and then open my eyes, I'll see him somewhere in the yard.

"Picasso! Picasso! Picasso!" I yell.

I open my eyes. Of course he's not in the yard. What was I thinking? It isn't like I'm standing on a magic rock.

Now I begin talking to myself out loud, which just goes to show you how nervous I'm getting. "Okay, Delilah," I say to myself. "You have only looked in the backyard. You have a front yard too, you know."

This thought doesn't calm me, though, because along the edge of the front yard is the driveway, and the driveway leads to the road, and the road is about the most dangerous place I can think of for a dog, especially one like Picasso, who, as appealing as he is, is not particularly bright.

I jog down the hill toward the house, and suddenly a whole list of not-too-bright things that Picasso has done begins to play in my mind. It's like I'm envisioning Picasso's bad report card.

For starters, when my family went to the shelter in search of a pet, we had intended to adopt an older dog, since older dogs have a harder time finding homes than puppies do, but we were stopped by the sight of a puppy (Picasso, obviously) who was barking at a bowl of water.

"What's he doing?" Mom asked the shelter manager.

The shelter manager's name was Brian. He shrugged. "He barks at it a lot."

"I think it's funny," I said. (I was eight.)

"Does he bark at other things?" asked my father.

"No. Just the water bowl," Brian replied.

Picasso looked at us briefly, pawed at the bowl, and barked twice more.

So we adopted him and brought him home, and I tried to come up with an explanation for his behavior. "Maybe he sees himself in the water. Maybe he's barking at his reflection," I said.

"Maybe," my father replied. And then I distinctly heard him whisper to my mother, "Picasso isn't the brightest dog."

Sadly, it was true. Picasso grew up a little and stopped barking at water bowls, and my mother even fondly pointed out to whoever would listen that he'd been housebroken far more quickly than either Anthony or I had been toilet-trained. On the other hand, we once lost track of Picasso at a state park, and while we called and shouted and frantically yelled, "Treat, Picasso!" he joined up with another family, and almost went home with them. When we caught sight of his flag tail disappearing down a path, we ran to him and hugged him and kissed him, and he gave us a look that plainly said, "Oh, were you gone? I found these nice people who had hot dogs."

"He'll do anything for a hot dog," I said later to my parents. "That's why he was going to go home with that other family."

"He's not too bright," my father whispered to my mother.

Picasso's report card is looking worse and worse, because now I also remember his problem with hiding. Every so often, Picasso tries to hide for one reason or another, usually when we have company and he doesn't want to meet anyone new. This is how a not-very-bright dog hides: with his head and front feet behind one of the dining room curtains and his tail and entire rump sticking out in full view. Once when he was hiding like this, a visiting six-year-old went shrieking into the dining room, saw Picasso's rump, and patted it, and Picasso jumped a mile because he wasn't expecting it. He was so sure he was well hidden.

So you can see why the thought of Picasso on the road is alarming. I increase my speed from a jog to a full run, and since I'm running downhill, I can barely stop myself when I reach the front yard. I actually have to grab at the side of the garage as I fly by in order to slow down. Then I stand in the middle of the yard and catch my breath and listen for Picasso sounds again. Nothing. Just the Wilsons' tractor.

"Picasso?" I call. "Picasso?"

Horrible, horrible images are creeping into my mind. I picture Picasso lying by the side of the road, unmoving. I picture a pack of coyotes taking him down. I picture someone driving along the road and luring him into a car with a piece of hot dog and selling him to a lab where unspeakable experiments are performed on him for the rest of his life, which is very short.

Picasso is plainly not in the front yard, so I run to the road and look up and down it as far as I can see, which isn't very far, since we live on a curvy, wooded country road. But at least there are no furry bodies anywhere. I don't know whether to be relieved or more frantic. Where is Picasso?

I listen to the sound of the tractor, and now I picture Mrs. Wilson riding around and around as she mows the field, and that makes me picture Cynthia Wilson behind the wheel of the Wilsons' Prius. Cynthia is seventeen and has just gotten her driver's license. I don't know much about cars—or Cynthia—but I have a feeling that Cynthia is looking for any possible excuse to get the Prius out on the road.

I jog across the Wilsons' front lawn and ring their bell. My fingers are crossed that both Cynthia and the Prius are at home. Cynthia answers the door, which is good, but I don't see a car anywhere.

"Hey, Cynthia," I say.

"Hey, Delilah. What's going on?"

This is a fair question, since there aren't any Wilsons my age and I don't have much reason to show up on their doorstep.

I think for a moment. "I heard you got your license."

Cynthia beams at me. "Yeah. I got it on Friday."

"That is so cool." (I have no idea if seventeen-year-olds say "cool.") "I can't wait until I can drive. Anyway, I was wondering . . ."

"Yeah?"

"If you could take me for a dr—" This is probably the lamest thing I've ever suggested, but the fact that Cynthia doesn't even wait until I've finished the sentence before she makes a grab for the car keys just goes to show you how eager she is to show off her new skill.

"Sure!" she exclaims. "Come on!"

In about one second, we are sitting in the Prius (which was in the garage), and about one second after that, we're nosing onto the road.

"Where do you want to go?" asks Cynthia. "Into town?"

That would be the logical destination, but I'm forced to say, "Let's just drive around here a little." There is absolutely no way I'm going to admit that the first time I was left alone and in charge I immediately lost our dog. My parents must never know about this.

"Seriously?" asks Cynthia.

"Yeah. Up and down the road and, oh, maybe out Carter Lane a little way." (Picasso and I sometimes take walks along Carter Lane, so he's familiar with the road, and he likes it because once he found part of a hamburger under a laurel bush.)

"Really? Because I'm allowed to drive into town."

"No, here is good."

So Cynthia starts speeding along our road, and I say, "Could you please slow down?"

"You don't get carsick, do you?"

I don't, but I reply, "Yeah," and look all sheepish.

Cynthia slows down, and I open my window and peer carefully at the ditch that runs along the road. I try to see into the woods too. I really want to call, "Picasso! Picasso!" but of course that would give things away.

After we've gone about a mile and a half, I say, "Okay, now could you turn around, please?"

"Here?" (We're in the middle of nowhere, but I don't think Picasso could have gotten this far already—unless he's been dognapped.) "There isn't anywhere to turn around," Cynthia points out.

Something springs to mind. All I know about driving is the stuff my mother shouts at other drivers when she gets frustrated behind the wheel. Things like "Use your signal. Your signal! You have a signal, don't you? Or am I just supposed to guess which way you're going to turn?" And "Go ahead, take up both lanes. It's fine with me. The road was made for you and you alone. Don't worry about anyone in any of the other cars." Also once I heard her shout, "Are you kidding me? You're going to make a K-turn here, in the middle of the road? Well, go ahead, take your time. No one else is in any rush. It's all about you."

"Did you learn how to make a K-turn?" I ask Cynthia now.

Cynthia brightens. "Oh! Yeah! I did. My dad says I do them really well."

"Could you show me?" I ask, trying to appear fascinated and scan the woods for Picasso at the same time.

Cynthia wrenches the wheel around, and pretty soon we're heading back the way we came and I'm checking the ditches on the other side of the road, which, thankfully, are free of dog bodies. Eventually I see the turnoff for Carter Lane, so I say, "Hey, could you demonstrate a left-hand turn? You could turn there, onto Carter."

"Sure!"

More cruising along, more searching for Picasso, more pretending to be impressed with Cynthia's driving ability, and eventually the flawless execution of another K-turn.

"Wow," I say, shaking my head. "I hope someday I'll be as good a driver as you." I gaze meaningfully at Cynthia until my eyes are drawn to a flash of tan—a moving flash of tan—through the trees a little ahead of us. I stare hard and realize that the lean haunches belong to a deer, which glances at me before crashing out of sight.

"Thank you," Cynthia replies.

She gives me a grateful smile, and I feel like a horrible person. Then I think about Picasso and feel even worse.

"You're welcome," I say anyway. "Well, you probably want to get back home. Thanks for the demonstration."

Cynthia expertly parks the Prius in the Wilsons' garage, and I lope across the road and up my driveway. I have absolutely no idea what to do next.

I fix myself some lunch. Then I sit on the front porch for a while. I remember the time Picasso poked his head through the railings to get a better view of a Pop-Tart that Anthony had accidentally dropped over the side and how he barked and sniffed and

barked some more before realizing that he couldn't pull his head back out.

"Dad! Picasso's stuck!" I had yelled into the house.

"Why am I not surprised?" replied my father, appearing at the screen door and surveying the situation.

Dad had to get his saw and remove part of one of the railings in order to free Picasso, and he wasn't happy about it.

The railing has never been repaired. I kick my foot through the space.

"Picasso!" I shout, but without any conviction.

The phone rings, and I nearly fall down the porch steps—that's how nervous I am now. I tear inside. Maybe someone has found Picasso. I don't even care if it's Cynthia Wilson and I have to confess the real purpose of the driving demonstration.

I snatch up the phone without looking at the Caller ID display. "Hello? Hello?"

"Hi, honey," says my mother's voice. "Just checking in. Everything all right?"

"Well," I say, and luckily I don't get any further before I hear a lot of static and some whooshing and crackling noises.

"Uh-oh," says Mom. "I think I'm breaking up." (*Whooooosh.*) "I'm not" (*crackle, crackle*) "be using my cell phone." (*Creeeak, crackle, crackle.*) "So we'll see you—"

The line goes dead.

"When? You'll see me when?" I cry. I shake the phone as if that will restore our connection. I'm not even sure where Mom was calling from. For all I know, they're on their way home. I imagine Dad turning onto our road two miles from here where it intersects with the highway and then screeching to a halt as Picasso saunters out of the woods.

I return to the porch, where I look toward the road and yell, "Picasso! You'd better come back right now, or you will be in very, very big trouble. And I mean it!"

Of course nothing happens. I stomp around to the backyard, stand in the middle of it, and am about to yell Picasso's name in a crabby and annoyed manner, when suddenly I remember last winter when I had the flu and Picasso spent nearly two weeks sleeping at my side. While I coughed and sneezed and burned up with fever and shivered with chills, Picasso lay peacefully on my bed. He didn't care when I tossed back the covers and started sweating, and then hugged him to me five minutes later when I was cold. He did avoid the mound of tissues that piled up when I was too weak to aim for the wastebasket, but he didn't seem to care that I had bad dreams (the kind that make you shout yourself awake) or that I smelled (a combination of sweat, cough medicine, and nose spray) or that I also had bad breath. He lay with his head on my knee and snored, day and night, until I was well.

"Picasso, where are you?" I say. I don't even bother to shout.

Now how long has he been missing? I look at my watch. Close to three hours.

This is very, very bad.

I plop down in the grass, which is starting to turn brown. It's only July third, but the last few weeks have been hot, not to mention entirely free of rain, and my parents are worrying about a drought and whether our well will go dry. I pull a fat blade of brown grass off of its stem, arrange it between my thumbs, and blow. The sound it makes is pathetic.

I'm beginning to think that I am pathetic too when something drifts to me on a little breeze and I lift my nose in the air and sniff just the way Picasso does when someone opens a package of hot dogs.

Then I realize that I actually do smell hot dogs, or something cooking on a barbecue—hot dogs, hamburgers, steak, vegetables. It's hard to tell. But this is when it dawns on me that this is Fourth of July weekend. As if to drive the point home, just as I'm getting to my feet, I hear a *pop, pop, pop* in the distance. Fireworks. I ignore the fireworks, though, and concentrate on the smell. Someone is having a cookout nearby. And if I can smell the food, then Picasso can certainly smell it (if he's still nearby). All at once, I know what I must do. I have to figure out who's having the barbecue, and then I have to crash it.

For the second time that day, I dash through our yard and down to the road. When I reach the end of our driveway, I stand there and pretend I'm Picasso. I sniff the air again. Left or right? I can't tell. Picasso would be able to follow an odor the way I follow a trail through the woods, but I have no idea which way to go. Eventually I turn right, since we have more neighbors in that direction.

I walk about half a mile, the smell goes away, and I don't hear or see anything that would indicate a party, so I turn around, walk back, pass my driveway, and continue in the other direction until I notice a mailbox with a dinky red balloon tied to it. The balloon is so small that I'm not surprised I didn't see it when I was driving around with Cynthia. I pause and listen. I hear laughter. I hear voices. I hear something clinking. At the end of the long driveway I see cars. And I definitely smell hot dogs.

This is it. I have outwitted Picasso. (Of course, he isn't very bright.)

I turn up the driveway and tiptoe along the edge of it toward a small white house with another dinky red balloon, this one fastened to a lamppost by the front door. I picture myself returning home with Picasso and making a beeline for the refrigerator, where I will add hot dogs to our shopping list. As long as we always have hot dogs in the freezer, I think, I will never be in this situation again. The only thing I'll have to do the next time he disappears is heat up a hot dog and wave it around in the yard.

I stand at the top of the driveway and try to figure out how, exactly, I will lure Picasso back to our house, considering that I haven't brought his leash with me. (Maybe *I'm* not too bright.) I could ask someone to give me a hot dog, I think, and I could feed him little bits of it as we walk home.

I tiptoe on around to the backyard, where the party is in full swing. So many thoughts about getting Picasso home are whirling around in my head that at least a full minute goes by before I realize that Picasso is no-where in sight. He's not begging from any of the guests who are sitting in lawn chairs with plates of food in their laps; he's not under a table guiltily eating a stolen hot dog; he's not even waiting by the grill.

I skirt the yard, trying to stay out of view. I look and look and look.

The number of dogs at the party is zero.

I wonder if anyone would notice if I sud-denly yelled, "Picasso!" but I really don't see the point.

He isn't here.

I walk back to the road and amble along toward my house. I don't even bother to hurry. Why should I? Picasso has been missing for hours, and Mom and Dad and Anthony will probably be home any minute.

I have blown the biggest opportunity of my entire twelve-year-old life.

I near my driveway. Across the road, I see Cynthia hosing down the Prius in the Wilsons' driveway. I wave sadly to her, and she gives me a little wave back. She must think I spend all day roaming aimlessly around our neighborhood.

Finally I turn right and walk up my own driveway. I watch my feet and notice that I have a hole in the toe of my left sneaker. I need new shoes. I'll probably have to buy them myself. After today, my parents will never give me another nickel.

I reach the top of the driveway, eyes still downcast, and this is when I trip over Picasso. He's sitting under the basketball net, tongue hanging out, giving me a doggie grin.

Picasso lets out a yip, and I let out a scream. "Picasso!"

He gets to his feet. I crouch down and

check him over thoroughly. He looks just fine.

"Where on earth were you?" I cry. I fling my arms around him and hug him, thinking how nice it is that he's hugging me back. Then I realize that Picasso isn't hugging me, he's sniffing me. I smell like barbecue.

Picasso gazes into my eyes and produces an award-winning belch.

I take him inside and direct him to his water bowl. He has a long, sloppy drink. Then I snap his leash onto his collar and lead him to the front porch. We're sitting there in a relaxed fashion when a car turns into our driveway. Mom and Dad and Anthony pile out, Anthony waving his arm around, showing off his cast like he has just had a great adventure.

"Hi, honey!" calls my mother. "How was your day?"

"Fine," I say, getting to my feet.

Picasso stands up, too, and sticks his head through the porch railings. He tries to back up and can't.

"Picasso just got stuck again," I announce.

My father closes his eyes briefly, then opens them and looks at the place where he has already removed one railing. "Why couldn't he have put his head there?" he asks, and huffs inside to find his tools.

The God of the Pond

by Valerie Hobbs

illustrated by Olga and Aleksey Ivanov

Bertha

What Emmy wanted more than anything, more than new ice skates, more than a job for her father, even more than to be tall, was to do a full flip jump. Just one perfect flip jump. Maybe even a not-so-perfect flip jump. Just as long as it was the real thing. As long as she leapt and turned in the air, landed on a back outside edge, and at least one person was there to see her do it.

Bobby. Bobby would be the perfect person. If she closed her eyes, she could see him standing right there at the edge of the pond, with his hands stuffed in his pockets, his bright blue eyes, and his cheeks pink from the cold. Emmy would leap, turn, and come down perfectly onto the ice, and Bobby would cheer and punch the air. "Yeah!"

Walking home, he might just take her hand. Perfect!

But life wasn't perfect, and Emmy knew it. She wasn't a baby. She was eleven, almost twelve. It was an actual fact that you didn't always get what you wanted, even if you asked God for it.

How many times had she prayed for new skates? A hundred?

Or you got what you asked for, but not exactly. Like praying for a dog and getting Bertha. Emmy had begged her parents for a dog for so long that she had almost given up. Then one day, one plain old, unsurprising day, her father had come home with a surprise.

Sweet, shy Bertha, whose time at the shelter had almost run out. Bertha, with her sad eyes and long, wet doggie kisses. Bertha, who wriggled all over with love.

Bertha, the chicken killer. Bertha, the dog no fence could keep in.

If life were perfect, Bobby would have the perfect grandfather, not Old Man Brennan. Mean Old Man Brennan with his hundreds of chickens.

Just this morning, she had opened the front door and there he had been.

"This your mutt?" he'd said.

Emmy had nodded.

Old Man Brennan had handed her the rope he'd tied to Bertha's collar.

"He got another one of my chickens," he'd said. "And if I find him after my chickens again, he's a dead dog." His words had come out in great white puffs.

Under his left arm, pointed down, was a gun with two long barrels.

"She," said Emmy. Bertha had pushed her

wet nose into Emmy's hand. Her skinny tail slapped against Emmy's legs.

Mr. Brennan's red face had creased up in a frown. "Are you sassing me, young lady?"

"No, sir."

"You tell your folks what I said. One more chicken, no more dog."

"Yes, sir," said Emmy.

Old Man Brennan had turned away, and Emmy quietly closed the door.

Her heart was beating as hard as Bertha's tail.

She shook her finger at Bertha. "You're a bad girl, Bertha," she'd said.

Bertha had done her little yip-yip. What's wrong? What's all the fuss about?

But Bertha knew. She had been grounded for a month, ever since she'd come home covered with feathers.

"No chickens. Do you understand?" Emmy had said.

Bertha had cocked her head, as if trying her best to do what Emmy said: understand.

"Did you hear me? NO CHICKENS."

Bertha had pawed Emmy's foot and wriggled her skinny backside. She smiled like no dog Emmy had ever seen. Pet me, pet me. I'm your best friend.

Emmy's mother had come out of the bathroom smelling like lemon, her favorite shower gel. "Who was that?"

Emmy's pulses were all on alarm. "Just the paper guy." She had not been able to look her mother in the eye, so she'd patted Bertha instead.

"Don't let Bertha out," said her mother.

"I didn't do it!" said Emmy. "It was Dad!"

Emmy had put on her down jacket, hat, and gloves, and grabbed up her ice skates. "I'm going skating," she said. "Bertha's coming with me."

"Be careful," her mother said, which was what she always said, even in the dead of winter when the ice was rock hard.

Bertha had submitted to the muzzle and

the leash, her eyes dark and tragic. *Trust me*, her eyes said, even though she couldn't be trusted and probably knew it.

Bertha had pulled Emmy up the road that had been cleared the week before. Little mounds of crunchy, sooty snow lay along the side. It had been a long, cold winter with plenty of good days for skating, and Emmy had finally learned to do a half flip. Now, at winter's end, she was working on the full. If she did just one, she'd be the only kid besides Sara Stewart to do that trick. Sara actually did a triple once, but she was sixteen, a whole five years older than Emmy.

Emmy stood at the top of the hill, looking down at Brennan's Pond.

The boys had been busy with their brooms, and the ice was half cleared.

No Bobby.

Emmy's heart fell. She tried to tell herself that the day wasn't ruined, but it was. It had started out ruined.

Emmy tied Bertha's leash to a tree and took off her muzzle. Bertha whined and slapped her tail against the tree. Then she turned three times and plopped down on a patch of dirt to sulk.

Every inch of ice was scarred over with skate marks. Emmy stepped onto "the girls' side" and glided off. Turning, she looked back across the ice at Bertha, who was on her feet again.

Sara Stewart and a couple of her friends were coming down from the road, their skates slung around their necks. They all wore tights that looked brand-new and short skirts.

Emmy's tights had a hole in the knee from when she had taken a particularly bad fall, but her skirt almost hid it. She was never going to grow. All her life she would be four feet six inches, a shrimp.

Turning lazy circles, Emmy watched Sara

step onto the ice in her snow boots and jump a few times, then go a little farther out and do the same thing. She shook her head and went back to her friends. Emmy heard them shout, "The ice is no good!" But the boys waved them off and kept skating.

Emmy began skating back. She listened, as she hadn't earlier, for the ominous sound of ice breaking up. But the boys were still skating, slamming the puck and each other as if nothing in the world mattered but making a goal. She skated back to shore.

Bertha was busy strangling herself. She had run round and round the tree until her leash was wound tight. Emmy had a hard time convincing her that she had to go back the other way, and an even harder time trying to get her muzzle back on. Why the muzzle when poor old Bertha was on her leash? Emmy's mother was just being extra cautious, as usual.

Her father never was. He knew better than to let Bertha out without her muzzle, but he did it anyway. "What's a chicken or two?" he'd said the first time Bertha came home with feathers.

But her father had not seen Old Man Brennan standing on the porch this morning with a shotgun.

She was going to have to tell her parents.

But she couldn't. If she did, her mother would say it was "time." Time to find Bertha a good home somewhere else, a place where there were no chickens.

But she had to. If she didn't, her father would let Bertha out tomorrow, and Old Man Brennan would shoot her. Which was worse than Bertha living somewhere else, or even the shelter. Worse than anything Emmy could imagine.

All afternoon, as Emmy worked on an art project and Bertha paced back and forth behind the door, she thought about how to tell her parents.

At dinner, she couldn't eat. Every bite felt like a hockey puck going down her throat.

At last, she forced herself to say, "Um, this morning?"

Bertha gave a little groan, as if she knew what was coming.

Her mother smiled encouragingly. "Yes?"

Her father looked up from his potatoes.

"I meant to tell you this morning, only—"

Her mother's eyebrows came together. "Only what?"

"Well . . . the snow and all . . . and it is Saturday. . . ."

Which had nothing to do with anything.

Her mother tilted her head and did her little mother frown. "And?"

"Mom. Dad. Bertha killed another chicken."

"No!" said her mother.

"Huh," said her father, setting his fork down.

"Mr. Brennan brought her home on a rope, and he had this gun and—"

"What?" Her mother stood. Pushing back her chair, she stepped on Bertha's paw. Bertha yelped like she'd been shot. "I will not have guns in my house. What was that man thinking of! Guns around children!"

"Calm down, Alice," Emmy's father said.

"He wasn't actually in the house," said Emmy. "He was on the porch the whole time."

Her mother was wringing the life out of a dish towel. "As if that makes one bit of difference!" She grimaced and made up her mind. "It's time for Bertha to go," she said.

"No!" cried Emmy.

Her mother brushed the hair back from Emmy's face. "I'm sorry, honey."

Emmy jumped up and ran to her room. Slamming the door, she threw herself on her bed and cried until she made herself sick. It wasn't Bertha's fault. She loved to chase chickens the way Emmy loved to skate. It was in her blood.

It was all her father's fault. Why couldn't he just remember to muzzle Bertha?

Was it the war? The war in Iraq was the reason for everything else: why he couldn't sleep or keep a job, why he smoked, why his mind drifted off in the middle of a conversation.

So maybe it wasn't his fault. It was the war's fault. Or the president's fault. But Bertha could die, no matter whose fault it was.

Mr. Brennan's fault. He was the one with the stupid chickens. And the gun.

She had to help her father remember. When her stomach finally settled, she got up and dug out her felt pens. On two big pieces of paper, in giant red letters, she wrote REMEMBER THE MUZZLE.

Beneath the words, she drew Bertha with big, sad eyes. The first Bertha looked like a raccoon; the second one was a little better. She taped the signs next to the front and back doors, where her father couldn't miss seeing them. Before turning in, she set her alarm clock. At five A.M., she would get up, muzzle Bertha, and let her out. That would be her job from now on.

She would tell her father about the new plan, but he'd probably just forget.

She awoke to the sound of rain—4:40. She turned off her alarm and yawned. She closed her eyes. In five minutes she would get up and let Bertha out.

When she awoke again, the rain had stopped—6:10.

Bertha! She leapt out of bed and raced to the living room.

There was Bertha, asleep on her blanket. Her father was standing at the window, looking out, steam rising from his World's Greatest Dad coffee mug. According to him, a day could not begin without coffee.

"Did you let Bertha out, Daddy?"

"Hmmmm?"

"Bertha. Does she need to go out?"

Her father turned and smiled, as if he'd just woken up. "Good morning, cookie. You're up early."

Emmy joined him at the window. "It's stopped raining. Good."

"That's the end of the skating for this year," he said. He put his arm around Emmy, giving her a sideways squeeze.

Her heart tumbled downhill. One more day on the ice, and she'd have her flip jump. She just knew it.

They ate their Cheerios together. Then her father went out to his garage workshop, and she went outside. It was cold. Cold enough.

Well, maybe not cold enough. But cold. The sky was a frozen gray. Her breath came out white. A little voice inside told her that this would be her last chance, that she had to hurry.

She went back inside, dressed, and gathered up her skates. It was Sunday, and her mother was sleeping in.

Bertha was sleeping in, too. Was she sick? Emmy felt her nose. Bertha opened one eye, banged her tail against the wall, and went back to sleep. Emmy crept out the door.

The sun was just coming up, a soft orange smudge behind the leafless trees. Emmy hurried up the wet road. The sooner she got to the pond, the better. The air would warm up as the day went on, and the ice would begin to melt.

But for now, there was time. There had to be. Just one quick flip. One perfect, even not-so-perfect flip.

Rainwater glazed the pond. It had never looked so beautiful or so still, and Emmy had it all to herself. Stepping out onto the ice, she was Emily Hughes at Nationals, ready for her free skate. She glided off. Not a sound but the scritch and scratch of her blades. She would skate to the other side of the pond and back. By then, she would be warmed up. By then, Bobby might be coming down the hill and she would do her first ever flip jump.

On the pond's far end, water was seeping up through the ice. Water?

Emmy stopped. Her breath came short. She turned and began skating back fast to where the ice was safe.

She felt it before she knew exactly what was happening, a sickening lurch in the pit of her stomach as the ice cracked and began to give. Then, ever so slowly, as if it had all the time in the world, the black water rose up through the sinking floor and took her down.

Under the freezing, dark water Emmy thrashed in all directions, through her own bubbles, not knowing which way was up and out. Branches underwater, like withered arms, snagged her sleeve. But then her skates touched on something, just the tips of their blades, and she gave one huge push upward.

She broke through the surface, gasping, screaming. "Help! Help, somebody!"

Her jaw ached, her teeth began to chatter like a windup toy. She clung to a shelf of ice, afraid to look down. All that black water. Every prayer she ever knew rose to her lips.

If she weren't so cold, she could believe she was dreaming. She could wake herself out of this.

How had she let herself believe that a flip jump was worth more than her life?

"Help! Somebody, help!"

From the other side of the pond came a

familiar bark, and Bertha came racing across the ice, a brown blur, slipping and sliding, falling and getting back up, heading straight for Emmy.

"No, Bertha! Go back! You'll fall through!" But Bertha was determined. As the ice cracked around them, Bertha tugged on Emmy's sleeve with all thirty pounds of her might. She couldn't budge Emmy, who had begun to wail.

"Get help, Bertha," she begged. Bertha whined and pulled.

Someone was coming down the hill, a moving black shadow.

"Help!" cried Emmy through frozen lips. Her voice cracked. She was turning to ice. "Help me!"

Old Man Brennan stopped perfectly still at the edge of the pond, a black cutout silhouette stuck onto white paper. He looked down then, as if he'd lost something. Then he turned and went back up the way he had come. Bertha took off after him. Catching

up, she ran circles around his legs, barking and barking.

Emmy tried again to hoist herself out, but the ice broke under her weight. She thrashed in the water until she could grab on again.

Was this the way it happened? Was this the way she would die? Would Old Man Brennan let her freeze to death because of a couple of chickens?

Then she saw him coming back, trudging down the hill with his shotgun. Where was Bertha? Had he shot her? Was he going to shoot Emmy, too?

Was he crazy?

But there was Bertha, racing down the hill, past Old Man Brennan and onto the ice. She grabbed onto Emmy's sleeve again and, lowering her haunches, began to pull.

Old Man Brennan made his way toward them, slowly, carefully, testing each step, his face hidden in the collar of his jacket. A loose snap on his huge black boots rattled.

Kneeling, he began crawling on his hands and knees across the ice. He pushed the big barrel of the gun toward her. His eyes, shadowed under the brim of his hat, looked almost afraid. When the pipe—not a shotgun!—reached her, Emmy grabbed on like a fish biting bait.

Slowly, carefully, Old Man Brennan pulled Emmy out and over the ice. Then she was sitting on her bottom, curled up with her arms around her soaked tights and wailing like a wet baby while Bertha licked her face.

"Careful, now," said Old Man Brennan, helping Emmy to her feet. With his hands on her shoulders, he guided her back over the ice.

When Bertha saw that Emmy was safe, she took off, skidding and slipping across the ice and into the woods.

Old Man Brennan wrapped his jacket around Emmy and lifted her into his arms. "We've got to get you home," he said.

"Bertha's gone after your chickens," Emmy mumbled through Popsicle lips.

It was only fair to tell him.

"You almost lost your life, young lady," he said.

By the end of February, the ice was melting fast, and by March, it was gone. Emmy went to the pond to sit and think, no matter the season. She turned twelve in March, and there was so much to think about when you were twelve. She had grown almost an inch. There was hope. Sometimes she was by herself, and sometimes Bobby came down the hill and sat beside her on the log. They talked about school, their teachers, friends and family, the usual things.

They both missed skating and talked about his dreams of being on the Rangers and hers of being in the Olympics. Emmy hadn't done a flip jump after all, but she wasn't giving up hope. Some things took time, and flips were one of those things.

"How come your grandfather doesn't come down to the pond anymore?" said Emmy on one long and lazy afternoon, happy that she and Bobby had the pond to themselves.

"No ice," said Bobby. When he looked

over at her, Emmy saw a change in him. It was as if he'd thought of something he didn't like to remember. "When he was twelve, his little sister fell through the ice and drowned."

A chill ran through Emmy. "She drowned right here? In this pond?"

"Right here," he said. They both looked out at the greenish-black water as if they could see it happening. "My grandpa tried to pull her out, but he couldn't."

"So he watches you?"

"Sometimes he watches even when I'm not there. He's like the god of the pond."

Bertha lay with her muzzled snout on the log, right between them, as if she'd been sent by Emmy's mother to keep them apart.

"Your grandpa thinks I'm an idiot, right?"

"He says you're too brave for your own good. But I can tell that he likes you." Bobby patted Bertha, who was clearly in love with him. "At least Bertha hasn't killed any more chickens."

At the mention of her name, Bertha's tail thumped the ground.

"I put a sign on my dad's Mr. Coffee machine," said Emmy. "Now he never forgets."

By the middle of May, Brennan's Pond was warm enough to wade in, but the bottom was thick with mud that sucked you down, and nobody ever swam in it. There were cattails all along one side, leaves on the trees, birds that settled in the branches at dusk and gossiped about their day, frogs that blinked their big wise eyes. By August, Bobby and Emmy were holding hands, unless Bertha was there to nudge them apart.

Bertha kept catching chickens, but only in her dreams. Emmy could tell by her

scrambling feet and the smile on her face as she slept.

On December 21, the official start of winter, Emmy did a full, only-a-little-crooked, almost-perfect flip jump, and Bertha and Bobby and the whole hockey crew were there to see it happen.

Trail Magic

by Margarita Engle

illustrated by Olga and Aleksey Ivanov

Gabe

In my other life there were pit bulls.
The puppies weren't born vicious,
but Mom taught them how to bite,
turning meanness into money,
until she got caught.

Now I live in a high mountain cabin
with my brave forest ranger uncle,

and I only see Mom on visiting days,
when the heavy gate of a lowland prison
slides shut behind me, making me feel small
and trapped.

I'm not small—I'm almost twelve, the
    tallest boy
in my tiny, three-room mountain school.
Living in the forest feels like time travel.
Tío reminds me of heroes in ancient stories,
fearless people who knew how to fly,
talk to animals, and face any danger
without sinking into the huge
loneliness
of nightmares.

Tío takes me bird-watching and stargazing
in places without any traffic or lights.
He shows me how to survive lightning
    storms
and where to find roots and berries.
He patrols the Pacific Crest Trail,
where hikers from all over the world

walk thousands of miles, just to find
peace and quiet, luxuries I never imagined
in my old life of rage and pain.
Peace and quiet feel like a mysterious
sort of medicine.

Tío promises that someday I'll feel brave,
but I swear it isn't true.
I'm a coward.
I'm even scared of falling asleep.
I'm scared of dreams.

When my uncle is out making his rounds,
I'm alone in the cabin with his friendly
search-and-rescue dog, a shelter mutt
with the glow of a golden retriever,
the genius of a border collie,
and the name of a boy: Gabe.
Tío thinks dogs deserve human names
to remind us that they're alive,
with real feelings, like joy and pain.

Tío and Gabe and I are a team.
We serve hamburgers and wild berry pies

to backpackers who visit our cabin.
The hikers come from places like Iceland,
    Japan,
and Australia, talking with exotic accents
as they tell stories about other mountains
they've hiked—the Andes, the Alps, the
    Himalayas.
Listening to their adventures,
I imagine the size of the world.
No wonder I feel small.

Backpackers headed all the way from
    Canada
to Mexico are called thru-hikers.
They leave their everyday lives behind,
choosing trail names like Wolf, Wild Man,
Explorer, or Skywalker.
I imagine those trail names must help
the hikers feel free and heroic,
but when they ask me what trail name
I'd choose if I was old enough to walk
all over the world, I can't even begin
to imagine being that brave.

Strangely, I'm not afraid of dogs.
You'd think I would be, after all the fights
I've seen, all the growling I've heard.

Thru-hikers call my uncle a trail angel,
meaning a stranger who spreads trail magic,
which is any unexpected act of kindness,
like sharing food or finding the lost.
The Pacific Crest Trail passes through places
with names like Desolation, where
    exhausted hikers
sometimes lose their way.

That's when Gabe's amazing nose
goes into action, sniffing like crazy,
twitching so hard I can hear the air
    popping
in and out of his nostrils.

Dogs think work and fun
are exactly the same thing.
Gabe gets bouncy and excited,
but he's serious too, as if he understands

that search and rescue is a life-or-death
    game
of hide-and-seek.

Life-or-death games are all I knew
back in my old life, when I had to take care
of dogs that could have killed me.

Mountain chores are safe and easy.
All I have to do is weed the vegetable
    garden,
stack firewood, chop fruit for pies, and hide
way out in the forest, so Gabe can practice
finding a lost person.

When a wilderness area dog like Gabe is
    searching,
he runs back and forth in a big zigzag
    pattern,
sniffing the air until he finds my scent.
Then he turns and races back to alert Tío,
who praises him and tosses a squeaky toy.
Gabe's reward for winning at hide-and-seek

is playing fetch, only he can't work alone.
He needs guidance.
Without Tío's instructions,
Gabe would be as mixed up and confused
as a boy raised by pit bulls.
On the other hand, once Gabe understands
what he's supposed to do,
he moves like a shooting star,
a fiery streak of pure energy!

Once the life-or-death game
of hide-and-seek is finally over,
it's time to rest.

At night in the cabin, Gabe curls up
beside me, and I listen to his breath.
The unworried rhythm is like music,
helping me relax and forget to be scared
of memory-dreams that make the past
still seem real.

When Gabe dreams, his eyelids flicker,
and I imagine that I can see his thoughts.

Before the shelter, he must have been lonely,
just a puppy lost on a mountain road,
hoping to be found and rescued.
Now he finds and rescues lost people.
Some things in life actually do make sense.
So why can't I ever imagine my mom's
    thoughts?
The dogfights were ugly and noisy.
I didn't know how to make the meanness
    stop.
Drunk men came to bet money—scary men,
betting on scary dogs, but the next morning,
I had to feed those dogs and patch their
    wounds.
I took them for long, tail-wagging walks,
just like any other boy who had never
heard snarls or touched scars.

Gabe wakes me up out of the memories.
We stop dreaming, we get up, move around,
set ourselves free of the past.
The weather is clear and warm.
The forest is alive with clean smells,

pine, incense cedar, and wildness.
It's Saturday, no school, and Tío is already
out in the woods, working weekends
because it's just past summer, the busy
     season,
when even the most remote campgrounds
are crowded.

I take Gabe out for a run, feed him,
and heat up some leftover pie for myself.
There's no Internet or cell phone
     reception
up here, but I have a two-way radio
for checking in to let my uncle know I'm
     fine.
The problem is, today he's patrolling
on such a remote peak that even my radio
won't reach him.

I'm not fine.
Memory-dreams have a way of leaving
a bitter aftertaste, like strong medicine.
To get away from the creeping sadness,
I take my radio out to the garden,

where I can pretend Tío is close.
I pretend the thorny weeds
are alien invaders and I'm a superhero,
chasing them back to their own planet.

Gabe tries to help, but he digs up
Tío's prize heirloom tomato plants,
along with the giant alpine dandelions.
So I stop hoeing and just blow a bunch
of dandelion fluff up into the sky.
It makes me feel babyish with hope,
but I have to admit I love to watch
all those wispy wishes twirl and rise.

A call comes in on the radio,
but it's not my uncle—it's a search,
a real search, not just practice.
There's a lost child, a little boy
who wandered away from a campsite.
What were the grown-ups doing?
How could they fail to pay attention?
Gabe stares up at me with eager wolf eyes.
He recognizes the radio's automated voice
calling for volunteers to join the search.

He knows words like *deploy* and *urgent*.
Gabe is just as much of a natural-born trail
    angel
as my uncle—I'm the only one who doesn't
    know
how to help.

Vermilion, that's where the radio tells
searchers to meet and be deployed,
sent out to various portions of the area
where the lost boy might be found.
Vermilion isn't too far. I could make it
on the ATV, a super-cool all-terrain vehicle
that looks like a golf cart and drives
like a motorbike.

I'm not supposed to take the ATV
past the driveway, but I do know how,
and this is an emergency, hide-and-seek,
life or death.

Tío would disapprove.
Or would he?

Isn't he the one who always
insists that I can be brave?
I could do it, with Gabe's help
I could find that little lost kid.
I'd be a hero.
I'd be a trail angel,
filled with magic.

Gabe's eyes urge me to go, go, go!
He sits beside me on the ATV while I talk,
reminding him that we can't really search
because I don't have the CPR training
or any of the dog-handling skills Tío has
      studied
and mastered, day after day, year after year.
We'll just watch.
We'll just be heroic observers.
We start gliding, slowly at first, then faster,
until we're on a narrow dirt road,
and then we've reached Vermilion,
a lively rest stop where two trails meet
and all the thru-hikers have to take a ferry
across Edison Lake.

There are dozens of people milling around,
some on horseback, leading pack mules
and llamas loaded with bundles.
I feel like I've landed in a faraway country
where animals are still a huge part
of daily life.

Gabe is crazy with excitement.
I hold on to his leash, so we can hang out
near a table where sheriffs are giving
instructions to all sorts of search-and-rescue
volunteers—mounted posses, dog teams,
ATV teams, and plenty of ground
    pounders,
people on foot who just walk around
trying to spot footprints in meadow grass
or pine needles, or on the mud
of slippery creek banks.

When Gabe bumps my leg with his nose,
I'm sure I can hear his thoughts.
Go, go, go, find, find, find!
But he isn't wearing his orange vest

with SEARCH DOG written on the sides,
and I'm not carrying a GPS for mapping
the area of interest, a circle that grows wider
and wider as minutes pass.
What if the little boy is still wandering
farther and farther, getting more and more
lonely and lost?

I try calling my uncle on the radio,
just in case he might be close enough.
Nothing.
Why did Tío choose this crazy day
to leave me alone without contact,
without any way to communicate
and ask him for help?
I recognize the dogs and handlers,
but they're too busy to notice me.
The handlers are volunteers, but they wear
official-looking uniforms, and they carry
heavy backpacks filled with emergency gear,
in case the search goes on overnight.
They have first aid supplies and space
    blankets,

food, water, matches. . . .
All I have is my uncle's dog.
If I found a lost, scared little boy,
I wouldn't be much use.
I'd be helpless,
not heroic.

Thru-hikers weave in and out of the crowd
of searchers, some talking English,
others chattering in their own languages.
There's a chaplain in a sheriff's uniform,
praying with people who must be the lost
    boy's
desperate, anxious, guilty family.
I feel like I've gone traveling to some
    faraway,
scary planet, even though I'm just a few
    miles
from the safe, quiet cabin.

Next thing I know, I really have gone away.
I don't know if it's courage or foolishness.
All I know is I want to help, I have to try.

Gabe whines beside me on the seat of the
    ATV
as I race it out onto a little side trail
that none of the searchers have reached yet.
Pretty soon, we've left the crowd behind.
We're in unfamiliar country, seeing plenty
of tracks, but none of them are human.

I park in a meadow, get off, and turn Gabe
    loose.
He goes into his zigzag search pattern,
expecting me to guide him
to the right areas, but all I can do is hope.
I have no idea where to search.
I don't know the right commands.
I can't read Gabe's movements.
It's like I'm illiterate in the mysterious
language of dogs.

We pass the musky scent of a bear den.
There are piles of colorful bear scat,
red poop next to Manzanita bushes,
blue piles near ripe elderberries.

I don't know what I was thinking.
This isn't a dog movie where the kid
turns into a hero because his puppy
knows the way.

Gabe is already frustrated.
He wants me to tell him what to do.
He knows his job, but I don't know mine.
So I get on the radio and try to call Tío.
That's when I find out the battery has died.
Now I'm scared beyond belief.
So is Gabe.
He smells my fear and makes it his own.
We climb back onto the ATV, but as soon
as I try to spin a U-turn and head home,
we flip over, and even though we're both
alive, we're bruised and scratched,
and the ATV is stuck upside down
in soft sand.
I feel as panicky
as I used to when the pit bulls
were fighting to entertain
human bullies.

What have I done?
How could I be so selfish?
Gabe is worried and whiny,
and his fear is my fault.
Worst of all, we aren't any use
when it comes to my far-fetched
daydream of becoming heroic
by helping
that lost little kid.

We have to walk now.
It's farther than I thought.
Gabe is thirsty, so we find a stream,
but once we've branched away from our trail,
I can't find my way back.
Gabe's sense of smell could lead us,
but I don't know how to tell him
what we need.
I make up my mind
to take dog training classes,
and pay more attention
to my surroundings,
and visit Mom more often,

now that I know
what it feels like
to do something dumb
and mess up.

If you get lost in the woods,
you're supposed to stay in one place
and wait to be found, but most people
just slide into a deeper and deeper panic,
and that's how I feel now, crazy with fear,
even though fear makes everything
worse, a lot worse. . . .

Gabe is hungry.
He chases a dragonfly, but he can't catch it,
and even though I know he loves berries,
I'm afraid to go near bear-scented bushes,
so we just nibble a few round, bitter leaves
of miner's lettuce, both of us wishing
for Tío's burgers and pie.

A helicopter whirs far overhead,
but I don't have a signal mirror,
and I know they're looking

for the other lost boy.
No one knows that I'm gone yet.
No one's searching for me.

Later, after I've run in circles
and confused Gabe, the cloudy truth
starts to get clear.

We'll be out overnight.
It's already twilight.
If I had a trash bag, I could fill it
with pine needles to make a sleeping bag.
If I had a fish hook . . .
If I knew how to find my way
by following stars . . .
If I had common sense . . .

Gabe keeps one side of me warm.
Looking up, beyond windblown trees,
we watch the half moon, wondering
what we'll do if the weather turns stormy,
if lightning strikes, if Tío loses custody
because I made him seem
like an irresponsible foster parent. . . .

Gabe is the first one to hear the shriek.
It sounds like a cross between a huge bird
and an eerie ghost in an old horror movie.
I know what it is, because my uncle
has described it a million times.
A mountain lion.
Or La Llorona, a mythical woman
who screams because she can't
find her children.
Tío says you can't tell mountain lions
and the Weeping Woman apart
just by sound, you have to see tracks,
but there's no way I'm getting up
to follow eerie moonlit footprints.

What would I do if I actually spotted
a mountain lion, anyway?
Tío has told me, over and over:
stand tall, wave a branch, be enormous,
never crouch or run, don't look like prey.

Gabe is silent.
He's holding his breath.

He knows the sound of a predator.
Or a mythical being.
He probably smells whatever it is.
He could tell me which direction to go
if running away was an option.
We lie still.
We don't breathe.
I wonder if Gabe can hear my thoughts
the way I imagine that I can hear his.

Somehow, we survive until morning.
Then we walk over rocks, between shrubs,
and past purple bear scat, even though I
    know
we should stay still, be patient, wait. . . .
By now there must be two searches,
one for a boy too young to know better
and one for a big boy who got careless.
Tío must be going crazy.
I'll be grounded forever, if I even get to stay
and live with him until college, like we'd
    planned.
Forestry, that's what I was going to study

if I'd been smart enough to stay out of
   trouble.

Gabe is up and gone.
I try to follow, but he races so fast
that I trip and fall, then scramble back up,
wishing, wishing, GIANT wishing
that I'd followed the rules.
A weight knocks me down,
swipes my breath, closes my eyes,
and when I open them, all I can see
is the dusky gold of a mountain lion's coat.
But it's Gabe, slamming against me,
alerting me, letting me know he's won
the life-or-death hide-and-seek game.
I smile.
I walk calmly.

There he is, the little boy, sound asleep,
tucked way under a twisted, wind-stunted
scrap of splintered pine tree.
No one could have spotted him
from a helicopter.

Without Gabe, I would have walked
right past him and seen nothing.
Gabe's nose found him.
Now it's up to me to carry him
out into the open, yell, wave my shirt,
stay in one place, and wait to be found.

Orange vests.
Four-legged trail angels.
It happens just like it's supposed to.
Dogs find us, people rescue us,
the little boy's mom cries, thanks me,
and tells me she loves me,
while Tío hugs me and admits
that he's furious.

The next few days aren't easy,
but nobody sends me away.
The cabin is crowded with thru-hikers
from Belgium, France, and New Zealand,
everyone calling me Wizard.
The trail name sticks, and even though I
    know
I'm not really a trail magician yet,

at least I do have hope.
Maybe I'll make it to college after all,
study forestry, and find some way
to repay my uncle for his trust.

When Mom gets out of prison,
I plan to ask Tío to invite her
up to the cabin to meet Gabe.
Together, Gabe and I can help her
clear up a few cloudy truths
about brave dogs
and scared boys.

Things People Can't See

by Matt de la Peña

illustrated by Olga and Aleksey Ivanov

Peanut

The day after Chico lost his dog, Peanut, he was beaten in a fight at school.

At least the fight part was something he could've predicted. Chico was new at the private junior high on the hill. He was the scholarship kid who got bused in every morning from the wrong side of the freeway. The outsider whose old man worked the endless flower fields behind Home Depot.

"See all them poinsettias?" his dad had just told him in Spanish at parent-teacher night. He was motioning toward the dense row of Christmas-colored flowers circling the two-story, brick library.

Chico nodded as they walked the wide path that cut through the heart of his new school.

"Every single one of 'em, boy. I raised it up from a tiny little seed. Like a pea in the palm of your hand."

Chico nodded some more, but in truth he wasn't thinking of pea-sized seeds or greenhouse-grown poinsettias. Nah, he was too busy watching his new classmates watch him and his dad.

He was seeing, for the first time, how they saw him.

And he felt ashamed.

The Fight

Calling it a fight, actually, was a bit of a stretch. More like Chico acted a fool and got jumped.

He was walking across the field on his way to first period, minding his own, reminiscing about Peanut, when he spotted a pack of kids following him with their eyes.

"Hey!" one of them yelled.

Chico kept walking.

"New dude!" another voice called out.

Chico gritted his teeth.

He was in no mood. He'd just lost his dog, man. His closest friend in the world. And he was working on zero sleep. He'd spent half the previous night stalking the neighborhood, calling Peanut's name, whistling, peeking over backyard fences. The remaining hours were spent crying into his pillow like a punk little kid.

"That's rude, bro!" he heard another voice yell. "People are trying to talk to you!"

Chico slowed to a stop, imagining the

inside of these rich kids' heads. To them he was a fly in the lemonade. A smudge on the screen of a brand-new laptop. He was their gardener. Their cleaning lady. The smiling busboy who collected dirty plates at their fancy restaurants.

In other words, Chico told himself, he was nobody.

He spun around quick with a chip on his shoulder. Marched toward the pack with clenched fists, shouting, "Who you talking to?"

The pack seemed caught off guard.

"Slow down," a guy named Gabe said, raising his hands and backing up.

"What's your problem?" another kid said.

"Maybe *you're* my problem," Chico told him.

They all looked at each other.

A few smiled.

Like Chico was funny.

Like Chico attending the school on the hill was a big joke.

That's when David Winters, Mr. Popularity, said, "Why the attitude, compadre? We just wanted to ask you a question."

Chico took another step forward. "What'd you just call me?"

There were six or seven of them. All dudes. All staring at him. Daring him.

One guy got off his beach cruiser and let it fall to the grass.

"You heard me," David said, smiling.

"You heard the man," another guy chimed in.

Then David said it again: "Compadre."

None of the fragmented thoughts flashing through Chico's mind told him to walk away. Nah, he'd seen the way they looked at him at parent-teacher night. Looked at his old man. They thought they were better.

And worse than that, a tiny part of Chico thought they were right.

That's the part that swung a closed fist at the closest kid. David Winters. Blasted him in the cheek.

David stumbled backward but didn't go down. He reached for his face. Checked fingers for blood that wasn't there.

Chico stepped forward, connected again. This time in the gut. David went down on one knee. When he looked up at Chico, his eyes seemed innocent.

A second of silence followed the body blow. It felt like minutes. Everybody looking at each other, trying to process, trying to imagine what was happening, Chico's chest going in and out and in and out, his mind unable to stick with one thought.

Then they were on him.

All seven of them.

Gabe held his arms back as David shoved his face, smacked him in the side of the head, in the ribs. Somebody kicked out Chico's legs, sent him sprawling to the ground. The pack's weight crushing down on him. Tweaking his neck. Making it impossible to breathe.

Under the pile, in the darkness, Chico secretly begged for more.

He knew something these rich kids didn't.

He deserved this beatdown.

For losing his dog. For coming to this private school in the first place.

Go on! he screamed inside his head. *Hit me, punk! Do it!*

But the barrage of flying fists had already stopped. The weight had lifted. He could breathe again.

Chico leapt to his feet, ready for more. But instead of locking eyes with Gabe and David Winters and everybody he was fighting, he found two male teachers grabbing arms and pushing people away.

"All right," the one with the clipboard said. "Somebody's gonna tell me what happened. Otherwise I march every single one of you to Principal Van Buren's office."

"What's it gonna be?" the whistle teacher said. "Who started it?"

"We need answers, gentlemen."

Without thinking, Chico stepped forward. Said it was him.

What did he care?

Maybe they'd do everybody a favor and kick him out of school. Send him back where he belonged, the public junior high down the street from the greenhouses.

With his friends.

With people like him.

The Inheritance

When Chico's grandmother, on his mom's side, passed she left him two things:

A bond for his education.

And her dog, Peanut.

She left the bond because she believed a

kid with grades like Chico's should be able to attend the best school around. From her hospital bed she arranged for him to take the pre SAT, hoping he might score high enough to be admitted to the private school on the hill.

Not only did Chico score high enough to get in, his score was so freakishly high they offered him a full scholarship through high school.

"What if I don't wanna go?" Chico asked his old man on the bus ride home from his grandma's cremation.

"Oh, you're going," his dad answered in Spanish.

All their conversations went like this. Chico spoke English, and his old man would answer in Spanish. They could both speak the other's first language, but they were embarrassed by clumsy accents.

"What about my friends?" Chico said.

"Make new ones."

"What about the money, then?"

"We'll save it for your college."

Chico rolled his eyes. He was pissed.

But he was something else, too. Something he couldn't put his finger on.

Minutes passed. The bus lurched forward and stopped, lurched forward and stopped.

Finally his old man cleared his throat, said, "I made a promise to that woman, Chico. I ain't going back on it just 'cause I got a kid who's *un miedica*."

"I ain't scared," Chico shot back.

His dad looked at him, grinning.

Chico shook his head and turned to look out the window. The poor side of the freeway flashing past. Boarded storefronts and tagged windows, old Mexican men pushing carts overflowing with bottles and cans and dirty blankets.

He glanced at his dad on the sly. Guy never made it passed sixth grade, but he was right. That was the exact feeling Chico couldn't name.

He was scared.

A month later, as Chico walked onto campus for the first time, he would remember the name his old man had called him on the bus that day. Scaredy cat. Because even though he was now an official student at the school on the hill, he still felt like an imposter. Like at any second security would come barreling around the corner in their golf carts, tackling him onto the wet lawn, pulling their canisters of mace.

Peanut

Nothing really changed when Chico's grandma left him her old dog. Peanut had already been living with them for two years, since his grandma first found out she was sick.

Chico's dad wasn't too excited with the arrangement. Peanut dug holes in their tiny backyard. And dog food, even the generic kind, he constantly reminded Chico, cost money. They could barely afford to feed themselves.

And it's not like Peanut was the cute and cuddly type. Nah, according to everybody in the neighborhood, including Chico, Peanut was the craziest-looking animal they'd ever laid eyes on.

First off, he took the term "mutt" to a whole other level. He was a mix of ten, maybe fifteen, different breeds. Everything from pit bull to poodle. He was knee-high, with long, spindly legs, an oversized head, and teeth so buck and crooked he could hardly close his mouth. Chico's friend Marco swore Peanut was too ugly to be a hundred percent dog.

"Is it me," he once asked with a serious face, "or does that mutt got some kind of reptile thing going on?"

"It's them bulging eyes, bro," Danny Muñoz agreed. "Look how far apart they are. Like a lizard."

"At the same time," Marco said, "he sort of got this wolf thing happening, too. Don't he look like a wolf, D?"

"His dad was probably a wolf," Danny

said. "And his moms was an alligator. He invented a new breed, man. A wolfigator."

He and Danny Muñoz touched fists, and everybody laughed and laughed and laughed. Except Peanut, who stared up at the three of them with his tongue going, oblivious to the bad-mouthing, happy to just be hanging out.

Peanut was old, too.

Chico assumed he had arthritis 'cause every morning it took him almost a full minute to get to his feet. Chico's grandma swore he'd once had a nice, shiny brown coat. But now Peanut was a poofy purple-gray, like old-lady hair. Except on the top of his head, where he was balding like a man.

And Peanut had a terrible problem with gas. He'd sound off all through the night.

But it wasn't the sound that killed Chico. It was the toxic smell. Some mornings, he'd wake up literally suffocating.

Chico's old man tried tying a small air freshener to Peanut's collar, but the gas smell was too powerful. Chico had to hold his breath whenever he sat down to pet his dog. And even then his eyes would still burn.

None of it mattered, though.

To Chico, Peanut was the greatest dog a kid could ever ask for. In fact, Peanut was more than just a dog. He was family.

That's why Chico swore he'd never stop looking.

He'd tape a handwritten sign to every lamppost in America if that's what it took.

Peanut Situation Goes from Bad to Worse

Soon as Chico got home from school, on the day of the fight, he tossed his bag on the couch and canvassed the neighborhood again, calling Peanut's name, knocking on doors, taping his flyers to any flat surface he saw.

But still.

There was no sign of his dog.

When he finally made his way back home, he found his old man in his usual spot. In front of the TV, dirty work boots kicked up on the coffee table, watching his favorite show, *Cops*, and drinking a beer.

"Yo, Pop," Chico said, "you got any idea what happened to Peanut? I looked everywhere."

His old man shrugged, continued working a toothpick in his teeth.

"It's been two whole days," Chico said. "I don't know what I should do."

His old man just sat there, never took his eyes off the drunk trucker getting patted down on TV. When he finally spoke, he told Chico in Spanish, "Your school called."

Chico froze.

"Said you got in some trouble. That right?"

It was Chico's turn to shrug.

He'd been hoping his old man would avoid this call, like he avoided just about every call from outsiders, by pretending he didn't understand English.

"A fight, Chico?" His dad stood up, snatched Chico by the chin, and looked over the scrapes and bruises on his face. He shook his head. "They told me next time you're gonna be suspended. That happens, you know what I'm gonna do, right, Chico?"

"What?"

"Kick your skinny butt myself. Then send you back to Tijuana to live with your Auntie Mariposa. How's that sound, Muhammad Ali?"

Chico didn't say anything.

When his old man turned back to the TV, shaking his head, Chico went to his tiny room and threw himself onto the futon bed.

He pulled down the two pictures he had pinned to his corkboard. The first was him and his mom. Weeks before she passed. Chico was little, barely a kid yet. His mom had a tiny smile on her face, but her eyes were made out of pain. The mini version of Chico in the picture was oblivious to this pain. He was caught in the camera's flash laughing. Like a clown.

The second picture was him and Peanut.

Taken a few months ago by Marco, outside the greenhouses. Chico's hand on his dog's balding head. Bucktoothed Peanut gazing up at Chico like he was the greatest.

Like Chico would always protect him.

Except he hadn't.

Chico thought back to the day the picture was taken, how after Marco went home, Chico sang the national anthem in Peanut's ear. It was their silly ritual. He didn't even remember how it started. Whenever Chico went after the high notes, Peanut would howl at the moon, like he was singing, too. Both of them so off-key Chico imagined windows shattering all around the neighborhood.

Chico lay there on his futon bed, staring at these two photos, one after the other, thinking of his mom and his grandma and his howling dog and the fight at school and his greenhouse friends and his old man's boots on the coffee table. He felt so confused it was like he was lifting out of his own body. Like he was float-ing up toward his bedroom ceiling, looking down at himself. Who was this lonely kid lying on this unmade futon bed? Holding these worn photos in his greasy fingers?

He snapped back to reality when he realized his old man was standing at his door, watching him.

Chico sat up.

His dad took a swig from his can of beer, wiped his mouth with the back of his hand. "Listen, boy," he said.

Chico was listening.

"Nobody walked that dog."

"What?"

"Nobody fed that dog. Nobody filled them holes that got dug up."

Chico looked at his old man, standing in his doorway, gripping a can of beer.

Then it hit him, what his old man was saying.

He choked on his own breath.

His dad took another swig, walked away shaking his head.

The next morning, Chico worked up the

courage to ask directly. Just before his old man got to the front door, he said, "Yo, Pop."

His dad looked over his shoulder.

"You took Peanut somewhere?"

"Had to," he said.

Like a punch in Chico's gut. "Where? The pound?"

His old man shook his head, switched his lunch box from one hand to the other.

"Where, then?"

"A ranch in Fallbrook, about fifty miles from here. He'll be better off, Chico. He's with a bunch of other dogs just like him."

"But he liked it *here*."

His dad shrugged. "Now he can dig all the holes he wants."

After his old man went out the front door, Chico sat on the couch and looked at his feet. He couldn't move. He imagined arthritic Peanut trying to stand on a ranch somewhere in Fallbrook, sniffing for someone familiar, someone who might sing the national anthem in his ear.

David Winters's Girlfriend

Days later, Chico was at his desk during lunch.

He'd stopped going out on the lawn with everybody 'cause it was awkward sitting alone. Plus, he could just as easily eat in the classroom. His teacher didn't care. And this way he didn't have to fight the glare from the sun reflecting off whatever page he was reading in his book.

Today, though, Chico wasn't reading.

He was staring at one of the flyers he'd made for his lost dog. Before he knew his dog wasn't actually lost but given away.

"Excuse me," he heard a girl voice say behind him. "You're Chico, right?"

Chico spun around.

Meagan Marshall, David Winters's girlfriend. She was wearing a black sweatshirt with the school emblem and a short denim skirt. Her long blond hair was so shiny and pretty up close it didn't seem real.

"Listen," she told him, "I'm sorry about what happened with you and David the other day. How he called you 'compadre' and all that." She smiled, added, "Even though technically you did throw the first punch."

Chico looked at Meagan. He couldn't think of anything to say, so he nodded.

"Anyways," she said. Then she looked down at his lost-dog flyer, asked, "Is Peanut your dog or something?"

Chico covered the flyer with his notebook.

"You lost him?"

"Sort of."

She frowned. "How do you sort of lose your dog?"

"My old man," Chico said. "He gave him away to a ranch."

"Why?"

"So he could dig all the holes he wants."

Meagan cringed.

Even with her face scrunched up, Chico thought, Meagan was still prettier than ninety percent of the girls at school.

"Do you have a picture?"

"A picture?" he said.

"Of your dog, Peanut."

"I think so."

"You're not very definitive with your answers, are you?"

Chico shrugged. He decided the pre SAT was ten times easier than talking to a pretty girl like Meagan.

"Bring one tomorrow," she said. "I wanna see what a dog named Peanut looks like."

Chico watched her gather her hair in a ponytail, wrap her black band around it, and pull it through.

"Anyways," she said again. "I just came in

here to apologize on David's behalf. Even though technically you started it."

"Okay," Chico heard himself say.

Meagan smiled and walked out of the classroom.

A Peanutless Existence

Over the next couple weeks, Chico kept seeing dogs.

Everywhere he went.

Boxers and terriers and pugs and golden retrievers and plain old mutts like Peanut. They were running wild near the greenhouses, stalking through the parking lot at the mall, they were on billboards advertising life insurance, on leashes at the park, they were sticking their heads out of passing trucks, chasing squirrels over fences and birds into trees.

Chico would sit and watch them and think of Peanut.

Once he tried humming the national anthem to himself, but he didn't even get to the high part. It wasn't the same.

Chico boycotted his old man for a while. Whenever the guy came home from work, Chico would get up and go to his room. Even when he didn't have any homework.

But the dad ban only lasted a few days.

One night he came into Chico's room while Chico was studying.

"What's going down?" he said in Spanish.

Chico lifted his chemistry textbook without turning around.

"Need help?" his old man asked.

Chico shook him off, but the dude sat down anyway, took the book out of Chico's hands, and started flipping through pages, nodding.

"It's about chemicals," he said.

Chico shrugged.

"Even water's made of chemicals," he said. "You know that, right, boy? It's called molecules. They all get attracted together with magnetism, and that's what makes the tap water you drink."

Chico stared at his old man.

The guy had no idea what he was talking about.

"Most people don't know that," his dad added, running a finger over the periodic table.

Chico studied him: sitting on the edge of his son's futon bed, flipping through the pages of a chemistry textbook he couldn't read, fingernails caked in dirt, shirt sweat-stained and worn thin from hard work.

An odd thought struck Chico.

Maybe his old man was lonely, too.

Chico cleared his throat, said, "Even tap water, Pop?"

"That's right, boy," his dad said, looking up. "Plants and animals, too. Everything in the world. It's all made up of things people can't even see."

Chico nodded.

His dad smiled, said, "See, boy? Your old man maybe works with flowers all day, but he gots a little knowledge, too."

"I know it, Pop."

He tossed the textbook back onto Chico's lap and stood up. Pointed at the book, then tapped his temple. "You remind me of your mom, Chico. She always liked to learn about stuff, too."

"She did?"

His old man nodded. "It's a good way to be."

Chico watched him walk out of his tiny room, knowing he could no longer be mad.

The Picture

Chico continued dining in at school. Table for one. Sometimes Meagan would pop her head in and ask if he brought the picture of Peanut. And even though it'd be burning a hole in his back pocket, Chico would tell her he forgot.

Two weeks after their initial meeting, though, Meagan walked all the way into Chico's classroom while he was studying and sat in the chair next to him.

She looked at him, said, "Well?"

"What?" he said.

"You bring the picture?"

Chico looked at his desk.

"Lemme guess," she said. "You forgot. Again."

Without really thinking about it, Chico pulled the picture of Peanut from his back pocket and laid it on the desk.

Meagan picked it up.

She covered her mouth and said, "Oh. My. God."

"I know," Chico said. "He looks kind of weird."

Meagan looked up at Chico and laughed. Then apologized.

She studied the photo again, said, "Is it me, or . . . ?"

"What?"

"Or does he sort of look like a wolf?"

Chico couldn't help himself. He cracked a smile.

"Right?"

"My friends say that he's part wolf and part alligator."

They both laughed.

Chico was slipping the photo back into his pocket when he heard a guy voice at the door. "Hey, Meagan."

It was Gabe. "We're going to the library," he said.

"The library?" Meagan said. "You guys?"

Gabe shrugged. "Baker won't give us an extension on that Civil War essay."

Gabe looked at Chico and then looked back at Meagan. "Anyways, Dave wanted me to tell you."

"Cool, meet you guys there in a few."

Gabe was already leaving when Meagan called out, "Gabe, wait!"

He popped his head back into the classroom.

"This is Chico," she said. "Chico, this is Gabe."

They both mumbled, "Hey."

Chico closed his textbook, and Gabe looked at Meagan and said, "We'll be in there."

And that was the end of it. Gabe left.

"See?" Meagan said. "They're not such bad guys."

Chico shrugged.

"Anyway, sorry I laughed at your dog. It's just his teeth. They, like, really stick out."

"I know."

"Like, far, though. I wonder if my mom would ever work on a dog. She's an orthodontist."

Meagan patted Chico's shoulder, got up, and grabbed her book bag. She gave Chico a little wave and walked out of the classroom.

The Wolf

A couple mornings later, there was a big rumor spreading around campus. A wolf was loose on the school grounds. Several groups of kids had spotted it on the field before first bell rang.

School security was out in full force, riding around the field on their carts, checking inside storage rooms, behind the handball walls, up the hill. Principal Van Buren was walking through the halls gripping an electric megaphone.

Chico's first-period teacher, Mrs. Blizzard, explained how the private school had been built right up against the woods, where wolves still bred. Now that developers were pushing in on both sides, the wolves' natural habitat was getting squeezed.

"Doesn't surprise me at all," she said, closing her roll book and leaning against her desk. "Of course they were going to end up on campus eventually. They're looking for food."

A girl across the room from Chico, Sarah Knowles, raised her hand and asked, "Would a wolf hurt people?"

"Best to err on the side of caution," Mrs. Blizzard said, looking out the window. "That's why they're keeping us inside until Animal Control arrives."

More hands went up, but before anybody was called on, the phone rang.

Mrs. Blizzard picked it up, and everybody

around Chico turned to one another and started talking about the wolf and whether or not they'd cancel school.

Chico was barely listening, though. He kept going back and forth on the thought stuck in his head. A wolf? Really? Or what if it was just a dog that looked like a wolf? Of course, Fallbrook was over fifty miles away. And there was the whole arthritis thing. But still. Imagine if it was Peanut!

The teacher hung up, shouted, "Class, please! Quiet down!"

The hum of conversation faded, and they all turned their attention back to the front of the room.

"That was Secretary Mulligan. Animal Control has arrived. Everything should be fine in a couple of hours. Now, please take out your readers and turn to page forty-seven."

The class groaned and started pulling out their books.

A few minutes into Mrs. Blizzard's lecture, Chico raised his hand and asked if he could use the bathroom.

"I don't know, Chico. They'd really like us to remain in the classrooms."

"It's an emergency, though," Chico said. "I'll hurry."

The teacher looked at her watch, then out the window. "The bathroom and back," she said. "Got it? No dillydallying."

Chico hustled out the door.

Instead of ducking into the bathroom two doors down from his class, he sped past it toward the field. He spotted a few men in safari-looking uniforms wandering around with walkie-talkies and a large net. The school security guards were right alongside them. Principal Van Buren was pointing up at the woods.

When everybody started toward the other end of campus, Chico snuck down onto the field and began a search of his own. He circled the new baseball diamond, ducked in and out of both dugouts. He walked the outside of the track. He marched up a bank covered in ice-plant flowers, peeked behind the rows of portable classrooms.

But there was no sign of any wild animal.

Chico was about to head back to class when he decided to check one last spot. Along the concrete wall just off campus, where he waited alone every morning for school to start.

Halfway up the stairs, he heard breathing.

Chico froze.

What if he was wrong? What if it really was an actual wolf? And it was looking for food?

He stood perfectly still for several long seconds, trying to decide what to do. His heart pounded inside his chest. On the other side of the field, he could make out the people from Animal Control and the security guards. They were leaning a tall ladder against the gym, which separated the east side of campus from the woods.

As Chico turned back around, he saw the shadow of a large animal head slowly peeking out from behind the wall.

His body went cold.

But then he smelled the horrible gas.

And he saw the crooked teeth.

Chico raced up the rest of the stairs as Peanut started patting his feet and moving his bald head around in excitement.

Chico slid to his knees and hugged Peanut, and Peanut licked his face and jumped up so his paws were on Chico's thighs.

Peanut smelled even worse than usual, but Chico didn't care. He rubbed his face all over Peanut's face. Hot dog breath in his ear. Sandpaper tongue. It was a miracle he had his best friend back.

He pulled away and looked at Peanut, said, "How'd you even get here, boy? I thought you had arthritis."

Peanut panted.

Chico's eyes burned.

He imagined the old dog limping along the sides of roads for over fifty miles, somehow finding his way here, to Chico's private school on the hill.

He leaned into his dog's ear and hummed

a portion of the national anthem. Peanut howled into the cloudless sky.

As Chico hugged his dog again, even tighter this time, he felt a couple tears sneak down his cheeks. He wanted to believe they were purely tears of joy, but he knew better. The toxic smell was also a factor.

Ditching School

Chico stood up, knowing he had a decision to make.

If he went to Animal Control, they might ship Peanut back to Fallbrook. He could leave school right now and walk Peanut home, but technically that would be ditching. His old man would flip when he got the call, maybe even ship him off to Tijuana. But could Chico really trust a hole-digging dog to stay hidden behind a wall until the end of school? There was no way he could let Animal Control snatch Peanut up.

Chico guided his dog back behind the wall and said, "Stay, boy."

They stared at each other.

"You hear me?"

Peanut panted, faded tongue bobbing over his buck teeth.

"I'm serious," Chico said. "Just for a minute. Don't come out."

Then he took off down the stairs, across the field, and up to the office, where he asked permission to go home. He was really sick, he explained to Secretary Mulligan. Maybe some kind of stomach flu. He was probably contagious.

But the secretary said they couldn't release sick students without a ride home. Especially with the wolf scare. "You're welcome to lie down in the nurse's office, though," she said. "And I can call home, see if your mother or father can come get you."

Chico considered this.

His dad wasn't near a phone. So that was out. And if he left without a ride, he might end up at Auntie Mariposa's in Mexico. But how could he just leave his dog sitting behind a wall all day? Even if he stayed put, Animal Control would eventually head in that direction. They'd catch him in their special net and take him away. Maybe to the pound. And what would the people at the pound do with a dog as old as Peanut? Put him to sleep?

"Honey?" the secretary said.

Chico looked at her, said, "I'll just wait in class, ma'am. I think my stomach's feeling better."

Meagan stopped Chico on his way back through the hall.

"Hey," she said, hanging halfway out of her classroom door.

"Hey," he said.

"Where you going? We're all supposed to be in our classrooms, you know."

Chico shrugged.

She tilted her head a little. "What's wrong?"

He whispered in her ear. "It's my dog. He came back."

"Peanut?" Meagan shouted. "Where? When?"

Chico put his finger to his lips for her to lower her voice. "Here," he whispered. "By the big concrete wall right off campus. Peanut's the wolf."

Gabe stepped out from behind Meagan, said, "What's going on?"

"Chico's dog," Meagan said in a quieter voice. "The one I told you guys about. He came all the way here from Fallbrook."

Gabe looked up at Chico. "He walked? That's, like, fifty miles."

"Exactly," Meagan said.

Gabe reached into the classroom and pulled another body toward the door. It was David Winters. "This guy's dog," Gabe explained, "traveled fifty miles to find him."

"Are you serious?" David said.

Chico nodded.

"You're taking him home, right?" Meagan said. "No way your dad could refuse a dog that walked fifty miles to find its owner."

Gabe opened his mouth like he was gonna say something, but right then the bell rang. The teacher inside the classroom shouted, "Only go from room to room, people! Field's off-limits!"

Meagan, Gabe, and David stepped out of the classroom. A few other people moved past them, headed toward other rooms.

"They told me I can't leave," Chico said.

"What do you mean you can't leave?" Meagan said.

"Secretary Mulligan. She told me I have to have a ride. Otherwise it's ditching."

David looked at Gabe and then looked back at Chico. "Let's go get your dog," he said.

Everybody turned to David.

"He came all this way," he said. "It's, like, special circumstances or something."

"Dave's right," Gabe said.

Meagan had a big smile on her face. She peeked into the class at her teacher, then turned to Chico and said, "Let's go."

The three of them were now looking to

him. Wanting to help. Chico could not believe it.

He started toward the field, and they followed.

At the top of the stairs they all stood staring at Peanut.

"Wow," Gabe said. "I've never seen a dog with a receding hairline."

Meagan laughed and said, "I told you guys."

Peanut went on his hind legs out of excitement, but as he did this, a very loud sound came from his backside.

David crinkled up his nose and turned to Chico. "Dude, did your dog just rip one?"

"He does that sometimes," Chico said.

Everybody shielded their noses with their hands. "Oh my God," Gabe said. "That's the worst thing I've ever smelled."

When the laughing died down, David patted Chico on the shoulder and said, "Lead the way, man. If you're getting in trouble for ditching, we're all getting in trouble."

"We're in this together," Meagan said.

"You sure?" Chico said. "It's on the other side of the freeway. Behind Home Depot."

"Near the flower fields?" Meagan said.

Chico nodded.

"We don't care," David said.

Chico tried to hide his smile as he took Peanut by the collar and they started walking.

"Does your dad work the flower fields?" Gabe said.

Chico nodded. "You know those poinsettias at school? Near the library?"

They said they did.

"My dad raised 'em up from tiny little seeds. Like a pea in the palm of your hand."

Everybody seemed impressed.

As they passed underneath the freeway, into Chico's side of town, he imagined how they must've looked moving down the middle of the rundown street. Chico leading his crazy-looking mutt by the collar. An arthritic wolf-dog that had somehow tracked him down from fifty miles away. Three white kids from the school on the hill. Escorting him.

Kids he'd fought with on the field less than three weeks ago.

He knew when his dad got home he'd have some explaining to do. He'd have to make a case for keeping Peanut. And he'd have to face whatever punishment his dad laid down for ditching school.

But they were gonna be okay, Chico decided.

All three of them.

Peanut and his dad and Chico.

Something about making new friends made him believe this.

Brancusi & Me

Written and illustrated
by Jon J Muth

Polaire

An Outing

Did you hear that!? It's not a chop. It's a crack! That is splintering of wood! And now comes the bad language. . . . "* # $ @ & !" Brancusi's voice. Yes! That means we will be going out! That's the third adze handle he's broken this morning. A walk! A walk! He has no more oak! We have to go to Old Man Berg's for ax handles!

Again, the voice, "Polaire! Get your shoes and coat!"

"Ha ha! Yes, you are so funny!" I bark. Brancusi says these things to amuse himself. He knows, of course, I am a dog and don't wear shoes. "Woof! I am ready! Ready ready ready! I am by the door! Let's go!" I say. This is wonderful! So many rare smells! We will pass through the park at exactly the right time. The second baguettes of the day will be baked, and children will be there!

We return home from our outing. That was magnificent! I shall be full for at least five minutes.

I love to hear him muttering under his breath. "The essence . . . not feathers, not a bird, but the essence. . . . What is the essence of a bird . . . ? Not to transcend the animal, but to reveal it more fully!"

I am lying on the concrete floor. He is standing with a stone file, creating a white fog of dust as he smoothes the marble.

"Master," I bark, "no one knows what you are talking about! What does this mean?! The 'essence'?"

"Flight!" he bellows. "Of course! It's flight!"

I can't help it, my tail is wagging/dusting the floor.

"Not the bird . . . but . . . *flight itself*!"

He looks down at me, pulls thoughtfully at his beard, then turns back to his work with the file.

I lick the bottom of his stool leg and watch as fine white particles catch the sunlight. Sometimes, when he is working feverishly, it gets so heavy, I can see sworls in the light.

When they sometimes turn into angels, I am up and barking. You must be vigilant with artists. You never know what their work will bring forth.

Woof! The dust has me sneezing again. I put my paws over my nose to try and stop it.

He laughs at this. He has a sweet laugh.

"Polaire! You are sneezing at my hard work." He crinkles up his eyes, and they sparkle from beneath his brows like a secret hidden in a dark forest. That's when I smell it: love. Even through the marble dust I can smell it. I can always smell it. And that makes my heart leap and fills every corner of the world.

If I'm lucky, that's when he comes in close and snuzzles me—his Romanian word—and no matter how much he washes, I can still smell the wood smoke in his beard. Smells like home. And the marble dust. Always the marble dust. My nose may not be able to smell as well as when I was a puppy, because

of the dust, but my ears are very good, and so are my eyes. I can see many things in the stone and many things in the wood. I try not to bark because it breaks his concentration. Then he puts me outside. The door is always open, but I know he would rather I stay outside if I am going to bark.

Sigh. There is much less to talk about outside. Rue de Ronsin has so little traffic. Crazy automobile drivers sometimes. Maybe one of Giacometti's cats will saunter by on a good day, and that can be a nice chase. Of course, I let Brancusi know when visitors are coming. Especially Duchamp. He always brings small sausages for me. Duchamp should come more often.

We enjoy Erik Satie's company very much these days. The music he and Brancusi play together is such fun: Satie playing that crazy old piano from the Russian painter in the next alley and Brancusi on a flute he carved himself.

Satie will come by the studio and play bits for Brancusi, sometimes working at the stunted piano all afternoon. Satie has been writing this sonata for a while, which he describes as a prayer. It has tender, sad passages and crashing desperate themes freely mingled, one after the other so splendidly, so powerfully, so naturally that it is no longer the sounds of music that fill the studio rooms, but the flow of Satie's memory, heard now for the first time. Satie's whole being seems to pour into this piece of music.

"Constantin"—this is Brancusi's given name, and Satie insists on using it—"I finally have a well-paying commission. It is for an opera. It is to be in the key of A and will revolve around the theme of a fairy tale. Anyone could write it. I am barely involved," says Satie. "The whole thing is outlined. Just a lot of labor, signifying nothing. But it is a big affair." The older pianist polishes his pince-nez glasses and plops them back on his nose. "Costumes, sets, so much time fiddling with this or that part because the soloist can't reach a note. Anyone could write it," he says, without a trace of pleasure in his voice. "And so I will spend the next year or more trying to help get this cement albatross off the ground."

Brancusi looks at his friend for a moment. He has been working on his magic bird—his *Maiastra*. "I have to remove a shadow from the neck of the *Maiastra*," he says. "It is important that a certain line stand out in relief." His eyes are watery. "A billion possible lines pass through a point, and I must choose from a billion lines . . . one . . . single line. No one knows where that line is but me. If I don't find it, it will never be found."

I look from Satie's face to Brancusi. In all Brancusi does there is a gentleness. Even carving the largest of stones there is an insistence of faith in the goodness of things. As his work progresses, he will stand face-to-face with some potential that only he can yet see. And when the work is finished and his sculpture stands in the room, the potential that he saw, now revealed to be the *one*—will be more real than all the others.

Satie looks at the younger Brancusi, who is focused intently on his seemingly perfect and finished sculpture.

For a long time that evening, when we are alone, a fire in the hand-built stove, Brancusi sits in a chair near my bed of woodchips just patting my head and thinking.

"Satie's music," he mumbles. "It's like a river flowing to all of his feelings. He is almost incapable of keeping it inside. That opera may lock it away. Satie is capable of showing us ourselves, what it is like to be here, alive, right now. But this opera will take much effort, and bring forth . . ."

Brancusi looks at me very seriously. "Polaire, what becomes of an artist when the necessities of the world drive him sane?"

The next day Satie visits. He brings biscuits. He has dropped the commission and will continue to work on his own music.

This is the effect Brancusi has on artists.

The Portrait

Brancusi is looking at me seriously. His sculpture of the magic bird—*Maiastra*—is behind him, framed against the bright window. It is too intense. I have to look away. He paces this way and stops. He paces that way and stops, never looking away from me. I show him my good side.

"What?! Master, what?!" I yip.

"Polaire," he says, "chisels cost money."

I sneak a look at him.

"Axes, saw blades, hammers, all cost money." He starts to walk around the room, rubbing his beard, woolgathering. "Not to mention food," he says.

"It's okay, mention food," I woof.

"True," he says, gesturing around the studio, "I can make most of the tools. . . ."

"And the food," I think.

"And I have made all of the furniture we need."

It's absolutely true, I think, looking at the large plaster table and the wooden stools and that comfy pile of woodchips.

Brancusi sits down heavily, as if he has been sentenced to the gallows. "We could use some money, so I am going to do a portrait bust," he says.

I'm not sure why, but I lay my head down in sympathy. I feel as if someone should come and tie a black veil over my head.

"Portraits are so difficult," he says sadly, looking at his shoes. "A portrait is an invitation to failure for an artist."

"Yes," I think. I put my head in his lap. "It is . . . wait, why?"

"We can never love the subject in the way the person asking us to do the portrait would want. If we are very lucky, we will succeed on the lowest level—it will *resemble* the subject." He says the word *resemble* like it tastes bad. His thick fingers stroke my white fur. "If we attempt the impossible, if we try to find a universal beauty underlying the distractions of outer appearance, if we try to capture some timeless essence, we will not be understood."

"Maybe you should stop complaining. Just do the bust, and see what happens," I think.

He looks at me. Marble dust flecks his eyebrows. His tiny eyes sparkle in a smile.

So the lady from Paris comes to our studio. . . .

I try to make her feel welcome once I realize she hasn't brought a bizarre and lazy animal with her. She is wearing a fur coat. She is a strange woman. I think she worries she is being followed. She keeps looking into all the mirrors. I want to tell her that I once barked at mirrors because I too thought something was there. Of course I was a pup then. She is a full-grown woman and should know by now there is nothing in a mirror!

My Brancusi is very charming, and in a few minutes, she is laughing and very comfortable. When she doesn't accept my offer of the bed of wood chips, I decide enough is enough, and I take my afternoon nap.

Weeks later, when Brancusi finishes the bust, even I am surprised. He has captured all that

strangeness in just three beautiful, simple shapes.

Saturday night is when we have visitors. I am near the fireplace helping to lick up the splashes of a very tasty stew, called *gulyás*, which Brancusi kindly sloshed over as he stirred the pot. There is a sharp rap on the door, and Marcel Duchamp's face appears.

"Maurice!"—this is what Brancusi calls all his most pure-hearted friends—"You have been away too long! How was America?"

"Excellent! And full of interest in your work," says Duchamp.

I lick the final delicious *gulyás* droplets as Duchamp gives Brancusi a great hug. "Look who is joining us this evening!" he says. Then Duchamp, with a lovely smell of sausages, waves around his elegant new walking stick. Erik Satie and a friend of his who is a poet step inside the studio, followed by some young dancers and a painter. The mirror lady is there. She is very happy. The Russian painter who gave us the piano and his little girl. She is very shy. I do my best not to look at her right away. They all enter and take their favorite places. More and more people seep in, giving the all-white cathedral-like space intimacy and warmth.

Duchamp holds his new cane up. "You must admire my new *whacking stick*!" he says with a funny American accent.

"I think you mean *walking* stick," says a guest with a slightly better accent.

Duchamp raises the stick, "No, no! Here, lean this way. I will demonstrate!"

I see the little girl cover her eyes with her hands, and I bark for the grown-ups to stop.

Can't they see they are frightening her?

Satie sits down at the piano.

Soon Brancusi has the little girl dancing with him and everyone is laughing. When the dance has ended and her shyness returns, I gently pluck a warm roll from the cutting board and give it to her. We spend the rest of the evening curled up together under the table, fast friends, dozing off now and then. That's how these evenings are.

And then, dawn at the windows; the night has gone. Most guests have left; stragglers are sleeping on couches and divans. I've finished eating the sausages and, sadly, most of Duchamp's coat pocket. Staying up late could be a bad habit. It clouds the senses.

The sun is rosy across the rooftops. I can hear the hotel on the boulevard waking up, the windows opening, flowers being set out, everywhere fresh scents, coffee, newspaper boys calling out the morning headlines.

My Brancusi is, on the other hand, working on his magic bird, his *Maiastra*. He stayed up all night after the guests had either left or fallen asleep, and I can see he is very tired. He steps back from the marble and sighs. For many minutes, he doesn't move. I hear someone snoring. Then Brancusi notices that

Duchamp has left his beautiful new wooden stick. He loves working in wood. It's a joyous material for him, I can see that. When I was a puppy I would chew the heavy scrap pieces. I think wood reminds him of when he was young. All the houses where he grew up were carved from wood. I've heard him tell this again and again to whoever will listen.

Then he looks at me with a grin and slips the walking stick behind his back. For a moment, he is young and mischievous. I think I see a young Brancusi's foxlike cunning. A few hours later, I hear the sounds of a flute from the carving room.

The Beginning of the World

Today he lifts a white dustcover and it softly falls away from a great long, graceful piece of marble like a fin, resting on its knifelike edge. I sit and look at the shape, hypnotized. Brancusi pushes gently on one end and it spins slowly round. It is so big and yet so thin it almost disappears as it turns.

"When you see a fish, you do not think of its fins and eyes and scales, do you?" His bright little eyes are twinkling. "You think of its speed, its floating, flashing body seen through water!"

He sits down on the bench next to me and scratches behind my left ear. We look at the fish slowly spinning; its surface catches the light and flashes like polished silver as it turns.

"I want to express just that," he says. "If I made eyes and fins and scales, I would trap the fish in a pattern or a shape of reality. I want just the flash of its spirit."

He holds my face and closes his eyes,
touches his forehead to mine. "Do you understand me?"

What can I say?

Contributors

Margarita Engle (author of "Trail Magic") is a poet and novelist whose work has been published in many countries. Her books include *The Surrender Tree*, a Newbery Honor book and winner of the Jane Addams Children's Book Award, the Pura Belpré Award, the Américas Award, and the Claudia Lewis Poetry Award; *The Poet Slave of Cuba,* winner of the Pura Belpré Award and the Américas Award; and *Hurricane Dancers*. Margarita enjoys hiking in California's Sierra Nevadas, where she helps her husband train his two wilderness search-and-rescue dogs, Maggi and Chance.

Valerie Hobbs (author of "The God of the Pond") has written many novels, including *Sheep*, a California Young Reader Medal winner. She lives in Santa Barbara and longs for a dog to walk on the beach. But Molly (aka Miss Bossy Cat) will not allow it.

Thacher Hurd (author and illustrator of "Patty") is the author and illustrator of many books for children, including *Bongo Fishing, Mama Don't Allow,* and *Art Dog*. Among his many honors are a Boston Globe–Horn Book award and a *New York Times* Best Illustrated Book Award. He lives in Berkeley, California.

Olga and **Aleksey Ivanov** (illustrators) immigrated to the United States from Russia in 2002. The husband-and-wife team received a classical art education in Moscow and have collaborated on more than eighty children's books, including *The Tall Book of Mother Goose* and *Charlotte's Web*. They live and work together in their studio near Denver, Colorado.

Ann M. Martin (author of "Picasso") is the author of many novels, including *A Corner of the Universe,* winner of the Newbery Honor; *Everything for a Dog;* and *Ten Rules for Living with My Sister.* Ann lives in upstate New York with her beloved dog, Sadie, and several rescued cats.

Jon J Muth (author and illustrator of "Brancusi & Me") is the author and illustrator of several books for children, including the Caldecott Honor winner *Zen Shorts* and *Come On, Rain!,* which won the Gold Medal from the Society of Illustrators. He lives in upstate New York with his wife, Bonnie, and their four children.

Wendy Orr (author of "Dognapper") has written more than two dozen children's books, including the Rainbow Street Shelter series, *Mokie and Bik,* and *Nim's Island.* She lives with her family in Australia, near the sea. Her dog friends Max, Harry, and Pippa all helped to inspire her story.

Matt de la Peña (author of "Things People Can't See") is the author of four critically acclaimed young adult novels: *Ball Don't Lie, Mexican WhiteBoy, We Were Here,* and *I Will Save You.* He's also the author of the picture book *A Nation's Hope: The Story of Boxing Legend Joe Louis,* illustrated by Kadir Nelson. Matt lives in Brooklyn and teaches creative writing at New York University.

Pam Muñoz Ryan (author of "Because of Shoe") has written more than thirty books for young readers, from picture books to young adult novels, including the award-winning *Esperanza Rising, Becoming Naomi León, Riding Freedom, Paint the Wind,* and *The Dreamer.* She has two dogs, Buddy and Sammie.

Mark Teague (author and illustrator of "Science Fair") is the author and illustrator of many award-winning books. His most popular titles include the How Do Dinosaurs series by Jane Yolen and his own LaRue books. In 2009 he published his first novel, *The Doom Machine.* Mark lives in upstate New York with his wife, Laura, two daughters, two dogs, two cats, and several chickens.

Go Fish!

Ann M. Martin

© Dion Ogust

Where did you get the inspiration for your story, *Picasso*?

My story was based on an experience I had with my own dog, Sadie. But I have to say up front that Sadie is nothing like Picasso, the dog in the story. Picasso is described as not terribly bright, and Sadie is quite intelligent—timid, but intelligent. I always thought that if she went to school, she would be the kid in the first row answering all the questions and turning in beautifully executed projects on time, complete with artistic covers and tables of content. Also, she would answer every extra credit question.

But back to the story. One day, my intelligent, well-behaved dog disappeared just the way Picasso did. I let her out of my sight for only a few minutes and she took off. I have no idea where she went. She'd never disappeared before. I called and called for her. I walked all around my yard and into the woods behind the yard. Finally I got in my car and drove around the neighborhood. I phoned neighbors and told them to look out for her. I drove around the neighborhood again. An hour later I got home and found Sadie sitting in the driveway. I still have no idea where she went, but she looked very pleased with herself. I think she had a happy adventure.

What is your favorite type of dog?

I don't have a favorite breed. Sadie is a mutt—excuse me, a mix. And I don't know what she's a mix of. People say she looks a little like a cocker spaniel and a little like a golden retriever and a teensy bit like a saluki (a breed I had never heard of until someone said, "Your dog looks like a saluki"). Sadie has the build of a greyhound and, as I mentioned, is extremely intelligent. I've heard that mixes are the healthiest dogs and live the longest, so I suppose that any mix is my favorite type of dog.

If you were an animal, what would you be?

I would like to be a wild animal—if I could live in my natural environment, free from poachers.

What is your favorite animal movie?

My favorite animal movie is *The Yearling*, even though it's very sad. It's based on one of my favorite animal books.

What is your funniest real-life animal story?

One night I had company over for dinner. I was just telling

my guests how well-behaved my cat Woody was when Woody jumped onto the dining room table, stole a piece of chicken out of a serving dish, and ate it under the table while the guests watched.

What advice would you give to future short-story writers?

Writing takes practice. You may not be a great author right now, but you can write well if you work at it. Writing each day will keep you "in shape," like an athlete getting ready for a big event.

~~~~~~~~~~~~~~~~~~~~~~~~~~~~~~~~

Margarita Engle

Where did you get the inspiration for your story, *Trail Magic*?

Trail Magic was inspired by long hours spent helping my husband train his search-and-rescue dogs, Maggie and Chance. I hide in the wilderness so the dogs can practice finding a "lost" person. To them, it's a great game of hide-

and-seek. For a hiker who is actually lost, it would be life and death.

What is your favorite type of dog?

Search-and-rescue dogs are my favorites, because of their dedication to life-saving work. They can be any breed or cross-breed. Maggie is an Australian shepherd/Queensland heeler, and Chance is a yellow Labrador retriever.

If you were an animal, what would you be?

I have always wanted to be a wild horse. There is no sight more spectacular than a herd of mustangs, galloping!

What is your favorite animal movie?

I loved *The Black Stallion*, but I actually loved the book more than the movie.

What is your funniest real-life animal story?

Our friend's parrot landed in my hair and refused to leave. My natural frizz must have looked like a nest!

What advice would you give to future short-story writers?

Know the ending before you start. In a short story, you don't have room to explore. You need a direction of travel within the miniature world of your plot.

Valerie Hobbs

Where did you get the inspiration for your story, _The God of the Pond_?

I had a chicken-stealing German shepherd when I was young. She was the sweetest girl, but she did love her chicken!

What is your favorite type of dog?

For fun, a border collie; for comfort, a golden retriever.

If you were an animal, what would you be?

A bird. Definitely. A crow or a hawk. I want to be up there in the sky, checking everything out and then soaring off into the clouds.

What is your favorite animal movie?

Rio.

What is your funniest real-life animal story?

I made the mistake of feeding a mother skunk and her seven little babies. They were cute! But she never went away, and we have lived with generations of skunks ever since.

What advice would you give to future short-story writers?

Close your eyes and "see" the story happening on film, then open your eyes and write what you saw.

THACHER HURD

Where did you get the inspiration for your story, *Patty*?

From something that happened when I was young and we were living in Vermont. Our dog, Patty, really did get into a porcupine and a skunk on the same day. What a mess that was, and what a big stink.

What is your favorite type of dog?

Golden retrievers, because they seem like the friendliest

dogs in the world. Sometimes almost foolishly friendly. Golden retrievers seem full of love for everything in the universe.

My neighbors when I was a kid had a golden retriever they named Rivers because she peed a lot when she was a puppy.

If you were an animal, what would you be?

A snow leopard in the Himalayan mountains in Tibet. I would love to roam the highest mountains in the world, my sharp eyes missing nothing, my thick fur coat keeping me warm through the winter.

What is your favorite animal movie?

Hmm. I'll have to think about that one.

What is your funniest real-life animal story?

This isn't funny, particularly, but when I was about five we drove across the country from where we lived in California to Vermont, where my parents had an old farm. We drove in an old station wagon. (This was in the early 1950s, before everyone flew everywhere.) We had just gotten through Nevada, heading east, when a little lizard appeared on the dashboard of our car. Somehow in Nevada the lizard had crawled up into our car and decided to stay, or maybe he was asleep when the engine started up in the morning and couldn't get out of the car in time.

We thought he would disappear the next time we stopped for gas. But after we had stopped, he once more appeared on the dashboard. And every day after that we saw him for a little while—always on our dashboard. We drove across Nebraska, Iowa, Illinois, Ohio, and all the other states. Eventually we got to Vermont and he was still with us! What a heroic and brave lizard he must have been to last all that way. When we got to Vermont, he disappeared. I wanted to keep him for a pet, but he was gone before I could catch him. He must have gone off into the field to find other lizards. I always wondered what happened to him.

What advice would you give to future short-story writers?

Find a beginning that is exciting. Find a twist at the end.

<hr />

Jon J Muth

© Bonnie Muth

Where did you get the inspiration for your story, *Brancusi and Me*?

The inspiration for *Brancusi and Me* came from seeing a

photo of Brancusi and his dog, Polaire. Brancusi was a pretty mysterious figure in the art world and he lived alone, so I started to wonder what kind of relationship he and Polaire had had. It must've been very close.

What is your favorite type of dog?

Dogs that are goofy and friendly are my favorite. The kind that wag their whole body when they are happy. Since most dogs I've met are pretty goofy, I guess I like most dogs.

If you were an animal, what would you be?

If I were an animal, I would be a heron. I like to sit still a lot and herons are pretty still, but they also like to fly!

What is your favorite animal movie?

My favorite animal movie is *Hidalgo*, about the American rider and his mustang, Hidalgo, racing across the Arabian desert.

What is your funniest real-life animal story?

I once had a cat who would always use my sock drawer as a litter box. No matter what I did, she would find where I hid my socks and use that drawer. Before I discovered what was going on, many friends thought I had very smelly feet. And some of them still don't believe the story!

What advice would you give to future short-story writers?

Short stories tend to be most powerful when they are about one thing.

Wendy Orr

Where did you get the inspiration for your story,
Dognapper?

My previous dog, a dachshund called Max, was a great digger. When he stayed in a boarding kennel, he actually dug
out of his pen and into the next one. (Which, luckily, also
had its gate closed and didn't have another dog in it!)

However, if Max was a great digger, then Harry, a poodle cross I have now, is a champion digger. The only thing
he likes more than digging is his pug–King Charles Cava-
lier cross girlfriend, Pippa. When he sees her, he leaps up
and down as if he's on a trampoline, with his golden ears
flapping. . . .

So I mixed all the dogs up and added Gus the German
shepherd—although Gus was actually the name of one of
my parents' dachshunds!

What is your favorite type of dog?

Whichever one I have. So maybe my favorite would be a

dachshund–poodle cross, but I'm not quite sure what that would look like!

If you were an animal, what would you be?

I'd love to be something fancy and elegant like a dolphin, but really, I think I'm a goofy, loving Labrador.

What is your favorite animal movie?

The Black Stallion.

What is your funniest real-life animal story?

Our border collie, Bear, was my husband's working dog on our farm, and so he was used to jumping fences to go where he needed to herd the cows back to the dairy. When we moved to a few acres on the edge of a village, he absolutely loved being a house dog and going for walks to outdoor cafés. And because he could jump any fence (and quickly learned to open the doors in the house), his favorite thing was going to the café by himself—and barking at the door till they came out and fed him. It always worked!

What advice would you give to future short-story writers?

Read your story aloud to someone when you're finished. If there's a part that you don't feel happy reading—maybe it feels a bit boring, or a bit confusing—it might mean you need to rewrite it.

Matt de la Peña

Where did you get the inspiration for your story,
Things People Can't See?

I grew up in an environment very similar to the setting in
this story. Greenhouses surrounded me. I went to a "good"
school just like the main character and at first I felt out
of place. I also like the idea of a smelly dog being able to
bring kids from different backgrounds together.

What is your favorite type of dog?

I love labs. Black Labs and white Labs. I also love pugs.

If you were an animal, what would you be?

I'd be a monkey, I think. I'd like to hang out in trees and
throw bananas at humans.

What is your favorite animal movie?

I'm gonna go way back on folks here. *Old Yeller*. I love that
movie. Chokes me up every time.

What is your funniest real-life animal story?

The dog in the story is based on my dog in real life, who was also named Peanut. Just like in the story, my Peanut was one of the most unattractive dogs in the history of the world. His teeth stuck out. His hair was coarse. And he had a serious problem with passing gas. Let's just say Peanut knew how to clear out a room!

What advice would you give to future short-story writers?

Try to make all your characters complex. The best bad guy is at least a little bit likable. The best good guy has at least one or two flaws.

~~~~~~~~~~~~~~~~~~~~~~~~~~~~~~~~~~~~

Pam Muñoz Ryan

Where did you get the inspiration for your story, *Because of Shoe*?

Dogs often bring people together, like matchmakers. I

wanted to create an instance where this might happen.

What is your favorite type of dog?

A mutt. Our family dogs have always been adopted from shelters.

If you were an animal, what would you be?

A dolphin.

What is your favorite animal movie?

When I was a girl, I loved the television series *Flipper*. As a (sometimes) grown-up, I love the movie *Seabiscuit*.

What is your funniest real-life animal story?

When my daughter was in preschool, we let her adopt two ducks that had hatched in her classroom incubator. We told her she could name them anything she wanted. My husband and I coached her about names that "went together," like Salt and Pepper, or Romeo and Juliet, but she wasn't interested in any of our ideas. She announced one morning, "I thought of names for my ducks, and . . . the names go together!" She named the ducks Stick and Branch.

What advice would you give to future short-story writers?

Even though a short story is, well . . . short, it still needs a beginning, a middle, and an end.

Mark Teague

Where did you get the inspiration for your story, *Science Fair*?

I believe I was sitting around feeling like a dog. Also, I had a deadline.

What is your favorite type of dog?

I have a pit bull and a Boston terrier. I tell the Boston terrier I prefer pit bulls, but that's mostly just to annoy him.

If you were an animal, what would you be?

I really don't want to be anything but human. In fact, my story is a cautionary tale on this very theme.

What is your favorite animal movie?

I cannot recall a single animal movie. There was a TV show called *Lassie* when I was a kid. I didn't like it.

What is your funniest real-life animal story?

My animal stories tend to be either unbelievable (because they aren't true) or of the "I guess you had to be there" variety. I much prefer the stories in this book.

What advice would you give to future short-story writers?

Be outrageous. Make up events that nobody would believe and make them believable. Don't worry if it doesn't make sense. You can fix anything you don't like in your second draft. Or your third. Or your fourth . . .

THE BEAST WITHIN
A TALE OF BEAUTY'S PRINCE

THE BEAST WITHIN
A TALE OF BEAUTY'S PRINCE

BY SERENA VALENTINO

SCHOLASTIC INC.

ISBN 978-0-545-83353-0

12 11 10 9 8 7 6 5 4 3 2 1   15 16 17 18 19 20/0

Printed in the U.S.A.   40

First Scholastic printing, January 2015

This book is set in Garamond 3.

Dedicated to my dearest love, Shane Case
—Serena Valentino

CHAPTER I

THE WITCHES IN THE ROSE GARDEN

The Beast stood in his rose garden, the overwhelming scent of new blossoms making him slightly dizzy. His garden always seemed to have a life of its own, as if the twisting thorny vines could wrap themselves around his racing heart and put an end to his anxiety. There were times when he wished they would, but now his mind was filled with images of the beautiful young woman inside his castle: Belle, so brave and noble—willing to take her father's place as a prisoner in the castle dungeon. What sort of woman would do that—give up her life so easily, sacrificing her freedom for her father's? The Beast wondered if he was capable of such a sacrifice. He wondered if he was capable of love.

He stood there looking at the view of his castle from the garden. He tried to recall how the castle had looked before the curse. It was different now—menacing, and alive. Even the spires of his castle seemed to consciously pierce the sky with a violent fervor. He could only imagine how the place looked from a distance. It was tall and imposing and perched on the top of the highest mountain in the kingdom, and it appeared as though it were cut from the very mountain itself, surrounded by a thick green forest filled with dangerous wild creatures.

Only since he had been forced to spend his life hidden within its wretched walls and on its grounds had he done such things as take in his surroundings this way—actually see and, indeed, *feel* them. He now contemplated the moonlight casting sinister shadows on the statues that flanked the path leading from the castle to his garden—large winged creatures more frightening than anything from the ancient stories the tutors of his youth had made him study. He couldn't recall these sculptures being there before the castle and its lands were enchanted.

There had been many changes since the witches had brought their enchantments. The topiaries, for example, seemed to snarl at him as he prowled the labyrinth on evenings like this, attempting to take his mind off his troubles.

He had long since gotten used to the statues' watchful eyes glancing at him when he wasn't looking at them directly—and their slight movements he caught only out of the corner of his eye. He couldn't escape the feeling of being watched, and had almost gotten used to it. Almost. And the grand entrance of his castle seemed to him like a gaping mouth prepared to devour him. He spent as much time outdoors as possible. The castle felt like a prison, and as large as it was, it confined him, choking the life out of him.

Once, when he was still—dare he think it!—*human*, he spent much of his time out of doors, stalking wild beasts in his forests for sport. But when he himself turned into something to be hunted, he shut himself away in those first years, never leaving the West Wing, let alone the castle.

Perhaps that was why he now detested being withindoors: he had once spent so much time locked away by his own fear.

When the castle was first enchanted, he thought that his mind was playing tricks on him—that simply the idea of the curse had driven him mad. But he now knew everything that surrounded him was alive, and he was fearful any further misdeeds on his part would send it into a frenzy, and his enemies would make him suffer even more for the pain he had caused so many before he became a beast. The physical transformation was only part of the curse. There was much more, and it was far too frightening to think of.

Right now he wanted to think of the only thing that could calm him even slightly. He wanted to think of *her*.

Belle.

He looked upon the lake to the right of the garden, the moon creating beautiful silver patterns on the rippling water. Apart from his thoughts of Belle, this was the only tranquility he had been afforded since the curse. He spent many hours here, careful not to catch sight of his own reflection, though sometimes he was tempted. He was fully aware of the revulsion it would bring.

He had been almost obsessed with his reflection when the curse began to take hold, and he quite liked the little changes in his appearance at first, the deep lines he mused had made his young face more fearsome to his enemies. But now . . . now that the curse had overtaken him completely, he couldn't stand the sight of himself. Every mirror in the castle had been broken or shut away in the West Wing. His terrible deeds were engraved on his face, and that sent a hollow, wretched feeling deep into his gut, sickening him.

But enough of that.

He had a beautiful woman within his walls. She was a willing captive, someone to talk to, and yet he couldn't even bring himself to face her.

Fear.

It gripped him again. Would his fear now keep him outside, where once it had shut him *in*? Fear of going withindoors and facing the girl? She was a wise woman. Had she no idea his fate was in *her* hands?

The statues watched, as they always did, when he heard the click of tiny boots on the stone path heading in his direction, disturbing his musings. . . .

The odd sisters! Lucinda, Ruby, and Martha, an indistinguishable trio of witches with inky-black ringlets, a milky pallor with the texture of bleached driftwood, and red baby-doll lips, were standing before him in his rose garden. Their faces were glowing in the moonlight like those of ghosts with mocking expressions. Their finery glittered like stardust in his dark garden while the plumage in their hair made their birdlike gestures all the more grotesque. There was a nervousness about them; they were seized by a constant series of little twitches and gestures, as if they were in continuous communication with each other even when they weren't speaking. They seemed to be taking measure of him. And he let them. He stood in silence, as he often did when they came to him, waiting for them to speak.

They appeared whenever they pleased and always without warning. Never mind it was his castle, and his gardens. He had long before given up on insisting that they appear at his will. He soon discovered his own desires were of no consequence to them.

Their laughs were shrill and seemed to mock the tiny glimmer of hope the witches detected within his dark and lonely heart. Lucinda was the first to speak, as was their custom. He couldn't help being transfixed by her face when she spoke to him. She looked like an odd doll come to life, with her porcelain skin and ratty clothes, and her unfaltering monotone voice only made the scene more macabre.

"So, you've captured yourself a pretty little thing at long last."

He didn't bother asking how they knew Belle had come to his castle. He had his theories on how they always seemed to know everything about him, but didn't care to share them with the sisters.

"We're surprised, Beast," said Martha, her pale blue eyes watery and globelike.

"Yes, surprised," Ruby spat with an eerie wide grin animating her too-red lips morbidly, like a dead creature brought to life by evil incantations.

"We expected your condition to have progressed by now," said Lucinda, her head cocked slightly to the right while she looked at him. "We dreamed of you running in the wood hunting smaller prey."

Ruby continued, "We dreamed of hunters tracking you down."

Martha laughed and said, "Hunting you like the beast you are and mounting your head on the Huntsmen's Tavern wall."

"Why, you're even wearing clothes, we see. Holding on to the last shred of your humanity, is it?" they said in unison.

The Beast did nothing to betray his terror—terror not of the witches' magic but of his own threatening nature, of which they were reminding him. They were holding a mirror up to the monster within, which was longing to escape. It was a beast that wanted to kill the witches and everything else in its path. He longed to see blood and bones, to taste their flesh. If he tore at their throats with his claws, he'd never have to listen to their shrill taunting voices again.

Lucinda laughed.

"Now *that* is what we expected of you, Beast."

And Martha said, "He will never capture Belle's heart, Sister, no matter how desperate he is to break the curse."

"He's too far gone now, I daresay."

"Perhaps if he showed her how he once looked, she may have pity on him," Ruby said as a maddening cacophony of laughter filled the rose garden.

"Pity him, yes, but love him? Never!"

The Beast used to hurl insults back at all of them, but it seemed only to fuel their passion for cruelty, and he didn't dare stir up his own anger and desire for violence, so he just stood stock-still, waiting for their little torture session to end.

Martha spoke again. "In case you've forgotten, here are the rules, Beast, laid out by all the sisters:

You must love her and that love must be returned with true love's kiss, before your twenty-first birthday. She may use the mirror as you do, to see into the world beyond your kingdom, but she must never know the details of the curse or how it's to be broken. You will notice she sees the castle and its enchantments differently than yourself. The most terrifying aspects of the curse are reserved for you."

The Beast stared blankly at the witches.

Martha smiled creepily and continued, "This is your one advantage. The only thing in this castle or on its grounds that will frighten Belle is your visage."

Lucinda chimed in. "When was the last time you looked upon your reflection, Beast? Or saw to the rose?"

There had been a time when the rose wasn't out of his sight. Lately he tried to forget it. He had almost expected the sisters' visit this evening would be to inform him that the last petal had fallen off its enchanted stem. But they were just here to mock him, as always, to tempt him into violence, and they'd love nothing more than to see his soul further besmirched.

Lucinda's cackling voice brought him out of his reverie. "It won't be long now. . . ."

Martha continued, "Not long at all, Beast."

"Soon the last petal will fall and you shall remain in this form with no chance of transformation to your former self."

"And on that day . . ."

"We will dance!" they finished in unison.

The Beast finally spoke. "And what of the others? Are they to remain as they are, doomed to enchantment as well?"

Ruby's eyes widened in wonder. "Concern? Is that what we detect? Isn't that odd?"

"Concern for himself."

"Yes, for himself, always himself, never others."

"Why would he concern himself with servants? He never gave them a second thought, unless it was to punish them."

"I think he's afraid of what they might do to him if he doesn't break the curse."

"I think you're right, Sister."

"I am also interested in seeing what they'll do."

"It shall be a gruesome spectacle indeed."

"And we shall take much pleasure in bearing witness to it."

"Don't forget, Beast, true love, both given and received, before the last petal falls."

And with that the sisters turned on the heels of their tiny pointed boots and clicked their way out of the rose garden, the sound fading little by little until they vanished into a sudden mist and the Beast could no longer hear them at all.

Chapter II

The Refusal

The Beast sighed and slumped down on the stone bench in the shadow of the winged-creature statue hovering above him. Its shadow mingled with his own—his face and its wings—merging into what looked like a Shedu, the winged lion from ancient myth. It had been so long since he'd seen even his shadow that he hardly knew what he looked like, and this shadow stirred a great interest in him.

With an infusion of light the shadow faded into nothingness. Remaining was a new stark-white statue, wearing a passive expression. It was neither male nor female—not as far as he could surmise, anyway—and it was standing completely still with a small brass candelabrum in one hand, candles burning, while the other hand pointed toward the castle entrance. It was as if the stone figure was commanding him back to the castle, back into the gaping mouth.

He feared if he returned, the castle would at long last devour him.

He made his way back, leaving the silent statue and the sisters' taunting words in the garden. The light from the candelabrum looked tiny now, like fireflies in the distance.

The statue would make its way back to the castle in its own time, more than likely when the Beast was far enough away. They never moved or came to him while he was looking at them directly; they were always sneaking up on him while his attentions were elsewhere. It frightened him, really, to know they could come up to him at any time and do with him what they would, but that was yet another portion of the curse he had to contend with.

He thought about what the sisters had said, and

wondered how Belle saw the castle's enchantments and how its cursed servants appeared to her.

As he made his way through the foyer toward the dining room, he stopped to listen to the muted voices coming from Belle's chamber but couldn't quite make out what was being discussed. He was creeping down the hallway, hoping to get a peek at whom she was speaking to, when he heard a gentle-man with a French accent inviting her to dine. She slammed her door and refused.

"I won't! I don't want anything to do with him! He's a monster!"

Monster! His anger got the better of him. "If she won't dine with me, then she won't eat at all," he growled, turning the corner and half expecting to see another of the living statues standing there to torment him, but the only evidence of anyone hav-ing been there at all was the small gold candelabrum he'd just seen in the rose garden, now extinguished, with a tiny ribbon of smoke curling up from the smoldering wick.

"She thinks I'm a monster!" he fumed.

He felt his anger mounting, raging out of
control as he stormed his way to the West Wing.
Monster! His claws gouged the wooden banister as
he went up the long stairway, wishing it was flesh
and blood, not splintering wood.

Monster!

There was very little light in this part of the
castle. It was completely dark apart from the moonlight that came through the tattered red draperies
of his bedroom. Leaning on the far wall were stacks
of different-shaped mirrors covered in white moth-
eaten cloths. Among the mirrors were portraits,
some of which had been destroyed by his anger and
frustration, the visages mocking him as the witches
had, taunting him with his former likeness.

Monster!

He couldn't light a fire in the staggeringly large
fireplace or the torches on the wall brackets. His
paws couldn't master tiny things like matches, and
the servants weren't allowed into the West Wing.
Not even the sisters came to this part of the castle.
He had escaped their mockery for long stretches

of time when he spent most of his days here in the beginning—hiding away, letting his anger swell to epic proportions, fearful of what he was becoming, yet intrigued concurrently.

It had been that way at first, hadn't it? Intriguing. The subtle differences in his features, the lines around his eyes that frightened his foes when he narrowed them. Using a look rather than words to strike fear into his enemies was very useful indeed.

He *had* looked upon himself in the mirror in those days, trying to distinguish which sorts of deeds caused the most horrific alterations in his appearance. Knowing that this was a degenerative curse that wouldn't abate.

The sisters seemed to know of his compulsion and teased him about it, saying he would suffer the fate of their cousin's second wife if he wasn't careful. The sisters were always talking nonsense, always speaking in fragments, and suffered from fits of laughter so severe he hardly knew what they were on about most of the time. He was not sure even they were aware. Could it all be the rambling of maddened minds? Here he was—taunted by insane crones. *He*, who had once been a prince.

Once. And now . . . now he couldn't even venture out of his gardens or approach a wounded stranger who might wander from the forest to his castle in the night without sending him running in fear.

What did Belle think of what little she saw of him by dungeon torchlight? But he knew, didn't he? She'd called him a monster! Leave her to the servants, then; let them weave tales of his dastardly deeds! Let them confirm how vile and ugly he was. He cared not! After all, he was a monster. And monsters knew not feelings, especially the sentiment called *love*.

His anger and confusion were quelled as his head spun from exhaustion. He sat on the bed, wondering what to do next. The sisters implied that the girl was his only hope of escaping the curse. Liars! He could make her fall in love with him easily enough if he looked as he once had—handsome, well groomed, some might say arrogant.

Women were easily managed then. A few flowery words of love, feigning some interest in what she had to say, perhaps showing a pretense of vulnerability and the girl was his. And often he didn't even need to resort to such nonsense; only if the girl was exceedingly beautiful would he bother to try to win her admiration. Typically, his looks alone were enough to catch them spellbound.

But the way he looked now . . . He had no idea how to go about this with Belle. He pushed himself onto his feet, feeling the rough and tattered sheets with the pads of his paws. Perhaps he *should* let servants in to make the bed, dust the windows, and mop the floors. To have him live more like a human being than the monster he had become.

He stood on shaking legs, still dizzy from the rush of animal anger he'd felt when he heard Belle call him a monster. He moved to the mantel, where he kept the enchanted mirror the sisters had given him long before. He stood there for a moment, taking a deep breath before he looked at himself. It had been far too long since he had seen his own

19

reflection. He had to see how his odious deeds had etched themselves upon his face.

His paw rested on the sheet that was draped over the frame. Then, in one movement, he tore the sheet away and tossed it aside, revealing the looking glass and the tarnished reflection that stared back at him.

Monster!

The only indication of what he had once been was his soulful blue eyes, which teemed with humanity. Those hadn't changed. They were still his.

But in all other respects, he had become exactly what he had feared. And, indeed, it was worse than he ever could have fathomed.

His knees buckled as his world started to close in. His scope became narrower until he found himself in utter darkness, spiraling into a vision of his past—of himself as he'd once been, before he became a monster. Before he became the Beast.

Chapter III

The Prince

Before the curse, life had been good to the Prince.

To hear the sisters tell the tale of the curse would be to hear a story filled with examples of what a terrible person he was, a list of his misdeeds, tallied one by one, each of them worse and nastier than the one before, until the sisters swooped down on him with their spell, deforming him into the pathetic beast now lying on his bedroom floor before his mirror.

Eventually, that is indeed how the story will go. But the sisters won't be able to spew that part of the tale at first. Not until the Prince has had his say, a chance to tell you how much fun he had.

Because there was a time when things were good.

It was a time when the Prince was just an arrogant young man, full of pride and keenly aware of his station in life. What young prince hasn't found himself in exactly the same place? What do you think other princes are like? Are they just charming men venturing off hither and thither in search of sleeping brides to awaken with love's first kiss? Do you fancy them as dandy gentlemen while they slay dragons and vanquish foul, murderous stepmothers? Perhaps they do that sort of thing without the slightest bit of ego or aggression? One moment they're hacking their way through enchanted killer thornbushes only to find a fire-breathing dragon primed for murder on the other side, and the next they're expected to waltz with their new brides in pastel suits and golden sashes.

And what is up with those sashes, anyway? Horrible!

Our prince didn't want anything to do with that romantic poppycock. He wanted a different sort of life, and he learned early on he didn't have to slay a fire-breathing beast to get a fair maiden to kiss him. Though swaggering in with the corpse of a giant elk or a fearsome grizzly bear slung over his shoulder for Old Man Higgins to stuff and mount on the tavern wall did get him his fair share of smooches from the young ladies—and as dangerous as it might have been at times, it was a far cry from poison apples, stinky dwarfs, or being burnt alive by an evil fairy queen. He'd take hunting and philandering over that stuff any day.

Life was good; everyone loved and worshiped the Prince and he knew it.

As he sat in his favorite tavern, his clothes covered in earth, grime, and the blood from his latest kill, he couldn't have been more handsome. Or at least that was what he thought. The tavern was his favorite haunt. It had most everything he loved in one place. The wood walls were so crowded with the forest beasts he'd slain that Old Man Higgins laughed and teased him as he poured him another beer.

"I'm going to have to build a larger tavern, Prince!"

And it was true.

The only person who killed almost as many animals as the Prince was his good friend Gaston, who slammed a handful of coins onto the bar, startling poor Higgins before he could finish pouring the new round of drinks. "Drinks are on me tonight, Higgins! In celebration of the Prince's engagement!"

The men cheered and the barmaids wilted into tears, their bosoms heaving heavy sighs of disappointment. Gaston seemed to enjoy the spectacle as much as the Prince did.

"She is the most beautiful girl in the village! You're a lucky man! I'd be jealous if you weren't the very best of my friends!"

That he was. Gaston's best friend.

They had always been alike, Gaston and the Prince, and the Prince supposed that was why they had enjoyed each other's company so well. Or perhaps he had felt it was better to keep his competition close at hand. But then again, he wondered if that was how he'd actually seen it then.

The Prince couldn't help laughing sometimes while listening to Gaston go on about himself, bragging about his cleft chin, showing off his hairy chest, and singing his own praises up and down the town's main thoroughfares.

However, there was another side to the Prince's old friend, a vindictive cruelty about him.

Yes, they were very much alike, Gaston and the Prince, and that is what brought them together.

Gaston was the first to let the Prince know his fiancée, Circe, was from a poor farming family, in an attempt to prevent the Prince from shaming himself by marrying someone so low. *Of course* he couldn't marry her, no matter how beautiful she was. How could his subjects take the daughter of a pig farmer seriously as their queen? The servants wouldn't respect her, and she wouldn't know how to act in diplomatic situations. No, it would be a disaster. It would be unfair to his subjects and to her, and most of all to him. He didn't need anyone to tell him it was a poor idea; he came to the conclusion himself the moment he discovered her station in life.

Then the decision was made.

He couldn't marry the girl.

The Prince sent for his fiancée the next day. Circe looked beautiful when she stepped out of the carriage to meet him. Her light blond hair and shimmering silver dress glistened under the morning sun as she stood in his rose garden. It was hard to believe she was a pig farmer's daughter. Perhaps Gaston was mistaken. Where would a girl on a pig farm get a dress like that? Ah. Gaston was playing his tricks again. Trying to put him off so he could have Circe for himself. That wicked butt-chinned brute. He would have words with him about this soon enough. But in the meantime he had to make amends with his beautiful Circe. Of course she had no idea he had intended to break things off, but he felt his heart had betrayed her.

"My darling, Circe, you look beautiful."

She looked up at him with her pale blue eyes, with a slight blush that did not diminish the light smattering of freckles across her button nose.

Adorable.

She was simply that, adorable. How could he have thought she was the daughter of a pig farmer? He couldn't fathom her mucking about with those dirty, horrible creatures.

Think of it! Circe feeding pigs! It was laughable when he saw her sparkling like a dew-dropped rose, like the princess she was about to become. He would make Gaston pay for causing him to doubt her.

"Come, my love, to the morning room. I have arranged something special just for you."

He didn't mention Gaston's trick to Circe; it was too nasty to repeat. There was no need to cause ill will between the two. Gaston would, after all, be his best man at the wedding. Yes, he was brutish, ill-tempered, and conniving, but he was still his closest companion. And he wanted his best friend to stand beside him at his wedding.

And there was something else. It would please the Prince to know Gaston would be seething with envy as he stood there, forced to watch the wedding proceedings, knowing his attempts to break the Prince's faith in Circe had failed and he could not have her for himself. Yes, that would be very satisfying. Perhaps after the wedding he should send Gaston away on some errand for the kingdom—something distasteful and below his rank, to show him not to interfere again.

Who could blame Gaston, really, for trying to spirit Circe away from him? She was the prettiest girl they'd ever seen, and Gaston was only giving in to her beauty and letting it taint his better judgment. It was quite funny when you thought about it—Gaston, the prince of Buttchinland, trying to take his Circe away! Who would have a commoner, no matter how close a royal family friend he might be, when she could have the prince who would one day be king of these lands?

The Prince decided to laugh the entire thing off and focus on what he loved: hunting, drinking, spending the taxes collected from his estates, and charming the ladies.

Oh yes, and there was Circe, but he loved her the

way one would love his castle, or his stable stocked with the finest horses. She was the most beautiful creature, and he treasured her for how her beauty would reflect on him and his kingdom. Sensible, he thought, and he felt beyond reproach.

The wedding plans continued even though Gaston kept on about Circe's family. Not a day or night went by that he didn't mention it.

"You're starting to bore me, Gaston, honestly! Going on about this pig farm thing as if it were actually true. Why don't you give up already?"

Gaston wouldn't let the issue alone.

"Come with me, good friend, I will show you!"

So they rode several miles, until they reached the little farmhouse, which was tucked away beyond the woods on an uncommon path.

There was his Circe. She was standing in the pen feeding the pigs, the bottom of her simple white dress caked with mud. Her hair seemed dull, and her cheeks were flushed with hard work. She must have sensed them looking at her, for she glanced up and noticed the expression of disgust on her beloved's face, leaving her stricken with horror and shame.

She dropped her pail and stood on the spot, looking at the two men.

She said nothing.

"Come out here, girl! Is that how you greet your guests?" the Prince barked cockily.

Her eyes widened as if she was coming out of a haze.

"Of course," she said meekly.

Then she walked out of the pen and approached the men, looking up at them, still astride their horses. She felt small and meek and unable to meet their disapproving gazes.

"Hello, my love, what brings you here?" she asked.

The Prince scoffed. "What brings me indeed? Why didn't you tell me your father was a mere pig farmer?"

Circe looked desperate and confused, hardly able to answer.

"What do you mean, my dearest?"

The Prince was enraged. "Do not play coy with me, madam! How dare you keep such a thing from me! How could you lie to me in such a manner?"

Circe crumpled in tears. "You never asked about my parents! I never lied to you! Why should it matter? We love each other! And love conquers all."

"Love *you*? Seriously? Look at yourself—covered in muck! How could I *possibly* love you?"

He spat on the ground and then turned his attentions to his friend. "Come on, Gaston, let's leave this stinking place. I have nothing further to say to this filthy farm girl."

And the two men rode off, leaving the beautiful maiden covered in mud and a cloud of dust kicked up by their wild horses.

CHAPTER IV

THE WITCHES' LITTLE SISTER

The Prince sat alone in his study, sipping a drink by the fireplace. Images of Circe haunted him. They flashed between the bewitching young beautiful woman he wanted to marry and the sickening scene he'd witnessed earlier that day.

He almost felt sorry for her.

Almost.

But he could not soften to her, not after she had tried to trap him into marriage by weaving such horrid lies. As he sat there, sinister shadows danced on the walls. These were created by the firelight and the giant antlers mounted on the wall above his chair. He remembered the day he'd killed the largest trophy—the great elk. He had almost been sad the day he finally took him down. He'd been tracking the beast for years. But when he'd killed him, he felt as if he'd lost an old friend. He sipped some more, remembering that hallowed day. Just then the porter poked his head into the room.

"Prince, sir, Miss Circe is here to see you."

The Prince sighed with annoyance. "I've told you, numerous times now, not to admit her! Send her away!" And he turned back to his musings.

The porter didn't leave. He stuttered his reply. "I haven't let—let—let her in, my—my lord, she is standing out . . . side, but refuses to—to—to go. She says she will not leave until you speak with her."

"Very well, then."

Putting his drink on the little wooden side table next to his chair, he stood with a heavy sigh and made his way toward the grand entrance.

There stood Circe, a pathetic little creature holding a single red rose, looking downright diminutive in the gaping arched doorway. Her eyes were sad, swollen and red from crying. She looked nothing like the ravishing beauty that had once stood in his rose garden all golden, silver, and light. If seeing her mucking around in the mud that day hadn't vanquished that memory from his mind, then this encounter most surely would.

He'd never again be tempted by memories of her beauty, trying to fool him into feeling sorry for the lying little creature! She had a ratty shawl around her shoulders that made her look like an old beggar woman. The light and shadow on her face made her look old and haggard. Had he not known it was her, he would have thought her an old beggar woman indeed.

She spoke with a small voice. She sounded like a little crow—her voice scratchy and hoarse from long crying.

"My love, please, I can't believe you would treat me so poorly. Surely you didn't mean the things you said to me earlier today."

She broke down sobbing, her tearstained and swollen face buried in her small white hands.

How could he ever have thought her adorable?

"I cannot marry you, Circe. You must have known that from the start. I'm guessing that is why you tried to keep your parents a secret."

"But I didn't know, my love! My darling, please take this rose and remember the days you still loved me. Won't you please let me come inside, away from this cold? Do you hate me so much?"

"Your beauty, which so captured my heart in my very garden, will forever be tarnished by the *grotesque* scene I witnessed today, and by *this* shameful display."

When Circe's shawl fell back, the Prince was startled to see, her eyes were no longer swollen and her face was not splotched and red from long hours of crying. Her skin was pale and glowing as if she were infused with moonlight—and her hair was bright and shimmering with little silver adornments, like sparkling bits of stardust were captured within. Her dress was opalescent silver, and everything about her seemed to glow with enchantment, but nothing shined brighter than her pale blue eyes. She had never looked so beautiful.

"I'll never be quite as beautiful again in your eyes because you think I'm the daughter of a pig farmer?"

Then he heard their voices, climbing out of the darkness, like a chorus of harpies swooping up from Hell.

"Farmer's daughter?"

"Our little sister?"

"Why, she is of royal blood. She is cousin of the old king."

He couldn't see who was speaking; he only heard three distinct voices coming from the darkness. Something about the voices unnerved him. No, if he were completely honest with himself, he would admit the voices frightened him. He wanted nothing more than to slam the door and hide within the walls of his castle, but he stood his ground.

"Is this *true*, Circe?" he asked.

"Yes, my prince, it is. My sisters and I come from a long line of royalty."

"I don't understand!"

Circe's sisters stepped into the light and stood behind her. Their grotesquerie made Circe's beauty even more pronounced.

It was startling, really.

It wasn't that they were ugly, the sisters; it was just that everything about them was so striking, and in such contrast to their other features. Each feature on its own could have been beautiful. Their large eyes, for example, might have looked stunning on another woman. Their hair, somehow it was too black, like one could become lost in the depth of the darkness, and the contrast of their bloodred lips against their parchment-white skin was just too shocking. They didn't seem real, these sisters. None of this did, because all of it was absurd. He felt as if he must be dreaming, caught in a nightmare. He was entranced by Circe's transfiguration, and it made him forget his earlier vow never again to think of her.

He was enamored with her beauty once more.

"Circe! This is *wonderful*! All is well, you're of royal descent, we can be married!"

"We had to be sure you really loved her," said Lucinda, her eyes narrowing.

"Yes, sure," said Martha.

"We wouldn't just . . ."

"Let our little sister marry a . . ."

"Monster!" they shouted accusingly in unison.

"Monster? How dare you!" the Prince snapped.

The sisters laughed.

"That is what we see—"

"A monster."

"Oh, others may find you handsome enough—"

"But you have a cruel heart!"

"And that is what *we* see, the ugliness of your soul."

"Soon *all* will see you for the cruel beast you are!"

"Sisters, *please*! Let me speak! He is mine, after all!" said Circe, trying to calm her sisters. "It is my right to deliver the retribution."

"There is no need for this," the Prince said, finally showing his fear—whether it be of the sisters or of losing the beautiful vision before him. "We can be married now. I've never seen a woman as beautiful as you. There's nothing to stand in our way. I *must* have you as my wife!"

"Your *wife*? Never! I see now you only loved my beauty. I will ensure no woman will ever want you no matter how you try to charm her! Not as long as you remain as you are—tainted by vain cruelty."

The sisters' laugh could be heard clear across the land on that night. It was so piercing it sent hundreds of birds into flight and frightened the entire population of the kingdom, even Gaston—but Circe continued with her curse while Gaston and the others wondered what ominous happenings might be afoot.

"Your ugly deeds will mar that handsome face of yours, and soon, as my sisters said, everyone will see you as the beast you are."

She then handed the Prince the single rose she had tried to give him earlier. "And since you would not take this token of love from the woman you professed to cherish, let it then be a symbol of your doom!"

"*Your* doom!" Martha said, laughing while she clapped her little white hands and hopped in her tiny boots with absolute glee.

"*Your* doom!" joined Ruby and Lucinda, also jumping up and down, making the scene even more confusing and macabre.

"Sisters!" Circe pleaded. "I am not finished!"

She continued, "As the rose petals fall, so shall the years pass until your twenty-first birthday. If you have not found love—*true* love, both given and received—by that day, and sealed with a kiss, then you shall remain the horrifying creature you'll become."

The Prince squinted his eyes and cocked his head, trying to comprehend the meaning of this riddle.

"Oh, he'll become the beast! He will!"

"No doubt! He'll never change his wicked ways!"

The sisters were again clapping and jumping in vindictive delight. Their laughter seemed to feed upon itself. The more they laughed, the louder it became, and the more insane the sisters seemed to be. Circe had to take them in hand once again.

"Sisters, stop! He has to know the terms of the curse or it will not be binding."

The sisters' laughter ceased at once, and they became unnervingly quiet, twitching with discomfort.

"Mustn't ruin his punishment!"

"No, mustn't do that!"

Circe, hearing her sisters' chatter again, gave them a reproachful look, silencing them immediately.

"Thank you, Sisters. Now, Prince, do you understand the terms of the curse?" The Prince could only look at the women in wonder and horror.

"He's struck dumb, little sister!" cackled Lucinda.

"Shhh," reminded Ruby as Circe continued.

"Do you understand the terms?" she asked him again.

"That I'm supposed to turn into some sort of beast if I do not change my ways?" the Prince said, trying to repress a smile.

Circe nodded.

Now it was time for the Prince to laugh.

"Poppycock! What sort of trickery is this? I'm to believe you've *cursed* me? Am I supposed to become so frightened that I fool myself into making something dreadful happen? I won't fall for it, ladies! If indeed you can be *called* ladies, royal blood or not!"

Circe's face hardened. The Prince had never seen her like this—so angry, so stern and cold.

"Your castle and its grounds shall also be cursed, then, and everyone within will be forced to share your burden. Nothing but horrors will surround you, from when you look into a mirror to when you sit in your beloved rose garden."

Lucinda added, "And soon those horrors will be your only scenery."

"Yes, I see you stuck cowering withindoors."

"Yes, fearful of leaving your own bedchamber!"

"Yes, yes! Too frightened to show your ugly face to the world outside your castle walls!"

"I see your servants seething with hate, watching your every move from distant shadows, sneaking up on you in the night, just looking at the creature you've become."

"And I see *you*," Lucinda said, "wondering if they'll kill you to free themselves from the curse!"

"Enough! That is but one path he may take! There is one last thing he needs before we go." Circe looked to Ruby.

"The mirror, please, Ruby."

Lucinda's face contorted even more freakishly than imaginable. "Circe, no! Not the mirror."

"It's our mirror!"

"Not yours to give away!"

"No, no, no!"

"This is *my* curse, Sisters, and on my terms. I say he gets the mirror!

"My darling," Circe continued, "this enchanted mirror will let you see into the outside world. All you need to do is ask the mirror and it will show you what you want to see."

"I don't like you giving away our treasures, Circe! That was a gift from a very famous maker of mirrors. It's quite priceless and very old. It's a mirror of legends! It was given to us before you were even born."

"And shall I remind you how you came to possess it?" asked Circe, silencing her sisters.

"Let's not bore the Prince with our family history, Circe," said Martha. "He can have the mirror, not only to see the outside world, but to see the hideous creature he's bound to become."

"Oh yes! Let him try to break the maidens' hearts after he's turned into the beast!" screamed Ruby, with Lucinda and Martha chiming in, "Let him try, let him try, to break their hearts and make them cry!" They were spinning in circles like toy tops, their dresses blossoming about them like mutant flowers in a strange garden, while they chanted their incessant mockery.

"Let him try! Let him try! To break their hearts and make them cry!"

Circe was growing impatient, and the Prince looked as if he was straddling amusement and fear.

"Sisters! Please stop, I beg you!" Circe snapped.

"I'm supposed to take this seriously? Any of this? Really, Circe! Do you think I'm an idiot like your cackling sisters here?"

Before the Prince could say any more, he found himself pressed firmly against the stone wall behind him, Circe's hand placed tightly around his throat, her voice a hiss like a giant serpent's.

"Never speak ill of my sisters again! And yes, you'd better take everything I've said seriously, and I suggest you commit it to memory, because your life depends on it. The curse is in your hands now. Choose the right path, Prince, change your ways, and you shall be redeemed. Chose cruelty and vanity and you will suffer indeed!"

She released him. He was utterly gobsmacked. Her face was very close to his and full of hate. He felt frightened, really frightened, perhaps for the first time in his young life.

"Do you understand?" she asked again, vehemently, and all he could mutter was "Yes."

"Come, Sisters, let's leave him, then. He will choose his own path from here."

So he did.

CHAPTER V

THE PORTRAIT IN
THE WEST WING

In the first few months there was no sign of a curse: no taunting sisters, no beastly visage, and no villainous servants plotting his death. The idea was laughable, really. His loyal servants growing to hate him? Ludicrous! Imagine his beloved Cogsworth or Mrs. Potts wishing for his death—utterly inconceivable! It was pure claptrap!

Nothing of which the sisters spoke came true, and he saw no reason to believe it would. As a result, he did not think he needed to repent, change his ways, or take anything those insane women had to say seriously at all.

Life went on and it was good—as good as it had

always been, with Gaston at his side, money in his pockets, and women to fawn over him. What more could he ask for?

But as happy as he was, he couldn't completely shake the fear that perhaps Circe and her sisters were right. He noticed little changes in his appearance—small things that made him feel his mind might be betraying him and he was somehow falling for the sisters' ruse.

He had to constantly—obsessively—remind himself that there was no curse. There were only his fears and the sisters' lies, and he wasn't about to let either get the better of him.

He was in his bedroom readying himself for a hunting trip with Gaston when the porter came in to let him know his friend had arrived.

"Send him up, then. Unless he wants to take breakfast in the observatory while I finish getting ready."

The Prince was in fine spirits and found himself feeling better than he had in a long time. But he couldn't for the life of him remember the porter's name. A bit concerning, but one of the advantages of being a prince is that no one questions you. So if others were noticing a change in the Prince, they didn't mention it.

"Are my things packed? Is everything ready for our stalking expedition?" he asked the porter.

"Indeed, my liege, it's all been loaded. If there's nothing else that you require, then I shall see to the other gentleman's things?"

The Prince had to laugh. Gaston a gentleman? Hardly! The porter was too young to remember when Gaston and the Prince had been boys. Some of the older staff would remember. Mrs. Potts would remember, to be sure. She had often recounted old stories about the boys as children, laughing at the memory of them running to the kitchen and pleading with her for sweets after their grand adventures, both of them covered in mud, tracking it throughout the castle, like little boys love to do, making a maid trail after them—a maid who muttered curses under her breath the entire time.

Curses.

THE BEAST WITHIN

Put them out of your mind. Remember something else.

Mrs. Potts.

She loved telling the story of how the boys had convinced themselves the castle grounds had been plagued by an evil dragon. On more than one occasion, the boys went off adventuring all day and were gone well into the night, making everyone sick with worry over what might have befallen them—and the two of them just waltzed right in as happy and gay as could be, without a care in the world, wondering what the fuss was all about.

That was how those boys had been. The Prince wondered how much they'd actually changed, though Mrs. Potts reminded him at every opportunity that both he and Gaston had changed a great deal. She often said she didn't see much of the little boys she once adored in either of them.

Changed.

He had changed, hadn't he? And not in the way Mrs. Potts feared. In other ways. She still loved them, though. She couldn't help herself. She probably even thought of Gaston as a gentleman. She always treated him as such. She saw the best in everyone when she could, and encouraged their friendship when they were young, even though he was the gamekeeper's son.

"It shouldn't matter who his father is, young master. He is your friend and has proven to be a very good one at that." He remembered feeling terrible for letting a thing like status make him reconsider a friendship with Gaston. None of that mattered, not now. Gaston had his own lands and people to work them—the Prince had seen to that—and that life when they were so young, when Gaston lived with his father in the stable quarters, it all seemed so far away and long ago.

Gaston's very voice interrupted his thoughts.

"Prince! Why are you standing there daydreaming when you should be readying yourself? We have a long journey ahead of us."

"I was remembering when we were young, Gaston. Recalling our earlier adventures. Do you remember the time you saved my life in the . . ."

Gaston's face hardened. "You know I don't like to talk about that, Prince! Must you always remind me that I am not your equal?"

"That wasn't my aim, dear friend."

"Nevertheless, it is the *result*."

The Prince felt scolded.

Gaston seemed to be lost in his own thoughts now, musing over the large portrait of the Prince hanging over the fireplace. "When did you sit for this portrait? How long ago was it? Five years?"

"It was finished only a quarter of a year ago. You remember, it was done by that wildly eccentric painter. He called himself the Maestro, remember? He seemed to live in another world altogether with his pretty speeches about preserving our youth and making time stand still through the magic of depiction."

"I do! Yes, he was very . . . uh, interesting."

"Interesting? You wanted to toss him out the nearest window, if I recall!"

The two laughed but Gaston seemed to be preoccupied with thoughts other than those about strange painters and their proclamations of preserving a moment in time.

"I suppose there is something to his insane ramblings, though. I do seem much changed since this was painted. Look, around the eyes in the painting. There is no sign of lines, but if you see here, it does look as though I've aged more than five years."

"You sound like a woman, Prince, worrying about lines around the eyes! Next you'll be wondering what color petticoat looks best with a blue dress. Shall I inquire with your fairy godmother?"

The Prince laughed, but it wasn't genuine. Gaston continued, "We have better things to do than waste the day clucking away like a couple of hens. Meet me in the observatory for breakfast when you're finished getting ready."

"Yes, feel free to start without me. I'm sure Mrs. Potts is in a tizzy that it's taken us this long to get down there."

The portrait was still bothering him. How had his eyes become so lined in just a few months? Was it possible they had looked like this at the time and

the painter wished to compliment him by making him seem younger? No, the Maestro was very
specific about preserving that moment in time.
Making it as pure and realistic as possible. Freezing
a moment that could never be diminished or altered,
preserving it for the generations so they might
evoke something of his memory once he was long
gone. So the man had said, almost word for word.
It seemed contrary to his annoying speeches and
proclamations for him to have painted the Prince
any differently than he had appeared at the time.
So Gaston was right? Had he aged five years in just
over three months? Or was Gaston simply being
mean-spirited because he'd reminded him of when
they were young?

Could it be . . . ? No. But what if . . . what if
Circe's curse was real?

Then he remembered the sisters' mirror. He had
tucked it away the night the fiendish harpies gave it
to him, and hadn't given it a second thought. Their
words started to ring in his ears and he couldn't take
his mind off the hellish thing. *It will show you as the*

beast you are bound to become! He walked over to the mantel. Sitting on top was a voluminous tortoise-shell cat with narrowed yellow eyes lined in black. She looked down on him, scrutinizing him as he looked for the button that opened the secret compartment within the fireplace mantel. The fireless pit was flanked by two griffons with ruby-red eyes that sparkled in the morning light.

He pressed one of the eyes inward, and it recessed into the griffon's skull. Each griffon had a crest on its chest; the crest on the griffon to the right popped out, revealing the compartment containing the mirror.

The Prince just stood there looking at it. The mirror had landed facedown when he tossed it in. He stared at its back side. It was seemingly harmless, a simple silver hand mirror almost entirely black now from tarnish. He reached in, grabbing the mirror by its handle. It was cold in his hand, and he fancied he could feel the evil of the sisters penetrating him by his simply touching it.

Fancy.

He held it to his chest for a moment, not wanting to look at himself, wondering if this was folly. He was letting the sisters get to him. He had promised himself he wouldn't surrender to fears and superstitions. Yet he found himself wanting to look into the mirror. And he was worried about what he might see.

"Enough of this foolishness!" He gathered his courage, lifted the mirror, and looked into it unflinchingly, determined to face his fears. At first glance he didn't seem much changed. His heart felt lighter and he indeed felt foolish for letting the sisters' threats invade his thoughts.

"Look closer, Prince." He dropped the mirror and was afraid he had broken it. Though it might have been a blessing if he had. He was sure it was Lucinda's voice he'd heard taunting from the black ether, or wherever she deigned to dwell. It was Hell itself for all he knew. Picking up the mirror with a shaking hand, he took a second look. This time he did see deep lines around his eyes. Gaston was right: he looked a good five years older after just a few months! The lines made his face look cruel. Heartless. All the things Circe said he was.

Impossible.

His heart started to pound like thunder. It was pounding so violently that he felt as if it would burst within his chest.

Then came the laughter. It surrounded him, cacophonous. The wicked cackling seemed to come from lands unseen; their voices, their vindictive words entrapped him, causing his anxieties to overwhelm him. His vision became narrowed, and soon all he saw were the cat's yellow eyes staring at him from the mantel. Then everything closed in on him and his world became black.

Nothingness.

He was alone in the darkness with only the sisters' laughter and his own dread to keep him company.

He woke what seemed like some days later, feeling as if he'd been beaten by a gang of black-guards.

His entire body ached and he could barely move.

The sisters had ensured his misery and compounded it with their laughter and taunting, leaving him ill and suffering.

"You're awake, sir!" said Cogsworth from the corner chair, where he had been sitting. "We were very worried about you, sir."

"What happened?" The Prince's head was still slightly befogged and he couldn't quite get his bearings.

"Well, it seems, sir, you were very ill, suffering from a severe fever. When you hadn't come down to breakfast, I came up to find you lying on the floor."

"Where's the mirror?"

"The mirror, sir? Oh yes, I put it in your dressing stand."

The Prince's panic subsided.

"Was it all a dream, then? All fancy brought on by worry or illness?"

"I don't know what you mean, sir. But you were rather ill. We're all very much relieved to hear you are out of the woods, as they say."

Cogsworth was putting on a brave face, as he

always did, but the Prince could tell he had been worried. He looked tired, worn, and uncustomarily rumpled. He was usually fastidious. It was a credit to his loyalty that it seemed he had been at the Prince's side during his entire illness.

"Thank you, Cogsworth. You're a good man."

"Thank you, sir. It was nothing."

Before Cogsworth could be embarrassed any further, the porter poked in his head sheepishly to say, "Excuse me, sir, it's just that Mrs. Potts wants Cogsworth down in the kitchens."

"Here now, I won't have Mrs. Potts telling me where I am needed!" grumbled Cogsworth.

"No, she's right, you look like you could use a good cup of tea," said the Prince. "I'm fine. Go to the kitchens before she waddles her way up here, getting angrier with each flight of stairs she has to take to reach us."

Cogsworth laughed at the thought of it. "Perhaps you're right, sir." He left the room, taking the porter along with him.

The Prince felt incredibly foolish for thinking

he had actually been cursed. As he looked out the window, the trees were violently swaying, dancing to a manic song only they were privy to. He longed to be out of doors, tracking elk and talking with his friend about anything other than the sisters, Circe, or curses—and as if by magic, there was a knock at the door. It was Gaston.

"My friend! I heard you were awake! That Cogsworth wouldn't let anyone in your room except Dr. Hillsworth, who just came downstairs to let us know you were finally on your way to health."

"Yes, Gaston, I'm feeling much better, thank you." Looking at Gaston, the Prince noticed he hadn't shaven in more than a few days, and the Prince wondered how long he had been ill.

"Have you been here all along, good friend?"

"I have. Cogsworth gave me a room in the East Wing, but I spent most of my time down in the kitchens with Mrs. Potts and the others." Gaston seemed almost like the young boy the Prince had befriended so many years earlier, his face tensed with worry over his friend's illness—and spending

60

his time in the kitchen like the other servants' children.

"Stay as long as you like. This was once your home, friend, and I want you to always feel it is such." Gaston looked touched by the sentiment but didn't say so.

"I'm going to make myself presentable before heading home. I'm sure things have gone to the winds without me there for so many days."

"Surely LeFou has it handled." The Prince tried not to look disappointed his friend was making plans to leave.

"Doubtful. He's a fool at best! Don't fret, my friend. I'm sure Cogsworth will be up shortly to keep you company and help you to make plans for the party we're throwing the moment you're well enough."

"Party?" the Prince asked.

Gaston gave one of his magic smiles, the kind that always ensured he would get his way. "Yes, a party, my friend, one that will be remembered throughout the ages!"

Chapter VI

Gaston's Grand Idea

Gaston's plan went directly into action only a few short weeks after the Prince's recovery. The entire staff was behind it and thought it was exactly the thing he needed.

"This is like a dream!" was heard throughout the castle by Mrs. Potts as she amended menus and made suggestions for little cakes to be served in the great hall.

Cogsworth had an extra bounce in his step but was too austere to let it be known he was pleased to have a bustling house again to take control of like a general at war. And that was how he directed things, ordering the staff hither and thither to ready the castle for the grand event.

The Prince, however, had needed some persuading before he agreed to such a party. Gaston argued that after the mishap with Circe and his long illness, the Prince deserved a thrilling diversion.

"What better way to find the most enchanting woman in the kingdom than to invite every fair and available maiden so you may have your pick? And all under the guise of a fanciful ball?"

The Prince didn't share Gaston's enthusiasm.

"I hate such events, Gaston. I see no need to stuff my house with frilly ladies prancing around like decorated birds."

Gaston laughed.

"If we invite every fair maiden in the kingdom, I daresay every girl will attend!" the Prince protested.

"That is my point entirely, my friend! No girl would pass up her opportunity to shine in the Prince's eyes."

"But that is what I fear! Surely there will be far more ghastly-looking girls than beautiful! How shall I stand it?"

Gaston put his hand on his friend's shoulder and replied, "No doubt you will have to wade through some ugly ducklings before you find your princess, but won't it be worth it? What of your friend who had such a ball? Wasn't it a great success after the matter of the glass slipper was sorted?"

The Prince laughed. "Indeed, but you won't catch me marrying a housemaid like my dear friend, no matter how beautiful she is! Not after the disaster with the pig keeper."

The talk went on like that for many days, until the Prince decided he would have the ball after all, and why not? Why shouldn't he demand the attendance of every available maiden in the kingdom? He and Gaston would make a game of it, and if he did happen to find the young woman of his dreams, then all the better. So it was decided. He didn't have to think any more about it until the night of the event.

In the meantime he did his best to dodge his servants, running about like wild geese being chased by hounds. He forgave their franticness and even grew to laugh when he heard Mrs. Potts padding her way down the hall to ask him this or that about what he'd like served. Meanwhile, the maids were polishing silver in the dining room, the grooms were readying the stables for the guests' horses, and the parlor maids were perched precariously on tall ladders, dusting the chandeliers and replacing the old candles with new. The house was abustle and he wanted nothing more than to get out of doors and do some hunting. But Gaston was out traversing his lands, dealing with one thing or another, and couldn't be bothered with trivial sport.

The Prince chimed the bell for Cogsworth.

"Yes, sir, you rang?" asked Cogsworth, knowing full well he had. The Prince always detested all this ceremony, but he let Cogsworth have his way. He remembered what his father—rest his soul—had said to him many years ago. He said everyone in the house, upstairs and down, had their places and their roles to play. To deny a man like Cogsworth his duty and remove him from his place was like taking away his sense of self and dignity. Cogsworth had treated him well for many years; he couldn't shatter the man's self-worth by treating him like family, even though that was how he had grown to think of him. It was an unspoken sentiment between them.

The Prince believed Cogsworth thought the same of him but was too austere to say so.

"Yes, Cogsworth, I would like you to arrange for the Maestro as soon as manageable. I mean to have another portrait."

Cogsworth rarely let his expression betray him. "Yes, sir, I shall send for him."

"What is it, Cogsworth? Don't you approve?"

It seemed he thought about it for a moment before answering, "It isn't my place to say so, sir, but if it was, I would mention how 'interesting' the household becomes when he visits."

The Prince had to laugh. He had thought Cogsworth was going to comment on how recently he'd had a portrait done.

"Indeed. He is a bit of a character, isn't he? He treats the staff well, though, doesn't he? You don't have a complaint on that account, do you?"

"Oh no, sir, it isn't that. A gentleman such

as the Maestro isn't the least bit challenging in that regard. No, sir, he's just an eccentric fellow, wouldn't you agree?"

"Yes he is, and very keen on himself and the impact his art makes on the world, I would say. Enough of that. I am sure you are very busy with all the details for tomorrow's event. I trust everything is in hand?"

Cogsworth looked positively proud, almost beaming. "Oh yes, everything is running like clockwork, sir. It's going to be a perfect evening."

"And Gaston, have you any word from him? He all but insisted I have this party and then took off to places unknown, leaving me here to dawdle my time away."

Cogsworth smirked. "Yes, sir, he sent word this morning ensuring he would be back tomorrow morning. In the meantime, I've asked the gamekeeper to ready for a day of stalking. I thought with the house in such a state you would be eager to get out of doors."

"Brilliant idea, Cogsworth! Thank you!"

On the following evening the castle was aglow with gold flickering light, which was dancing in the hedge maze, making the animal topiaries seem to come to life. Everyone would be arriving within the hour, but the Prince was finding a moment of quiet in one of his favorite places on the castle grounds.

The tranquility was shattered by Gaston's booming voice calling for him from the arched entryway covered in tiny pink blossoming roses.

"Are you in this damnable maze again, Prince?"

The Prince didn't answer his friend. He just sat there wondering what the night would bring. He had also been thinking of Circe and wondering if it was possible ever to find another girl who loved him as much as she had. There had been times he thought Circe was a dream and her sisters some sort of nightmare he had conjured in his own fevered imagination. He'd lost so much time already, it didn't seem reasonable to waste much more with thoughts of Circe, her harpy sisters, or curses.

"Your guests will be arriving any moment,"

Gaston shouted, "and though he wouldn't admit it, I think Cogsworth will blow a gasket if you're not there to greet them as they enter the great hall!"

The Prince sighed. "I'll be right there."

Gaston turned the corner, seeing his friend sitting near a towering topiary of a winged lion. "What's the matter? I thought this would liven your spirits! Every girl in three kingdoms is said to attend! It's going to be magnificent!"

The Prince stood, straightening his velvet frock coat, and said, "Yes, it will be. Let's not keep the girls waiting."

The girls filed in by the hundreds. So many of them! He didn't know there could be so many in all the world. All of them were decked out for the occasion. There were stunning brunettes with dark haunting eyes, pale and lovely blondes with perfect ringlets, striking redheads with jade-colored eyes, and everything in between. They all paraded past him, some hiding behind their fans and giggling, while others tried not to look the least bit interested in whether he glanced in their direction. Some seemed too nervous to keep from trembling, sometimes so violently they lost composure altogether and spilled their drinks.

There was one girl with auburn hair he didn't manage to see properly. She seemed always to have her back turned. She must have been very beautiful, because he caught the dirty glances she received from the other ladies as they passed her, and quite unlike the others, she didn't travel in a swarm of girls. She stood off—apart from most everyone— seeming not the least bit interested in the idle chatter of the fairer sex.

"Gaston, who is that girl? The one in the blue dress I saw you talking with earlier? What's her name?" Gaston pretended he didn't recall, annoying the Prince. "You know very well to whom I'm referring, man! Bring her over here and introduce me."

"You wouldn't be interested in her, trust me!"

The Prince raised an eyebrow.

"Wouldn't I? And why is that, my good friend?"

Gaston lowered his voice so those nearby wouldn't

hear. "She's the daughter of Cuckoo! Oh, she's lovely, yes, but her father is the laughingstock of the village! He's harmless enough, but fancies himself a great inventor! He's always building contraptions that clank, rattle, and explode! She isn't the sort you'd like to get mixed up with, good friend."

"Perhaps you're right, but nevertheless, I would like to meet her."

"I daresay you would find her very tedious with her endless talk of literature, fairy tales, and poetry."

"You seem to know quite a bit about her, Gaston," the Prince said with a comical, knowing nod.

"I fear I do! In the few moments we spoke just now, she prattled on of nothing else. No, dear friend, we need to find you a *proper* lady. A princess! Someone like the princess Morningstar over there. Now, she is a delight! No talk of books from her! I bet she's never read even a single book or had a thought of her own!"

The Prince thought that was a very good quality

in a woman. He could do enough thinking for both himself and his future wife.

"Yes, bring over the princess Morningstar. I'd very much like to meet her."

Princess Tulip Morningstar had long golden locks, with a milk-and-honey complexion and light sky-blue eyes. She looked like a doll draped in diamonds and pink silks.

She was remarkably beautiful—radiant, in fact. Everything about her sparkled, with one exception: her personality. But that didn't bother the Prince. He had enough personality for both of them. It wouldn't do to have a wife who took attention away from him.

Morningstar had a charming little habit of giggling when she didn't have something to contribute on a subject, which was most of the time. This made him feel like the best of tutors. Honestly, he could talk about anything and her attentions were never diverted from him; she just giggled.

He had already decided he was going to marry her, and judging by the sulky looks on the faces of the rest of the ladies in attendance, it must have been quite clear.

Gaston looked positively pleased with himself that he had helped arrange a perfect match for his friend. And for his part, he saw to it that the other ladies didn't go without a dance partner for very long.

It seemed to the Prince that Gaston must have danced with every girl there that evening—all except the inventor's daughter, who by all accounts didn't seem too pleased to be there to begin with, though he couldn't tell by the look on her face, because he hadn't, in fact, had a single clear glance at her the entire evening.

None of that mattered, though. He had his darling princess Tulip to look after now.

CHAPTER VII

THE PRINCESS AND
THE PORTRAIT

The Prince was more pleased than ever the Maestro was coming to do his portrait now that he'd made Princess Tulip Morningstar his fiancée. It would be an engagement portrait with the two most attractive members of royalty anyone had beheld!

The princess went back to her father's kingdom after the ball and awaited the various ceremonies, parties, and other trappings that would take place during their engagement, all leading up to, of course, the most majestic of weddings. She would, by custom, live with her family, visiting the Prince frequently with her nanny as chaperone, and sometimes also bringing her mother along as it suited her or the occasion presented itself.

This visit she would come with her nanny. Everyone was excited that the Prince had commissioned the Maestro to paint the portrait. He was the most celebrated painter in many kingdoms and was in great demand. Not since the renowned Master Maker of Mirrors had there been another artist who caused such a stir in the royal circles. Though his art could be brutally accurate, most gentry didn't seem to let that color their opinion of the man.

Princess Tulip showed up on a rainy afternoon, quite soggy. Though her hair was flat and her clothes were sticking to her, she somehow managed to look pretty, and quite worth rescuing from the elements. The Prince kissed her sweetly on the cheek and greeted her happily when she stepped out of the carriage.

"Tulip, my love! How was your journey?"

A grumble came from inside the carriage, and out popped what must have been his dearest's nanny.

"It was intolerable, as you can see! The carriage

leaked and I would be surprised if my darling girl doesn't come down with the nastiest of colds! I must get her into a hot bath at once!"

The Prince blinked a couple of times and smiled at the woman. She was impossibly old and lined like a little apple doll that had been moldering away on a windowsill. Her hair and skin were powdery white, and though much aged, her eyes were rather sparkling with life. This woman was a little firecracker.

"I am so pleased to meet you at last, Nanny," he said as she wrinkled her nose at him as if there were a foul smell about the air.

"Yes, yes, very pleased to meet you, Prince, I'm sure. But won't you please show us to our rooms so I can get this girl into a hot bath?" Cogsworth took things into order.

"If you will follow me, Princess, I will happily show you to your quarters so you may freshen yourself after your long journey."

And with that he took the ladies up the stairs and out of sight.

Well, the Prince thought, this visit will be

interesting with Nanny grumbling about. Perhaps he could get Mrs. Potts to divert her in the kitchens so he could have some time alone with his princess. He couldn't imagine what the week would be like with her around. His dread was squashed with the announcement of his other guest.

The Maestro!

He came promenading in with the dandiest of outfits—all velvet and lace in various shades of lilacs and blackberry. He had large sad eyes set into a slightly swollen face but seemed all the more handsome for it.

The Maestro looked as if he had a saucy story to share, and the Prince wondered if it would be unwise to seat Nanny and the Maestro at the same table that evening for dinner. His head spun at the thought of Nanny listening to the painter's outlandish stories. What he needed was Cogsworth. He would sort it all out.

And sort it out he did. Nanny dined with Mrs. Potts, Cogsworth, and the other staff downstairs at Mrs. Potts's invitation. It wasn't custom by any means for a guest to eat with the downstairs staff, but Mrs. Potts had a way with people, and by the end of the conversation, the two were swapping stories about the Prince and princess when they were young, determining which of them had been more insolent.

Meanwhile, dinner upstairs was delightfully charming. The servants had decorated the dining room splendidly. Rather than a large floral centerpiece, there were a number of smaller arrangements artfully placed on the table, evoking the feel of a garden infused with candlelight. There were many crystal bowls with floating flowers and candles, and the particular cut of crystal made an interesting use of the light, causing a fanciful effect of reflection on the walls and diners. It was quite beautiful. But not as beautiful as his darling love, the Prince thought. The Maestro broke the silence.

"To love in all its tantalizing and vexing forms!"

Tulip laughed behind her fan while the Maestro stood theatrically erect with his glass raised high in the air, waiting, it seemed, for someone to respond to his toast. The Prince feared the Maestro might stay there forever frozen in time like one of his paintings if he didn't say something quickly.

"Yes! To love," he said, and quickly added, "and to you, Maestro!"

Princess Tulip giggled again, warming the Prince's heart even more. He loved how sweet and demure she was, so content to sit idly, and always looking ravishing while doing so. He really couldn't have chosen a better maiden to be his bride.

"I couldn't be more pleased to have you, Maestro! I know you will capture the moment perfectly! We will look back on our engagement not only with fond memories but with . . . How was it you put it? Oh yes, our senses will instantly be assaulted with a profound and visceral recollection of that exact moment in time."

The Maestro looked pleased. "I'm honored you remembered my words so vividly!" He then turned his attentions to the young lady, hoping to bring about something of her personality.

"You must be brimming with utter excitement,

Princess, are you not?" The princess's eyes widened with wonder. She hardly knew what to say. "Oh yes, I am. I am very much looking forward to the wedding."

"Of course you are! But I was of course speaking of our painting! I will want to see an assortment of outfits from each of you for my approval, and we will need to discuss the topic of location. The rose garden seems like an enchanting setting, I would think! Yes, the rose garden it shall be! I have decided and there is no changing my mind!" He continued, "It seems every portrait that is painted with any real feeling is a portrait of the artist, and not of the sitter. I daresay you will both be magnificent!"

Tulip blinked more than a few times, trying to understand his meaning.

"Will you be in the portrait with us, Maestro?" she asked. Both gentlemen laughed.

Princess Tulip Morningstar didn't know if they were laughing at what she had said because it was clever or dull-witted, but she decided to act as though it had been the cleverest thing she could possibly have said, and hoped the topic would change to something she needn't partake in. The Maestro, seeing the dread in her face, added, "Don't fret, dear Tulip. I am so clever that sometimes I don't understand a single word of what I am saying."

To this the princess could reply only by saying, "Oh!" and then giggling some more, which seemed to please everyone, because they joined in her laughter.

The next morning the magnificent trio was found in the rose garden as the Maestro sketched and the lovers did their best to hold their poses without giving the master painter cause to become cross with them.

"Prince, please! This is supposed to be the happiest moment of your life and your face looks like you've been eating something sour! Why do you look so displeased? What could you possibly be thinking of that causes one's face to contort so?"

The Prince had in fact been thinking about the last time he was in the rose garden, the night he parted with Circe. The events had become blurred in his mind and he was trying hard to make sense of it all. Surely Circe had brought along her wicked sisters and they had proclaimed he was cursed for his misdeeds. He was certain he hadn't imagined it, but the curse itself, that was balderdash . . . wasn't it? Sometimes he couldn't help fearing it might be true.

The Prince was brought out of his thoughts by Cogsworth's voice.

"Lunch is served."

The Maestro slammed down his drawing coals, cracking them into tiny powdery bits. "Very well! I think I prefer to lunch in my room! Alone!" he huffed, and he stormed away, not uttering a single word of salutation to either of the happy couple. Rather than giggling, as we well know was Tulip's way, she wilted into a heap of tears at being scolded.

The Prince, it seemed, had his hands entirely full with the fitful Maestro, his weeping Tulip, and her sour nanny. How would the rest of the week go?

CHAPTER VIII

THE WILTING FLOWER

The next day Princess Tulip Morningstar and the Prince shared a very quiet breakfast together in the morning room. She didn't ask the Prince where he had been the night before, or why he had missed dinner. She had been forced to dine with the Maestro by herself and was mortified when he inquired where the Prince might have been and she couldn't answer. She wanted to rail on him, honestly. Inwardly she was seething, but Nanny warned her never to let her anger show. It wasn't ladylike to appear upset. Nanny said that far too often a woman unknowingly sabotaged herself when reproaching her husband for his misdeeds. To stay quiet and say nothing was reproach itself. But to say something only gave him reason to turn the situation onto the lady, claiming that she was overly emotional and making more of the situation than needed, causing him to become angry with her.

Tulip didn't understand this entirely, but she did notice that Nanny didn't follow her own advice, and thought perhaps that was why Nanny had never married. So she said nothing. The only sounds in the room were those of the dishes clanking and the birds singing outside the lovely morning room windows. The room was made entirely of paned windows and had the most breathtaking view of the garden. Tulip thought of herself in the future, sitting here looking out these windows by the hour, languishing. She wished the Prince would say something, anything to break this silence. She couldn't think of what to say; anything she said would surely sound reproachful, and her tone—she wasn't at all positive it could be tempered.

She just sat there drinking her tea and picking at her scone, waiting for him to speak. And while waiting, she thought about that girl she'd met at the ball. Oh, what was her name? It was pretty, rather musical. She was probably the sort of girl who would rebuke the Prince in a situation like this—demand, in fact, to know where the Prince had been the night before. Then again, the girl with the pretty name was probably not the sort of girl a prince would want to marry. She sighed. Her thoughts were halted with the sound of his voice at last.

"Tulip."

Her eyes brightened when she heard him say her name.

"Yes?" she responded, hoping he would at last make his amends for stealing away the previous night and leaving her alone to listen to the Maestro talk endlessly about his art.

"We'd better not keep the Maestro waiting."

Her heart sank.

"Of course, shall we go to the rose garden?"

"Yes, I suppose we should."

The rest of the week went on very much the same. Princess Tulip Morningstar pouted and played with the castle's cat, the Maestro gesticulated wildly while making grand speeches about art at every opportunity, and the Prince escaped every evening to the tavern with Gaston the moment they were done sitting for the Maestro.

On the day of the unveiling of the new portrait, quite a little family party had been arranged. Tulip was in better spirits to have her mother, Queen Morningstar, there, as well as some of her ladies to attend her. Also present was Gaston, as well as a few other close friends of the Prince's. King Morningstar of course couldn't take time away from his duties at court but sent along lavish gifts for both his daughter and his future son-in-law.

After they had feasted well on what was one of Mrs. Potts's most outstanding dinners to date, everyone went into the great hall to partake in the unveiling of the portrait. The great hall was filled with paintings of the Prince's entire family, including portraits of him that had been painted from the time he was a wee lad.

"Ah! I see you've hung the Maestro's portrait

here in the great hall, where it belongs. Good choice, old man!" said Gaston as he looked upon faces he had grown up with.

"Yes, I thought it was better suited in here."

A rather loud clearing of the throat was heard from the other side of the room, where the Maestro was standing. It seemed he thought the occasion required more ceremony and this idle chat was debasing the situation at hand. Thank goodness he wouldn't have to suffer this company much longer.

"Yes, well, without further delay, I would like to share the latest of my greatest treasures." With that, Lumiere pulled the cord, which dropped the black silk cloth that had been concealing the painting. The room erupted into a loud clatter of sighs and applause. Everyone seemed to be highly impressed with the painting, and the Maestro soaked in the praise that was being heaped upon him like an actor on the stage would—bowing at the waist and placing his hand upon his heart to indicate that he was very touched indeed.

No doubt he actually was.

The Prince couldn't help noticing how harshly he had been painted in the portrait. His eyes looked cruel, piercing, almost like those of a wolf seeking his prey, and his mouth looked thinner, more sinister than it had looked before. Gaston knocked the Prince with his elbow.

"Say something, man! They're expecting a speech!" he whispered in the Prince's ear.

"I couldn't have asked for a more beautiful portrait of my lovely bride-to-be!" the Prince finally uttered.

Princess Tulip blushed deeply and said, "Thank you, my love. And I, too, couldn't have asked for a more handsome and dignified visage of my prospective husband."

Dignified? Wasn't that a word one used for older men? Did he look *dignified?* His visage, as she called it, looked harsh and worn, not one of a man who had not yet reached his twentieth birthday, but one of a man well into his forties. This wouldn't do. *Dignified!*

The party was led out of the great hall and into

the music room, where a group of musicians waited to entertain the party. By all accounts the evening went on pleasantly enough, but the Prince couldn't take his mind off the painting. He looked so worn, so ugly. Had Tulip agreed to marry him simply because she would eventually be queen in these lands? Did she love him at all?

He couldn't see how.

He slipped away from the party to confirm the Maestro's rendition of him in his bedroom mirror. He just stood there staring, trying to find himself in the man staring back at him. Why hadn't anyone said anything? How could he have changed so much in so little time?

Later that evening, when the Prince's guests and staff were all tucked into their beds, the Prince stole out of his rooms and made his way down the long, dark corridor. He was fearful of waking Queen Morningstar. She would of course think he was sneaking into the princess's chamber, but that was the furthest thing from his mind now. When he passed Tulip's room, a creaking sound startled him, but it was only that blasted cat pushing the door open. He had no idea why the princess liked it so well. There was something sinister about the way the feline looked at him, and something eerie in her markings, which made her look like a creature that roamed cemeteries rather than castle grounds.

Well, if the queen did wake to find him prowling the halls, she wouldn't believe he was on his way to look at his painting again. He'd been sleeping fitfully and unable to rest, his thoughts consumed by that ghastly painting. Once he got into the great hall and managed to light the candles, he stood there staring at the painting again. He had indeed changed—that had been clear when he looked at himself in the mirror earlier that evening—but surely the Maestro had dramatized the changes. Just look at the difference between this painting and the last, which had been done less than a year earlier. There was no way a man could change so dramatically. He would never forgive the Maestro for creating the unfavorable rendering. He decided the man must pay for such an uncharitable act.

The beautiful orange-and-black cat seemed to be in accord with the Prince, because she narrowed her eyes in much the same way he did when he plotted his revenge.

At the Prince's encouragement, Cogsworth had all visiting guests packed and stuffed into the carriages very early the next morning. Mrs. Potts was disappointed not to have the opportunity to serve the guests breakfast before the start of their travels, so she packed a large trunk with lovely things for them to eat on their journey. The sun was barely visible, and the tops of the trees were obscured in mist. There was a terrible chill in the air, so it didn't seem unreasonable that the Prince was eager to get back withindoors, where he could warm himself.

He made his good-byes to his guests, thanking them all and bidding them farewell, with promises of love and letter-writing to Tulip. He sighed in great relief when the carriages drove away. Gaston, who had been standing silently at his side, finally spoke.

"So why was it you woke me at this ungodly hour, my friend?"

"I need a little favor. Some time back you mentioned a particularly unscrupulous fellow who can be called upon for certain deeds."

Gaston raised his eyebrows. "Surely there are ways to get out of marrying the princess other than having her killed!"

The Prince laughed.

"No, man! I mean the Maestro! I would like you to make the arrangements for me. The incident cannot be traced back to me, you understand?"

Gaston looked at his friend and said, "Absolutely!"

"Thank you, good friend. And once that is sorted, what do you say to a day of hunting?"

"Sounds perfect! I would like nothing more."

CHAPTER IX

THE STATUE IN THE OBSERVATORY

As Princess Tulip Morningstar's carriage rolled up the path leading to the Prince's castle, she thought there was nothing more breathtaking than the sight of the castle in wintertime. Her father's kingdom was beautiful, yes, but it didn't compare to the Prince's, especially when it was covered in pure white snow and decorated for the winter solstice.

The entire castle was infused with light and glowing brightly in the dark winter night. She had high hopes for this visit and wished nothing more than for the Prince to treat her with kindness and love like he once had. Surely the winter holiday would cheer his sour mood of late and bring him back around to the man she'd fallen in love with that dreamy night at the ball.

"Look, Nanny, isn't it beautiful the way the pathway is lined with candlelight?"

Nanny smiled and said, "Yes, my dear child, it's very beautiful. Even more lovely than I imagined it would be."

Tulip sighed.

"What is it, Tulip? What's troubling you?"

Tulip said nothing. She loved her nanny dearly and couldn't bring herself to ask her what she'd been rehearsing the entire way from her father's kingdom to their destination.

"I think I know, dear heart, and don't you fret. I won't give the Prince any reason to be upset this visit, I promise you. Nanny will keep her thoughts to herself this time."

Tulip smiled and kissed her nanny on her soft powdery cheek.

"That's right, give your old nanny a kiss and forget your troubles. It's solstice, dear, your favorite time of year, and nothing will ruin this for you, I promise you that!"

The carriage reached the front doors of the castle, where Lumiere was standing, waiting to open her carriage door.

"Bonjour, Princess! Aren't you looking as beautiful as always? It is so lovely to see you again!"

Tulip giggled and blushed, as she often did when Lumiere spoke to her.

"Hello, Lumiere. I trust the Prince is attending to more pressing matters than taking time to greet his fiancée, who has traveled across the country to visit him for the solstice?" grumbled Nanny. Lumiere took it in stride.

"Indeed, Nanny! If both of you will follow me, Christian there will take your luggage to your apartments in the East Wing."

Nanny and Tulip looked at each other in wonder. Usually they would be shown up to their rooms so they might refresh themselves after their long travels. But Lumiere ushered them past many vast and beautiful rooms until they finally arrived at a large door wrapped to look like an extravagant gift with a big gold bow.

"What is this?" Nanny snapped.

"Go inside and see for yourself!"

Tulip opened the giant gift-wrapped door to find a winter wonderland within. There was an enormous oak tree stretching to the very height of the golden domed ceiling. It was covered in magnificent lights and beautifully ornate finery that sparkled in their glow. Under the tree was an abundance of gifts, and standing among them was the Prince, his arms stretched out as he waited to greet her. Tulip's heart was filled with joy. The Prince seemed to be in wonderful spirits!

"My love! I am so happy to see you!" She wrapped her arms around his waist and embraced him.

"Hello, my dearest. You are in quite a state from traveling, aren't you? I'm surprised you didn't insist to be taken to your rooms to make yourself presentable before showing yourself."

The Prince scowled as if he were looking at a dirty servant girl and not the woman he loved.

"I'm sorry, dear, you're right, of course."

Lumiere, always the gentleman, and eager to please the ladies, added, "It's my fault, my lord. I insisted she follow me at once. I knew you were excited to show the princess the decorations."

"I see. Well, Tulip dear, soon you will be queen in these lands and, more important, queen in this house, and you must learn to decide for yourself what is right and insist upon it. I am sure next time you will make the right choice."

Tulip colored a deep crimson but found the most authoritative voice she could manage.

"Yes, my love and prince. Lumiere, if you will show Nanny and me to our rooms so we may ready ourselves for dinner . . ."

With that, she left the room without even a kiss for the Prince, for she was rushing to avoid letting him see she was on the verge of tears.

How dare he suggest she was unseemly to come into his company upon her arrival? Did she look so grotesque? Lumiere seemed to hear her very thoughts.

"As I said when you arrived, dear princess," he said, "you look beautiful as always. Do not heed the master's words. He has been rather distracted as of late."

Nanny and Tulip just looked at each other, wondering what this visit had in store.

CHAPTER X

THE OBSERVER IN
THE OBSERVATORY

It seemed to Tulip there were fewer servants than the last time she visited, though the castle didn't seem to suffer for it; it looked even more grand than usual, having been decorated for the solstice. Her favorite court companion, Pflanze, a beautiful black, orange, and white cat, was in attendance to keep her company. "Hello, beautiful Pflanze!" she said to her little friend, and she leaned over to pat her on the head.

"So you've named her? What a strange name. What does it mean?"

Tulip looked up to see the Prince standing over her.

"Oh! I don't know! I thought you came up with it. I was sure it was you who told me her name," the princess responded.

"It wasn't me. I don't even like the beast!" he said, giving Pflanze a dirty look as she gave him her customary side glance and adjusted her paws.

"Someone else must have told me, then," said the princess.

"Indeed! That is clear, someone else would have had to tell you! I could puzzle that out on my own! And like the featherhead you are apt to be, you've completely forgotten who told you. But clearly someone else told you!"

"Yes," said Tulip in the tiniest of voices, trying desperately not to let her lip quiver as he went on.

"Never mind! I see you've not changed for dinner yet! Well, we can't keep Mrs. Potts waiting. What you're wearing will just have to do! Come! I'll escort you into the dining room, even if you're not fit for the grand affair planned in your honor."

Tulip's heart sank and her face turned scarlet. She had, in fact, changed for dinner and made herself up considerably well—at least, she thought so. She was wearing one of her finest gowns and had thought she looked quite beautiful before she started down the stairway. She made a special effort to look flawless in light of what had happened upon her arrival. Now she wanted nothing more than to run away from this place and never come back again, but she was trapped. Trapped with this terrible prince! She didn't care how rich he was, or how massive his kingdom or influence; she couldn't stand the idea of being married to such a bully. How would she get out of it? She didn't know what to do. She decided to stay quiet on the matter until she could talk to Nanny.

After dinner Tulip asked the Prince if he'd like to go on a walk, and he agreed. He was being sullen and quiet but not cross, so for that, at least, she was thankful. They walked around the lake, which was frozen this time of year but still breathtakingly beautiful.

"Could you show me the observatory, sweetheart? The sky is very clear and I should like to see the view you've spoken of so frequently."

"If you'd like."

They walked the long stone spiral staircase until they reached the top floor of the observatory. Even without the telescope, the view was spellbinding. Tulip could see the entire sky through the glass domed ceiling. She felt as if the stars were winking back at her for how joyfully she looked upon them.

It seemed they were not the only ones who had decided it was a good night to stargaze. Someone was already looking through the telescope when they reached the top of the stairs.

"Hello! Who's there?"

The observer didn't answer.

"I said, who's there?"

Tulip was frightened, especially after the Prince motioned her to get behind him for protection—but as the Prince got closer to the intruder, he realized it wasn't a person at all, but a statue.

"What's this?" He was nonplussed. There had never been a statue up here before, and how on earth had someone gotten it up here without some sort of elaborate apparatus? There was no way something that heavy could have been brought up the stairs without his knowing.

Tulip started to giggle in nervous relief.

"Oh my! It's just a statue! I feel silly for being so startled!"

But the Prince still had a look of confusion on his face while she prattled on.

"But it does look kind of creepy, doesn't it? It almost looked like it was giving us a side glance when we walked in! And how odd a pose for a statue, leaning over looking into the telescope! It obstructs our ability to look through it completely! I'm sure this wasn't your idea, dear! Honestly, I don't think I like it. I can't tell if it's meant to be a man or a woman. Male or female, though, it does look horrified, don't you think? Like something terrible came upon it and turned it into stone?"

The Prince hardly heard what she was rambling; his mind was suddenly violated by terrible disembodied voices from the past.

Your castle and its grounds shall also be cursed, then,

and everyone within will be forced to share your burden. Nothing but horrors will surround you, from when you look into a mirror to when you sit in your beloved rose garden.

The Prince shuddered at the sound of the witch's voice ringing in his ears. Was he cursed after all? First the drastic change in his appearance and now this strange event?

His servants trapped within stone? He couldn't imagine what it would be like to be trapped like that. He wondered if the person trapped could hear their conversation. If the person was aware he had been entrapped in stone. The thought sent shivers up the Prince's spine.

"Darling, you look peaky! What's the matter?" Princess Tulip asked.

The Prince's heart was racing, his chest felt heavy, and it was hard for him to breathe. He suddenly realized everything the sisters had said was coming true.

"Tulip! Do you love me? I mean, truly love me?"

When she looked at him, he looked like a lost

little boy and not the spiteful bully he'd been to her as of late.

"I do, my love! Why do you ask?"

He grabbed her hand and held it tightly.

"But would you love me if I were somehow disfigured?"

"What a question! Of course I would!"

Her heart was again softening to the Prince. Not since the night they had met and he had asked her to marry him had he been so kind.

"You know that I love you, my darling! I love you more than anything!" he said desperately as tears welled up in her eyes at his sweet words.

"I do now, my love! I do now!"

Princess Tulip was happier than she had dared hope on Solstice Eve. She hadn't imagined such a turn of character in the Prince, but since that night in the observatory, he'd been nothing but sweet to her.

"Oh, Nanny! I do love him so!" she whispered while sipping her spiced wine.

"How quickly you pivot from one emotion to another, my dear!" said Nanny.

"But, Nanny! His disposition has fluctuated greatly from one moment to the next! But I do feel he's finally himself again."

Nanny did not look convinced.

"We shall see, my dear."

The Prince did look glad, Nanny had to admit, and he seemed to be falling all over himself to make Tulip happy. It was almost comical, actually, quite like a mockery of love. But her Tulip was happy, so she didn't press the matter or cast an evil eye in his direction. She did notice, however, Pflanze, who was perched on Tulip's lap, looking at the Prince with hateful eyes. Nanny had to wonder why that cat disliked him so. Perhaps she too saw through this ruse.

The Prince was very pleased with the Solstice Eve gathering. He was a bit exhausted by his attentions to Tulip, but he had decided there was no better way of breaking the curse than marrying Princess Morningstar. It was clear she loved him a great deal, so he was halfway there. All he had to do now was make the sisters believe he loved her, too.

Of course, there were indeed things about her that he loved. He loved her beauty, her coyness, and her keeping her opinions to herself. There was nothing he hated more than a girl with too many opinions of her own.

He liked that she showed no interest in books, and that she didn't prattle on about her pastimes. In fact, he had no idea how she spent her time when she wasn't in his company. It was as if she didn't exist when she wasn't with him. He imagined her sitting in a little chair in her father's castle, waiting for him to send for her.

He loved how she never gave him a cross look or scorned him even when he was in the foulest of moods, and how easy she was to manage. Surely that counted for something; surely that was a form of love, was it not? And he figured the sweeter he was to her, the more quickly he would reverse the curse.

So that was the aim of this visit, to show the sisters how much he loved Princess Tulip Morningstar. But how would he get their attention?

Oh yes, they had said the Prince and his beloved had to seal their love with a kiss. Well, that would be easy enough. He would just have to spirit her away to a romantic setting and *bam!* A kiss! A kiss she would never forget!

He arranged the entire thing with Lumiere, who was best at planning such romantic things.

"Romantic interludes," he called them. "Oh yes, Prince, she will melt into your arms in utter delight when she sees what we have in store for her, mark my words!"

"Wonderful, Lumiere. And Mrs. Potts—she's sorted a hamper for the picnic, has she?"

"Everything is taken care of, even the nanny. We invited her to a tea party downstairs so she will be very well occupied and you lovebirds will be able to fly free without worry of her watchful gaze."

The Prince laughed. Lumiere was always so poetic when he spoke of love, so devoted to the notion of it. The Prince couldn't go wrong with having him arrange this little escapade, and he was sure Tulip would be very happy.

CHAPTER XI

MORNING TEA

The following day, in the morning room, Tulip was working at some needlepoint while idly petting Pflanze as the cat pawed at some spools of thread that fell onto her red velvet cushion.

Nanny was talking, presumably to Tulip, about Mrs. Potts's cobbler and wondering how hard it would be to wrangle the recipe out of her, when Lumiere entered the room.

"Excuse me, lovely ladies, but my dear Tulip, could you possibly spare your nanny for a few moments? Mrs. Potts has arranged a little tea for Nanny downstairs. I think she is eager for your company, Nanny."

Nanny looked at Lumiere with a sly grin.

"And yes, Nanny, to be sure, she has baked a peach cobbler for the tea. She knows how fond you are of her cobblers."

Nanny smiled. "Tulip, dear, you wouldn't mind, would you? You won't feel too lonely if Nanny slipped away for a spot of tea with old Mrs. Potts?"

Tulip grinned at her nanny and said, "Of course not, I have Pflanze to keep me company." And then, looking at Pflanze, she added, "Don't I, sweet girl?"

Pflanze just looked at Tulip with her large black-rimmed golden eyes, tinted with tiny flakes of green, and blinked them slowly at her as if to say, "Yes."

"See! I will be fine! Go have your tea!"

And off Nanny went.

Tulip didn't know what she would do without Nanny. But she knew once she was married, she couldn't justify having her in the household. She would, of course, have a lady's servant—someone to do her hair, to help her dress, to arrange her jewels— but it wouldn't be the same. She couldn't imagine sharing her feelings with anyone but Nanny. Perhaps since she and Mrs. Potts had become so friendly, it wouldn't seem strange to keep Nanny on. She would have to talk to her mother about that when she returned from her trip. But what if her mother was unable to spare Nanny or thought it was somehow inappropriate for Tulip to bring her along? That was just too dreadful to think of now.

The Prince peeked into the room, taking Tulip's mind off her future household concerns. She knew he didn't like Pflanze sitting on his fine cushions, but she couldn't help indulging the creature, and he didn't seem to notice.

"Hello, my love. I have a little surprise for you. Do you think I can steal you away while we don't have Nanny to worry about? She's always snooping around and wondering where you are."

Tulip's face transformed into something shining and bright. She couldn't remember ever being so happy, not even when her father gave her Cupcake, her favorite horse. Oh, Cupcake! She couldn't wait to see her again. She wondered if the Prince would object to Cupcake's coming to live here once they were married. So many things to think about.

"Darling?" His voice brought Tulip out of her deep thoughts.

"Oh, yes, dear, I'm sorry. I was just thinking about how much I love you! And how sweet you are for asking Mrs. Potts to invite Nanny for tea so we could have some time together alone."

The Prince smiled. His featherhead had puzzled out his ruse. What a surprise.

"So you worked out my clever scheme? Aren't you a cunning girl?" he said. "Come now! I have something I would like to show you."

"What is it?" Tulip squealed like an excited little girl.

"You will just have to wait and see, my love, but first you will have to put this on."

He handed her a long white piece of silk.

She looked at him queerly.

"It's a surprise, my love. Trust me." He helped her tie the blindfold and led her to what she was sure was the courtyard. He let go of her hand and gently kissed her on the cheek. "Count to fifty, my dear, and then take off the blindfold."

He could see she was frightened.

"My dear, you're trembling. There's nothing to fear. I will be waiting for you at the end of your journey."

"My *journey?*" Her voice sounded small and confused.

"It won't be a long journey, my princess, and the way will be quite clear. Now count to fifty."

She could hear his footfalls moving farther and farther away as she counted in her mind. It was silly to be so frightened, but she hated nothing more than the dark. Nanny had tried everything, but Tulip's relentless fear of darkness never diminished. She tried not to count too quickly so she wouldn't ruin the Prince's surprise, but found herself becoming too fearful of the confining darkness. "Forty-eight, forty-nine, fifty!" She ripped the silk sash from her eyes. It took a moment for them to adjust before she saw the path laid before her. The tips of her toes touched the scattered pink rose petals that had been strewn across the courtyard to create a path that led right into the hedge maze. Her fears fluttered away as she quickly walked upon the petals, eager to venture into the maze constructed of animal topiaries. The petals led her past an exceptionally large serpent, its mouth gaping wide and bearing long, deadly fangs. The serpent twisted its way around the corner, revealing a part of the maze she'd never seen. It was a replica of the castle, almost exact in every way, except without the many griffons and gargoyles perched on every corner and turret. She imagined her future children playing here one day, laughing and making a game of the animals in the maze. What a lovely place this would be for children. She stopped her daydreaming and followed the rose petals past several whimsical animals, some of which she didn't know. She often felt cheated having been born a girl, not having had tutors like her brother had or the freedom to explore the world. Women learned of the world through their fathers, their brothers, and, if they were lucky, their husbands. It didn't seem quite fair.

She was accomplished for a girl—she knew how to sew, sing, paint watercolors, and even play the harpsichord fairly well—but she could not name all the animals in what would soon be her own hedge maze. She felt stupid most of the time and hoped others didn't see her in that light but feared they usually did.

"Never mind that," she said to herself, and was surprised to see that the trail of petals led out of the hedge maze and away from the mysterious animals that made her feel foolish and into a lovely garden she hadn't yet seen on her visits here.

It was enclosed with a low semicircle wall, and within were lovely bright-colored flowers. For a moment she thought she found herself stumbling upon springtide; it was such a remarkable sight, so bright and full of life in the middle of the wintery landscape. She couldn't fathom how the flowers thrived in such bitter cold. Scattered among the flowers were beautiful statues, characters from legends and myths; she knew that much from listening in on her brother's lessons with his tutors before

Nanny would take her away to practice walking.

Practice walking, indeed!

No wonder men didn't take women seriously; they had classes in walking while men learned ancient languages.

The garden was stunning, and very much like a fairy tale, filled with the cold blue light of the winter afternoon. Nestled in the center of the enchanted garden, all pink and gold, was a stone bench, where her dearest was waiting for her, smiling with his hand outstretched.

"It's so beautiful, my love! How is this possible?"

The Prince's smile broadened.

"I arranged flowers from the hothouse to be moved here so you may experience the joy of spring."

She sighed.

"You're amazing, my dearest! Thank you," she said coyly as she lowered her eyes to the flowers in the snow.

The Prince decided this was the moment—the moment when he would kiss her and break the curse.

"May I kiss you, my love?"

Tulip looked around as if expecting her mother or Nanny to jump out from the hedge maze or pop out from behind a statue, and then, deciding she didn't care if they did, she kissed him! And then she kissed him again, and again.

As they walked back to the castle, the Prince seemed happier and more at ease than she'd ever known him to be. It was all so unexpected—this day, his attentiveness, everything that had happened on this visit, really. She felt much better about their upcoming marriage. She had been so worried before, and now she could hardly recall why.

"Did you hear that, Tulip?" The Prince's mood shifted from gleeful to panicked.

"Hear what, dear?"

She hadn't heard a thing aside from the birds singing in the nearby snow-covered trees.

"That noise—it sounded like an animal, like a growl."

Tulip laughed, making a joke of it.

"Perhaps the hedge animals have come to life and they are going to eat us alive!"

The Prince looked as though he'd taken her jest quite seriously. His eyes were darting about as he tried to find the location of the wild beast.

"You don't really think there is an animal in here with us, do you?"

When she realized he was, in fact, serious, she became very frightened.

"I don't know, Tulip, stay right here. I'm going to check it out."

"No! Don't leave me here alone! I don't want to be eaten by whatever is prowling around in here!"

The Prince was becoming very impatient.

"You won't if you stay here like I've told you. Now be quiet and please do let go of my hand!"

He ripped his hand away from hers before she could comply with his request, and she stood there frozen in fear as he dashed off looking for wild beasts.

She sat there fretting for some time before the Prince came back for her.

"Oh my goodness!" she gasped.

He was badly clawed across his forearm. Whatever

had attacked him had clawed right through his jacket and left deep bloody wounds in his arm.

"My love, you're hurt!"

The Prince looked stricken and angry.

"Brilliant of you to have surmised that, my dear," he moaned.

"What happened? What attacked you?" she said, trying not to let his bad temper affect her.

"Clearly some sort of wild beast with sharp claws."

She knew it was better to ask nothing more than to provoke him into further bitterness.

"Let's get you back to the castle so we can have that taken care of."

They walked back in silence. She felt like his attitude toward her had completely shifted again. She tried to put it out of her mind, but she couldn't help feeling his anger was directed at her and not at the beast that had attacked him.

She wanted to cry, but she knew that would just make him angrier, so she walked back to the castle saying nothing, hoping his temper would improve.

CHAPTER XII

THE MYSTERY OF THE SERVANTS

Cogsworth did not greet them at the door as he normally did; instead it was Lumiere.

"Where is Cogsworth? I need him to fetch the doctor!" the Prince barked.

Lumiere looked worried, but not just for his master. It seemed as if something else was going on, something he dreaded telling the Prince.

"Of course, my lord. I shall take care of it."

As he was walking away to have one of the porters send a message for the doctor, the Prince said, "And send me Cogsworth!"

Lumiere stopped dead in his tracks and it took him quite a few moments before he turned around to respond.

"Well, sir, you see, we don't know where Cogsworth is."

"What on earth are you talking about, you don't know where he is? He's always here! Go and find him at once and tell him I need him! Never mind! I will ring for him myself."

He went to the mantel to pull the cord that summoned Cogsworth.

"Excuse me, sir, but he's not there. We've searched the entire estate and we cannot find him. We're all very worried."

The Prince was going out of his mind with anger.

"This is nonsense! Where on earth is the man? It's not like him to shirk his duties!"

"I know, sir, that is why we are all so worried. Mrs. Potts is in a heap of tears downstairs! She's had Chip looking everywhere for him. Everyone has been looking, sir. Do you recall the last time you saw him?"

He couldn't.

"Come to think of it, I have not seen him all day."

Tulip interjected, "This is very vexing, but I think we should call the doctor, don't you? I'm worried about your arm, my love."

Lumiere was rattled out of his panic for his friend Cogsworth and switched his focus to his master.

"Yes, sir, I'd better take care of that first thing, and then we will arrange another search for Cogsworth."

CHAPTER XIII

THE BOUNDER

The entire household was in a panic. Cogsworth was nowhere to be found, and now it seemed Mrs. Potts was also missing. "But, Nanny, it doesn't make sense! You were just having tea with her. Where in the world would she have gone off to?"

Nanny's eyes were red from crying.

"I don't know! I went to fetch us some more hot water for the tea. That Mrs. Potts is always bustling about, and I just wanted her to sit for a spell. You know that woman can't just sit down to enjoy a nice cup of tea without getting this or that for one person or another. But wouldn't you know it, once I returned with the water, she was gone! And the strangest thing, sitting there on the table was a pretty little teapot as round as can be!"

Tulip was confused.

"Nanny, you were having tea. I don't understand why a pot upon the table would be so strange."

Nanny said, "Ah, but you see, I had the teapot we were using, didn't I? To get the water. So why was there another just sitting on the table?"

"That is strange, I suppose."

Nanny's face crinkled up.

"It's more than strange, girl! Something is happening in this house! Something sinister! I felt it the first time we arrived and now it's getting stronger!"

Tulip wasn't going to let Nanny get her worked up with her superstitious nonsense. She'd done it far too often in the past, and she wouldn't allow herself to be swept away by it again. Not now.

"Oh, I know what you're thinking, girl! You think Nanny is an old foolish woman, but I've been on this earth much longer than most and I've seen things most people only dream of."

Tulip rolled her eyes, but Nanny went on.

"I'm telling you, I think this place is cursed." Both ladies looked up from their conversation when they heard Lumiere clearing his throat at the room's threshold.

"I just wanted you to know the doctor has left and the Prince is resting comfortably."

"Will he be okay?" Tulip asked, worried.

"Oh yes, he will be fine. He's recovering and exhausted, that's all. I'm sure he will want to see you tomorrow," he said, smiling in an attempt to lighten the mood.

"Tomorrow? Not today?" Tulip wondered, but she smiled back at Lumiere. She couldn't help it; there was something about him.

"You needn't fuss over us this evening for dinner," she said. "You can just bring us something on a tray. We can eat in our rooms or perhaps next to the fire in the sitting room. I'm sure everyone is in a tizzy down there with Mrs. Potts and Cogsworth missing. I don't want you worrying over us."

Nanny looked pleased with the job she had done raising Tulip; she sounded not only like a real queen but a very compassionate one at that. But the flirty little Frenchman wouldn't hear of serving guests on trays in the sitting room or any other room aside from the dining hall.

"Oh no! That will not do! If Mrs. Potts were here, she would blow her lid at the thought of you two eating off trays! And as for the menu this evening, never fear, we have something special planned for you!" He smiled another magical grin and said, "The dressing gong will be at six o'clock, dinner at eight o'clock. See you then!"

Then he was gone, likely dashing his way downstairs to arrange dinner and supervise the search for the missing servants. Tulip looked at her nanny coyly. "You don't think the two of them snuck off together? Cogsworth and Mrs. Potts? You don't think they're in love?"

Nanny laughed. "I wish it were as simple as that, my girl, but no. Neither of them gave me the slightest notion there was something between them. No, I fear something dreadful has happened to them."

Tulip rolled her eyes again. "Stop with all the talk of curses, Nanny! I won't have it!"

Later that night, in the main dining hall, you wouldn't have known two of the most important people on staff were missing. The room looked lovely, decorated with some of the hothouse flowers from Tulip's surprise earlier in the day, and the candles were sparkling brightly in crystal votive bowls, casting an unearthly light. The two ladies were enjoying their dessert when the Prince stumbled into the room looking half crazed.

"I'm happy you ladies are enjoying your meal while the entire household is falling into shambles around you!" He looked terribly worn, as though he'd aged several years from the ordeal. Nanny and Tulip just stared at him, at a complete loss.

"Have you nothing to say for yourself, Tulip? Sitting there stuffing yourself while my childhood companions are suffering such a terrible fate?"

Nanny spoke first.

"Here now! I won't have you speaking to her like

that. She's been worried sick over them and you. We both have!"

His face turned into something inhuman, something wicked and cruel. Nanny feared the Prince was losing his mind.

"Don't look at me like that, old woman! I won't have you casting evil looks at me! And you . . . !" He turned his anger on Tulip. "You lying strumpet, playing with my emotions, pretending you love me when clearly you do not!"

Tulip gasped and melted into tears at once, hardly able to speak.

"That's not true! I do love you!" The Prince's face was ashen, his eyes sunken and dark with illness, his anger growing with every word.

"If you loved me, truly loved me, then none of this would be happening! Mrs. Potts and Cogsworth would be here! The animals in the maze wouldn't have attacked me, and I wouldn't look like this! Look at me! Every day I grow uglier, more wretched."

Nanny put her arm around Tulip, who was crying so hard she couldn't breathe properly, let alone say anything in her defense. Though even if she had, he wouldn't have heard her; his anger was growing completely out of control.

"I can't stand the sight of you! I want you out of my castle this moment! Don't bother packing your things."

He rushed to the ladies, grasped Tulip by the hair, and pulled her toward the door, knocking over Nanny in the process.

"I won't have you in the castle another moment, do you understand? You disgust me!"

Tulip was weeping harder than ever, screaming for the Prince to let her go so she could see to her nanny, when Gaston came into the room.

"What on earth is going on here, man?"

He wrenched Tulip from the Prince's clutches and helped Nanny to her feet.

"What are you playing at, sir? Are you deranged?" Then, turning his attention to the ladies, he said, "Go to your rooms, ladies, I will take care of this."

The ladies waited in their rooms with their bags hastily packed. They had no idea what to think of the entire matter. Clearly the Prince was suffering from some sort of fever from his wounds and exhaustion. They sat in silence until Lumiere came into the room. His face looked grieved.

"Princess, I see you have packed your things. If you and Nanny could follow me, I will escort you to your carriage." He could see the numerous questions written on Tulip's face. "We think it's best you go home to your mother and father. The Prince will write you when he is feeling, more . . . like himself again."

Nanny spoke. "Yes, I think that is best. Come now, child, all will be well. I promise."

And the ladies walked through the castle and into the courtyard to meet the carriage with as much dignity and composure as they could gather in light of their terrible ordeal.

CHAPTER XIV

THE DESCENT

The princess never heard from the Prince again. The Prince had stopped raging on about spells and evil curses; he saw how they looked at him when he did. They thought he was mad. He couldn't blame them. He often thought himself mad. He almost wished he were. He had taken to keeping within-doors since he had chased Tulip out of the castle. He never left his room, didn't allow the servants to open the drapes, and lit only one candle in the evenings, saying the doctor advised it for his recovery. The only visitor allowed was Gaston.

"You're sure this is how you'd like to handle this, Prince?"

The Prince did his level best not to slip into one of the fits of rage that seemed to seize him so easily these days.

"I am quite sure, my friend. It's the only way. You're to ride out to Morningstar Castle to officially break off the engagement."

"And what of the marriage settlement? The king will be destitute without your promised arrangement."

The Prince smiled. "I'm sure he will. But that is what he deserves for flinging his stupid daughter at me! She never loved me, Gaston! Never! It was all lies! All a means to get to my money, for herself and her father's kingdom!"

Gaston saw he was getting worked up. He didn't bother arguing that he thought Tulip actually did love him. He had tried convincing him of that in the first few weeks of his breakdown. But nothing Gaston said convinced him. Something must have happened that day in the hedge maze to make the Prince believe Tulip didn't love him, and there was nothing anyone could say to convince him of the contrary. Whatever it was, Gaston had to trust that his friend was right. Tulip might have been playing him a fool all along. Frankly, Gaston didn't think she was smart enough to play such a clever trick; he hadn't marked her as a mercenary. He had thought he'd chosen so wisely when he originally made the match, and now he felt sorry for the trouble it had caused.

"I will ride out this day, my good friend. You just rest."

The Prince smiled a wicked smile that distorted his face in the vague candlelight, casting villainous shadows. It almost made Gaston frightened of his friend.

Chapter XV

The Hunt

The Prince hadn't left his rooms for months; he was held captive by his fear and anger, which were mounting by the day. The only servant he now saw was Lumiere, and he was rather oblique on matters of the household when the Prince inquired. He stood there holding a small gold candelabrum, making sure not to cast light on his master's face, or his own, for fear of showing the pure terror he was trying to conceal while looking at the Prince's form.

The Prince looked ghastly, pale and worn. His eyes were like black pits and his features were becoming more animal than human. Lumiere hadn't the heart to tell the Prince that everyone else in the castle had become enchanted after he broke Tulip's heart. It became clear to Lumiere that the Prince did not see the servants as they saw themselves. Whatever he saw was horrifying. He kept going on about statues moving about the castle, casting their eyes in his direction when he wasn't looking.

Lumiere and the other servants saw nothing of the sort, and not a single person on staff wished the Prince harm. Lumiere knew it was only a matter of time before he, too, was transformed into some household object like the others, and then his master would be left alone with only the horrors that were conjured in his mind.

Lumiere wished there was another way; he wished the Prince hadn't taken this path, dragging the entire household along with him into darkness. How he missed the young man the Prince had once been, before cruelty overtook him and besmirched his heart.

Mrs. Potts had reminded them with stories of what a promising young man he had once been, and Cogsworth still held faith the Prince would change his heart and break the curse; they all did. In the meantime, it was up to Lumiere to take care of him as long as he could.

"Won't you please go outside, Prince? You are withering withindoors. You need to see the sun and breathe fresh air!"

The Prince dreaded the idea of anyone seeing him as he was. After the ruin of Tulip's family, his malformation progressed beyond his wildest fears.

He looked like a monster.

Like a beast.

Clearly there was nothing he could do to break the curse; the sisters had lied. They had never intended for him to be able to break the curse; all his efforts with Tulip were in vain.

Lumiere was still standing there, waiting for his answer. The Prince was only reminded of that when he heard the man clear his throat.

"Yes, man, I heard you! I will go outside but not until nightfall! And I don't want anyone lurking in the halls to catch sight of me, do you understand? I don't want to see a single soul! If someone is afoot, they are to avert their gaze from me!"

Lumiere nodded in understanding.

"Shall I arrange dinner in the main dining hall, sir? It's been some time since we've had the opportunity to serve you at tableside."

The Prince felt sickened at the thought.

"We shall see! Now go! I want to be alone."

Lumiere left the room, stopping in the hall to speak to someone. The Prince got himself out of bed for the first time in weeks. His body ached and was stiff—so stiff he found it surprisingly hard to make his way to the door. But the voice sounded like Cogsworth's, and he desperately wanted to see him. When he opened the door, he expected to find the two men talking, but only found Lumiere.

"What is going on? I heard you speaking to someone!"

Lumiere turned around in fright.

"Only to myself, while I was winding this clock, sir. I'm sorry to disturb you!"

The Prince was losing his temper again, spiraling into a dangerous rage.

"Balderdash! I heard Cogsworth's voice!"

Lumiere looked sad at the mention of his name, but the Prince persisted. "You mean to tell me you weren't speaking to him? You haven't seen him at all?"

Lumiere, still holding his brass candlestick, calmly replied, "I can say with all honesty, sir, it has been some time since I've seen dear Cogsworth in the flesh."

Chapter XVI

The Sun Goes Down

Twilight was his favorite time, the in-between time when everything looked perfect and anything was possible, especially in spring. The darkening sky was lilac, making the moon all the more striking.

The Prince did feel better being outdoors, and Lumiere had made good on his promise. The Prince hadn't seen a single person while making his way out of the castle. Though he couldn't help feeling fearful someone could come upon him at any time. He decided a walk in the woods would be best. Once there, he felt more at ease. It was darker now, and the canopy of trees overhead obscured the light almost entirely except for little patches revealing a star-filled blanket of night. He had always seen well in the dark, but since he'd been in seclusion for so long, his eyes were even keener in darkness than before. He did feel quite beastly, actually, like a creature prowling in the forest.

Prowling.

Yes, that was exactly what he was doing, and he liked it. He almost felt more at home here than he did in his chamber. At times he felt like he couldn't breathe in his room, just sitting there, waiting for those sisters to swoop upon him like a pack of Gorgons. However, in the forest, everything felt right, somehow perfect, like home. Though he wasn't sure if that, too, was the lure of the witches. If they had somehow enchanted the forest to draw him in, make him feel more natural there, trap him in surroundings that would increase his beastliness. He suddenly wanted to flee home, to shut himself away, but something caught his ear.

He quickly hid behind a very large moss-covered tree stump to see what was coming. It was Gaston with his hunting rifle, but before the Prince could react, shots rained upon him, penetrating the tree trunk, splintering the wood and sending his heart into a manic rhythm he thought would kill him.

Something other than fear was growing inside him, something terrible and dark that obscured his fondness for, and even made him forget, his friend. Indeed, for a moment, this beast couldn't recall Gaston. There was some recollection, but nothing he could put his finger on. Then he remembered.

He felt different, like he was slipping into a deep, dark ocean; he felt himself drowning in it, losing himself completely while something else took over, something that felt alien yet familiar and comfortable at the same time.

Everything in his periphery narrowed, and the only thing he could focus on was Gaston. Nothing else existed; nothing else mattered but the sound of blood rushing to Gaston's beating heart. The sound enveloped him, matching his own heartbeat. He wanted Gaston's blood. He wasn't even aware that he rushed forward, knocking Gaston over and pinning him to the ground.

His own power frightened him; it was so easy to take a man down, to hold him there, rendering him defenseless. He wanted nothing more than to taste his warm salty blood. But then he looked into Gaston's eyes and saw fear. And he again recognized his friend.

Gaston was frightened. The Prince had not seen him look fearful since they were young boys.

He had been about to take the life of his best friend. A man who had saved his own when they were boys. He snatched Gaston's gun from his shaking hands and flung it far into the woods. He ran as fast as he could, leaving Gaston confused and alone and wondering what sort of foul beast had attacked him. He could only hope Gaston didn't know it was his old friend the Prince.

CHAPTER XVII

THE PRINCE IN EXILE

The Prince didn't leave his rooms after that night in the woods. He heard the commotion downstairs when Gaston burst into the castle, seeking help with his wounds. The Prince wanted to help his friend but knew Lumiere had it well in hand. The doctor was called, Gaston's wounds were attended to, and excuses were made for the Prince's absence.

"How did you explain the state of the castle?" the Prince asked Lumiere later, wondering how things must have looked to Gaston.

But it might not have mattered to Gaston—who, like the Prince, appeared to be losing recollection of the Prince's former life. In fact, even

149

the court was losing any awareness of Gaston, the Prince, and, in some cases, their own lives before the cursed transformation.

"A man came to the castle. A stranger, but so familiar," Lumiere had said, referring to Gaston. "He had been attacked in the forest nearby while hunting. And he apologized for intruding on a royal court, but needed help. He was mortally wounded."

"This man," the Prince said, "had he any idea what attacked him in the forest?"

"A beast, sir, that is what he said, some sort of animal. But like none he'd ever seen before."

Animal.

Beast.

Weren't those the words the witches used? The exact words? Those women were probably dancing with joy, chanting, and clicking the awful heels of their stupid little boots.

"Sir," Lumiere croaked, "might I suggest saying you prefer the castle to be left unoccupied and kept for you by the groundskeeper?"

"Have we a groundskeeper?" asked the Prince,

once again struggling for recollection.

"Yes, sir. Not in the traditional sense, but yes. We have everything. Everyone is here, sir, you just don't see them. Your every wish will still be attended to."

He looked lost in thought and confusion for a moment while the Prince waited for him to continue.

"And I don't know, sir, how long you will have me as companion. I don't know what will become of me when the curse takes its effects. But I will still be here like the rest, I'm sure of that. We will all do our best to make ourselves known to you when we can. To let you know you're not alone."

The Prince didn't know what to say.

"We just hope you're able to break the curse."

Something snapped in his mind; his eyes were wild and he verged on the edge of frenzy. *Break the curse! He hopes I'm able to break the curse!*

"As if there was a moment that went by that I thought of anything else but breaking this accursed spell! Get out of here before I strike you!"

Lumiere backed away with every spiteful word. "I'm sorry, sir! I didn't . . ."

"Get out now!" And that was the last the Prince, now the Beast, saw of Lumiere.

CHAPTER XVIII

THE ODD SISTERS' SPY

At the top of a grassy hill was a dark green gingerbread-style mansion trimmed with gold and with black shutters. Its roof stretched skyward, its shape resembling a tall witch's cap. Nestled within the house were the odd sisters, having their morning tea. Martha was bringing in a tray of hot blueberry scones when she heard Lucinda squeal with delight.

"She's here! She's here!"

All the sisters ran to the window, tripping over themselves to see who was there. She walked up the dirt path. Her beautiful golden eyes, lined in black, shined with little specks of green in the morning light as she made her way to the front door. Martha was there to greet her.

"Pflanze, hello! Ruby, quick, get her a saucer of milk!"

Pflanze walked in calmly among the frenzied squeals of excitement that surrounded her. She took her customary seat at the kitchen table, where her saucer of milk was already waiting for her.

Lucinda spoke first. "We've seen everything, Pflanze." She was shaking with delight, she was so excited!

"Yes, everything! We've seen it all!" said Ruby. "You've done well, our beloved!" They surrounded her, chattering away like little birds while she drank her milk. The heels of their boots where making a clicking sound on the wood floor as they sang Pflanze's praises.

Circe came into the room bleary-eyed to see why her sisters were in such a blissful tizzy at that early hour.

"Ah, I see, Pflanze has finally come home!" She stroked Pflanze on the head as she finished up her milk.

"And where did you get off to, pretty girl?"

Circe's older sisters looked at each other fearfully, which only succeeded in making them look guilty. It was rare Circe let them get away with their small deceptions. They found it very hard to keep secrets from their little sister. They were often up to some sort of skullduggery, anyway, so it wasn't a stretch when she'd ask what they'd been doing. It was almost as if they liked being caught by her.

"Or perhaps I should be asking you ladies what you've been doing?"

Lucinda put on the most innocent face she could conjure, but it didn't fool Circe. "Oh, don't try pulling that with me, Lucinda! I know when you've been up to your trickery. Now out with it!"

Pflanze looked up at the witches, all four of them, blinked slowly in thanks for the milk, adjusted her paws, and jumped down from the table. She was above such conversations. She curled up in front of the fireplace while the sisters had it out.

"So?" Circe had her hand on her hip, waiting for her older sisters to answer.

155

"Pflanze has been with the Prince, keeping an eye on him for us, that's all."

Circe rolled her eyes.

"I told you not to meddle with him. I told you to leave him alone!"

Martha almost knocked over the teapot in protest. "We haven't meddled, I promise! We've just been looking in on him."

Circe couldn't help asking, "And what did you see?" but she knew the moment she asked it was a mistake. The words rained down on her like a storm; she got caught in the flurry of their fragmented stories that they were all too pleased to share.

"Oh, we've seen everything!" "Nasty, terrible things!" "Worse than we imagined!" "Murder!" "Lies!" "He drove a girl to suicide!" "She jumped off the cliffs!" "Ugly, nasty, horrible beast!" "Broken hearts, romancing tarts!" "Ah, are we rhyming now? Lovely!"

Circe put an end to it before the rhyming continued. "No, no you're not! No rhyming!"

Much like everyone else, Circe found it hard

to follow her sisters when they got excited. You'd think after almost twenty years of living with them it would get easier, but as the years passed, their mania just made Circe's head spin more.

"Sisters, please, just one of you speak, and please tell it slowly and in a straight line."

The three witches were stone silent.

"I know you are capable of speaking normally, I've heard you do it! Please."

Ruby spoke. "He's turned into the Beast, as we thought he would. He almost killed Gaston while stalking in the forest."

Circe looked disappointed. "But he didn't kill him, so there's still hope?"

Lucinda's already pinched lips puckered even smaller. You could always tell how angry she was by how small her lips became.

"You still love him, don't you?"

Circe walked away from her sisters and sat on the chair next to the fireplace to be near Pflanze.

"I wish you could talk, dear Pflanze. I wish you could tell me what happened so I wouldn't have to suffer these lunatic sisters of mine!"

Martha chucked her teacup at the wall in frustration.

"How dare you?"

Ruby had tears flowing from her eyes. "I never thought to hear such words from you, little sister, not after everything we've done for you!"

Circe put an end to the theatrics at once. "Just stop! All of you! Stop! I'm sorry. I didn't mean it, it's just sometimes you do drive me to distraction! Of course I'm not in love with him, I had just hoped he would have learned his lesson. Changed his ways and made a better life for himself!"

Lucinda smiled at her little sister. "Of course, dear, you always cared about people, we know. Sometimes we forget that we are not alike. We care only for you. We love you for your compassion, we just do not share it."

Circe didn't understand her sisters. They lived in a world logical only to them, with their own twisted moral code. Often what they said made sense to her intellectually; other times their words simply confused her. This made her thankful for her capacity for compassion. Without it, she felt, she would be just like her older sisters.

"It's hard to feel sorry for those willing to fling themselves into disaster. They are their own undoing, my dear. They bring it upon themselves. They don't merit your pity."

Circe sighed, because she knew there was logic in her sister's argument; there was just no heart. They sat to tea, chatting about everything the Prince had done since she had last seen him, this time more calmly.

"He thought he could break the curse with poor Tulip, and she really did love him, adored him! But he blamed her when their kiss did not break the curse! Of course he didn't love her. Not really. Not true love. She loved him, true! But the curse dictates both given and received! He thought his selfish version of love would fool us, and he broke her heart in the process!"

Circe felt horrible for what had happened to Princess Tulip, and resigned herself to making things right for her and her family. Lucinda saw in Circe's face that she felt guilty.

"The Prince did that to her, Circe, not you!"

Circe sighed and said, "I know, but he destroyed her and her family trying to break the curse! My curse!"

Martha smiled at her little sister. "The old queen blighted the land and left a trail of disaster and death in her wake. Should we blame ourselves?"

Ruby laughed. "Oh, how she would have hated to be called the old queen! But that is what she has become so many years after her death: she's become the old queen of legend and myth! But we know the truth! We know she was real! The queen who ruined herself over grief and vanity."

Lucinda joined in the laughter. "Oh, she would have hated that name indeed! She would fling curses, and threaten to kill anyone who referred to her as such! But she's dead now! Dead, dead, dead! Fallen off the rocky cliffs!"

Circe remembered Tulip.

"So, it was she—Tulip—who was driven to

suicide? Who threw herself off the cliffs?" Circe asked.

"Oh, I think she did for the loss of her daughter and of herself. She drowned in her own misery and regret in the end. I almost felt sorry for her."

Circe wondered how many stories like this she hadn't heard from her sisters. It was clear they were not speaking of Tulip, but some queen who had thrown herself from a cliff.

"No, I meant Tulip. Your words led me to believe she'd thrown herself off the cliffs of her father's shores."

Lucinda answered, "She did, my dear, but was saved by our friend Ursula."

Circe glared at her sisters. "And what did the sea witch demand in return?"

Ruby looked hurt. "You think so little of the company we keep?"

Lucinda added, "And how would we know what Ursula took from her? We are not privy to the goings-on in every kingdom!"

Circe gave her sister a look as if she knew very

well that was a lie, and her sister relented, as they often did with their Circe. She was their one weakness. "She took nothing from her she actually needed."

Circe didn't look convinced. "I want you to make it right with Ursula! You give her something in exchange for whatever she took from Tulip! And I am going to sort out the kingdom's affairs!"

Lucinda looked deeply unhappy. "If you insist."

Circe narrowed her eyes. "I do! And, Sisters, we're to see that Tulip's beauty is returned to her without delay!"

Ruby was surprised their little sister had guessed what the sea witch had swapped for Tulip's life.

Circe smiled smugly. "Don't look so surprised! Ursula's beauty was ripped from her years ago, so it would stand to reason she would try to regain it by devious means! I think it's terrible what happened to her, but it doesn't excuse her actions!"

Lucinda spoke. "Doesn't it? Someone has stolen her beauty and absconded with her true voice. Her losses are too many to count. So much was taken from her and then scattered across the vast ocean so she may never find it again—and for what? A trifle!"

Circe rolled her eyes at her sisters again. "Ursula's deeds were not trifles!"

Lucinda continued. "Whatever our differing opinions may be, I will do what you ask because I love you far too much to watch you suffer and blame yourself for Tulip's unhappiness."

Martha looked panicked. "But what will we give her? Nothing too precious, nothing from the vault!"

Ruby was also in a panic over the thought of giving something away to Ursula. "Circe would have us give away all our treasures! First one of our enchanted mirrors, now what?"

Lucinda, who seemed unusually calm, quelled Martha's fears. "Don't worry, we won't part with anything too precious. I promise."

Then she looked to Circe. "I assume you will be off to Morningstar Castle straightaway?"

Circe had in fact decided she would venture out there right away.

"Yes, I will." Lucinda went to the pantry and pushed a few things about until she found what she was looking for: a little velvet drawstring bag.

"When you get there, go to the cliffs and give Ursula this. She will be waiting for you." And she added, "Tulip's beauty will be returned."

Circe smiled, transforming herself from her just-awoken disheveled state to one that was more than presentable for a journey to Morningstar Kingdom. "I'll be off, then. Don't get into any trouble while I'm away. It may be some time before I return."

CHAPTER XIX

THE WOLVES IN THE WOODS

The Beast woke on the floor in a room he seldom visited. It was dark except for the pink glow of the enchanted rose the sisters had given him on the night of the curse so long ago; its light was hazy under the protective glass dome that covered it, and its petals were few. His anger and anxiety seemed to have subsided after overhearing Belle refusing to dine with him. The maelstrom of his life had finally stopped spinning in his head, and he was able to focus on the present. The present. Belle. How long had she been here?

He could hear her in the hall. She was in the West Wing! She knew it was forbidden. He had told her so! It sounded like she was talking to Pflanze as

165

they made their way through the wing. Why did women insist on talking to cats as if they understood what they were saying? He could never grasp the concept. He hid behind a changing screen, waiting to see if she was going to enter the room. She did. His heart raced. She was drawn to the rose, spellbound by its beauty. Her curiosity pulled her to it as the Beast's panic rose, triggering his anger to dangerous proportions. He snatched the domed lid from her hands and slammed it back into place, making sure the delicate flower wasn't damaged. His anger raged. All he saw was Belle's terrified face.

"This room is forbidden! Now get out!" She stuttered, trying to find words to defend herself, but her fear took hold of her shaking body and she ran out of the castle and into the forest. She was alone and in despair. She didn't care any longer about her promise to stay in her father's place.

She wanted to leave, to go home. Her father would understand. Together they would find a way to defeat the Beast. She refused to be his prisoner one more night. She ran so far and so deep into the forest she could no longer see the sky overhead; the trees were tall and thick, and obscured every bit of light the moon might have lent. The tree branches looked menacing, like witches' hands seeking her death, and she heard howls in the distance. She was alone and afraid.

The odd sisters laughed and stomped their boots in outright bliss when they saw through Pflanze's eyes what was happening to Belle. The Beast had chased away any hope of breaking the curse. They sang and danced, laughing all the while. "The Beast chased away his chance to break the curse!" "The girl is going to die!"

If Circe were there, she'd want to help the poor girl, but her older sisters had something else entirely in mind. They were quite happy with themselves. They'd thought ahead; they'd thought to keep Circe busy with the sea witch. They'd asked Ursula to keep her there for as long as she could manage. They didn't want their little sister meddling in their plans. Circe didn't embrace death the way her sisters did. She wouldn't approve.

Lucinda took a little pouch that was tied to the belt around her impossibly small waist. Inside the pouch was a deep purple powder, which she sprinkled into the fireplace. A terrible black smoke rose from the fire, taking the form of a wolf's head. Its dead shadowy eyes glowed a blazing copper.

Lucinda spoke. "Send the wolves into the wood, scratch and bite until she bleeds, kill the beauty in the wood, make him regret his evil deeds!"

The witches laughed and watched the wolves advance on Belle. They encircled her, growling at her, showing their terrible sharp teeth. They snapped at her, one of them ripping her dress. She screamed.

This time the sisters said the words together: "Send the wolves into the wood, scratch and bite until she bleeds, kill the beauty in the wood, make him regret his evil deeds!"

Belle screamed again, keenly aware she was about to die. There was nothing she could do! She had nothing with which to protect herself. She looked for something, anything, that she could use as a weapon.

The sisters continued their chanting. "Send the wolves into the wood, scratch and bite until she bleeds, kill the beauty in the wood, make him regret his evil deeds!"

The wolves were upon her. How she wished she could see her father just one more time before she died; she couldn't bear to think of him living in a world without her. He would be lost.

"Send the wolves into the wood, scratch and bite until she bleeds, kill the beauty in the wood, make him regret his evil deeds!" The sisters were in a lunatic trance. Lucinda, delving even further into their manic frenzy, changed the chant: "Rip her throat, make her bleed, eat her flesh, my words you'll heed!"

Something flew past Belle—another wolf, she thought, but no, it was enormous. Far too big to be a wolf. She didn't know what was happening. But the sisters saw; they knew what it was.

"Rip her throat, make her bleed, eat her flesh, my words you'll heed!"

The creature was impossibly large and ferocious,

with huge talon-like claws and sharp terrible teeth. Belle was in sheer panic as the sisters' gruesome chant grew louder and more feverish.

"Rip her throat, make her bleed, eat her flesh, my words you'll heed!"

Belle didn't want to die. She'd hardly had a chance to experience life. So far she'd simply read about the many things she'd like to experience, but she hadn't yet had the opportunity to do them. She shut her eyes tightly, trying to be brave, trying not to regret her choices.

"Rip her throat, make her bleed, eat her flesh, my words you'll heed!"

The creature rushed past her, attacking the wolves, killing them all in a bloody slaughter. It all happened so quickly Belle hardly had time to react before it was over. She looked up and saw she was surrounded by blood. The earth was soaked in it; everywhere she looked she saw death. Blood, fur, and flesh. It was terrible. What sort of monster could do this? She wanted to run but saw the creature. He looked hurt. The monster that had saved her life was going to die; he was bruised and bleeding, and exhausted from the fight. Her heart went out to him. Something inside Belle told her not to run, told her the creature needed her help.

The sisters watched in shock, realizing their mistake. They should never have sent those wolves to kill Belle. The Beast was chasing her into the woods because he was angry; his rage would have overtaken him and he would have killed her himself. The wolves were a distraction. The wolves were their mistake. The wolves were dead and scattered on the forest floor. The wolves' blood was black and sticky on the creature's paws. The wolves would bring them together.

The witches' only solace was that Belle had seen the Beast for what he was. She had seen the violence he was capable of.

"She will be repulsed by him! Sickened by the death that surrounds him!"

But if any one of us were there, standing near that fire, and could see the looks on the sisters' faces, we would see the sister witches feared the contrary.

Why? Because they could see the look on Belle's face. They could detect her compassion for the Beast. After all, he had just saved her life. The odd sisters decided they needed to take further action.

"It's time to send Pflanze to see Gaston."

"Oh yes, Sister! I'm sure he would like to know where his dearest Belle has gotten off to!"

And Ruby added, "I bet he would, and I am sure if anyone could destroy the Beast, it would be him!"

CHAPTER XX

THE BEAUTY IN THE LIBRARY

Belle wasn't the sort of girl who got bored easily, but she found herself tired of being trapped withindoors. It was too cold to go outside, so she sat idly in the small study next to the fire, wondering when she would see the Beast.

She had grown less cross with him since he had saved her from the wolves, but she couldn't forget why she had run out into the forest, and into danger: his terrible temper. She played the scene in her head over and over. The wolves, the woods, the Beast, the blood. She had almost died that night because of his rage, and why? Because she touched his precious rose? Though her anger and fear hadn't stopped her mending his wounds, had it? She supposed it was the least she could do after he'd saved her life.

Oh, stop this! she thought. She spent far too much time thinking. That was all she did.

Think.

Analyze.

Brood.

She wondered how the women from the stories she loved to read could bear it. Sitting around all day so idle, just waiting to hear the day's news from men. But that was exactly what she was doing now, wasn't it? Waiting for the Beast. There was nothing for her to do in the castle, and she thought she would go mad from the banality. At least at home with Father she had her books, and she could help with his inventions. He needed her. She needed him. She missed him, and she even missed the people from the village.

It was true: everyone in the village thought she was queer for reading so much, and she didn't exactly behave like other girls. So what if she was more interested in reading about princesses than being one herself? She felt thankful her father always gave her the freedom to express herself how she wished and live her life the way she thought was right. He allowed her to be herself. Not many young women had that freedom, and she was starting to understand what a rare and beautiful life she had been living until recently.

Here she was stifled and alone.

The Beast watched her as she sat in the little red chair next to the fireplace.

She didn't know he was standing there. Her face was squished up in disapproval. Like she was reproaching herself inwardly. She was probably scolding herself for mending his wounds, but she couldn't know the truth. How could she?

She didn't know he just as easily could have killed her had the wolves not been there to distract him. Imagine it; imagine if he had killed her. How horrible, how utterly ghastly that he could do such a thing. Another terrible deed added to the long list—a list no doubt being tallied by those witches.

He was sure it would have been the final act of evil that would have pushed his dark heart into further decay, and the witches would be here now to mock him. He would have lost himself completely, if he hadn't already. Surely there was something left of himself. He wasn't entirely a beast now, was he? If he was, wouldn't he have killed her? He wouldn't have cared about breaking the curse. As it was, he needed her desperately. She was his last chance. He wasn't sure if he deserved this chance, but he saw Belle's arrival at the castle as a sign he should try.

How could he possibly make himself love her? Truly fall in love with someone like her? She was nothing like the girls he fancied. She was beautiful, yes, but not the in ways he usually admired. It would never work, and even if he did fall in love with her, how could she ever fall in love with him?

It was hopeless.

He was loathsome.

He saw that now, for the first time. He saw how vile he'd become, and he felt he deserved Circe's punishment.

Perhaps this, right here, was his punishment: never knowing what it was to love.

Belle looked up at him and smiled. He hadn't expected that. "Belle, will you come with me?" She raised one eyebrow and gave him a sly smile like she didn't trust him.

"Okay."

They walked past the vestibule and into a long passageway she hadn't yet seen. It was sparse except for a small red velvet bench and a lonely gargoyle statue, and at the end of the passage was a large arched doorway. When they reached the door, the Beast said, "Belle, there is something I want to show you." He started to open the door but stopped himself. He was surprised by his nervousness.

"But first you have to close your eyes."

She gave him that look again, like she didn't trust him. Honestly, how could she? he thought, but she did seem intrigued and slightly more comfortable in his company, which gave him hope.

"It's a surprise!" he said, and she closed her eyes. She could feel the passing of his hand in front of her face to be sure she wasn't peeking. Both of them were so untrusting of each other. He took her by the hands and led her into what seemed like a vast open space. She could tell by the sound her footsteps were making.

"Can I open them?" Her voice echoed. If she hadn't known better, she would have thought perhaps they were in a cathedral.

"No. No. Wait here!" He released her hands. She heard a swish and then felt warm sunlight on her face.

"Now can I open them?" He was actually enjoying this, giving her this gift, and he found himself smiling for the first time in ages.

"All right, now!" he said, and she opened her eyes, which widened at the remarkable sight. "I can't believe it! I've never seen so many books in my entire life!" The Beast hadn't expected to feel this way, hadn't expected what it would mean to him to make someone so happy.

"You—you like it?" he asked, and she did, more than she could express.

"It's wonderful!" she said, happier than he'd ever seen her before.

"Then it's yours." And he felt something completely unexpected. What had started out as a way to bring them closer together for the sake of breaking the curse turned into something else, something he didn't understand.

He loved making her happy.

"Oh, thank you so much!" Books! Books made her happy. She wasn't like any girl he'd ever known before, and he thought perhaps he liked it. In fact, he was sure he did.

Chapter XXI

Beauty and the Beast

The odd sisters were in a panic. Even they could see Belle was warming up to the Beast, and the Beast— well, he was experiencing something quite unique to him and utterly terrifying to the witches.

They had to do something.

They had their hands full keeping watch over Belle and the Beast, and now Gaston as well, since they had sent Pflanze to keep an eye on him. They were so consumed they never left the house for fear they'd miss an opportunity to sink their claws further into the Prince's withering heart.

"Just look at them playing in the snow!" hissed Ruby.

"Disgusting!" spat Martha.

"Look at the way she looks at him! Peeking at him coyly from behind that tree! You don't think she's falling in love with him, do you?" screamed Lucinda.

"She couldn't possibly!"

The sisters spent all their time now spying on Belle and the Beast, and with each day their panic grew. It was becoming painfully clear they were falling in love!

"Those damn servants aren't helping. They contrive romance at every opportunity!" squealed Ruby.

Ruby, Martha, and Lucinda must have looked a mess when Circe returned from her visit to Morningstar Castle. When they heard her come in, the three of them turned as one, startled to see their little sister standing in the doorway. "Oh! Hello!" they said together, looking frightfully tired and rather crazed from long nights of fretting, spying, and plotting.

Circe could see something was amiss.

"What is all this?" Circe asked.

Lucinda tried to put on her best face, though having not seen herself in a mirror for several days, she had no idea how frightful she looked. "What do you mean, dear?" she said with a twitch and sputter.

Circe narrowed her eyes, looking as though she was scanning her for some shred of the truth.

"This place! It's a disaster! What on earth have you been up to?"

The odd sisters just stood there. For once they had nothing to say. Lucinda's ringlets were tangled much like a bird's nest, with little bits of dried herbs and candle wax stuck within them, while Ruby's red silk skirt was covered in gray ash and the feathers in her hair were sticking out at even stranger angles than usual, and poor Martha—her face was smudged with some kind of orange powder.

They all stood there before their little sister acting as if their appearance was as normal as could be—like Circe was stupid or didn't have eyes in her head to see they were up to some sort of trickery.

"Spell-work, I see!" Circe scolded. "You know,

whatever you're doing, I've decided I don't want to know! Honestly, I don't feel like dealing with whatever it is! So, is anyone going to ask me how it went with the sea witch?"

Ruby croaked her reply: "And how was it, dear? Did you send our greetings?" Circe gave a start at the sound of her sister's voice but kept her questions about what they'd been doing to herself.

"She's very well, and was quite pleased with the exchange." She went on, "You know, out of all your strange friends I like Ursula best. She's very amusing."

The sisters laughed, croakily, their voices wrecked from their endless chanting.

Circe couldn't keep herself from asking this time, "Seriously, what have you been up to? Look at yourselves. You're a mess, and what happened to your voices? Why are you so hoarse?"

The sisters looked at each other, and with a nod from Lucinda, Ruby took a necklace out of her pocket.

"We got you this!" She dangled the pretty little

necklace from her fingertips, swinging it back and forth in an attempt to distract her. It was a beautiful necklace, braided silver with light pink stones.

"Yes! We got you a present, Circe!" said Martha as Circe narrowed her eyes at her scheming sisters.

"Do you think I'm stupid and so easily distracted?"

Martha frowned theatrically. "We thought you would like it! Try it on!"

Lucinda ran toward Circe like an excited little child, her pale face haggard and her red lipstick smudged. "Yes, try it on! I think it will look lovely."

Lucinda went behind Circe to put it around her neck. "Okay, fine! Let's see what it looks like if it will make you happy," Circe said.

And when Lucinda fastened the clasp, Circe slumped into her sister's waiting arms. "That's right, little sister, sleep!" The three witches carried Circe into her room and placed her on the soft featherbed, where she slept blissfully so her sisters could continue their fiendish deeds undisturbed.

"We will wake you when it's over, our sweet

little sister, and you will thank us for avenging your broken heart."

"No one hurts our little sister!" *"Shhh! You'll wake her!"* "Nothing will wake her, not until we take the necklace from her pretty little neck. . . ." "She won't be angry with us, will she?" "Oh no, she couldn't be, we're doing this for her own good!" "Yes, *her own good*!"

Chapter XXII

The Enchanted Mirror

The sisters had seen enough of Belle and the Beast over the past several days to know where this was heading; what with their daily frolics, bird-watching, and disgusting looks of tenderness, it was all the sisters could do to keep themselves from retching. If either of them got the nerve to kiss, it would be over. The curse would be broken. Thank Hades Belle and the Beast were each too bashful to make the first move, so for now the witches' curse was safe. What they needed to do was focus their attentions on someone who could rip Belle and the Beast apart before disaster struck—and that was when they had their idea.

They gathered again near the fire, this time tossing in a silver powder that sparked and made a putrid smell.

"Make her miss Father dear, show Belle her greatest fear."

The witches' laughs grew into a cacophonous maelstrom that traveled with the winds to the Beast's enchanted castle, casting an ill omen over the lovers holding hands in the moonlight.

The sisters watched.

"Belle, are you happy here with me?" The Beast's large paws enveloped her little hands as he waited for her answer.

"Yes," she said, turning away.

"What is it?"

She looked heartbroken.

"If only I could see my father again, just for a moment. I miss him so much."

"There is a way," he said.

The sisters were still watching and holding their breath.

"He's taking her into the West Wing!" Ruby

whispered, as if the two lovers could hear the sisters' remarks.

"Show her the mirror!" Martha screamed.

"Calm yourself, Sisters. He'll show her the mirror," Lucinda said, smiling, as they watched to see what would happen next.

"Shhh!" Martha hissed. "He's saying something!"

"This mirror can show you anything, anything you wish to see."

The sisters had to cover their mouths to muffle the squeals of glee threatening to burst from their tiny ruby-red lips.

"Take it! Take the mirror!" Lucinda screamed, trying to will Belle into taking the enchanted mirror from the Beast. "She took it!"

"I'd like to see my father, please," Belle said as she looked into the little hand mirror.

The sisters chanted their wicked words one more time.

"Make her miss Father dear, show Belle her greatest fear!"

Their cackles echoed across the lands, and along

with them, their foul magic. Belle felt a terrible chill. "Oh, Papa! Oh, no! He's sick, maybe dying, and he's all alone."

Ruby knocked over the scrying bowl, its water spilling over the gingerbread house's hardwood floors. They could no longer see Belle or the Beast or force their will upon them.

"Martha, quick, get more water!" Martha took the silver bowl and filled it with water, splashing some on her way back to her sisters, who were now on the floor anguishing.

"Here! I have it!" she yelled. "Look! They are starting to appear! What's happening?" Ruby was slamming her fists on the wet floor again and again so violently her hands started to bleed.

"Ruby, stop! She's leaving! She's going to her father! He's released her!"

Ruby's face was streaked with black tears. "But did he give her the mirror? Is she taking it with her? We were unable to finish the incantation!"

Lucinda looked up at her exhausted sisters, worn from long days of witchery. "Not to worry,

Sisters, she had the mirror when she left."

Ruby smiled a mischievous grin. "Everything is in place, then. Perfect." The sisters' odious laughter filled the room as they focused their attentions now on someone who wouldn't need much persuading to commit a bit of chicanery.

Chapter XXIII

The Witches' Plot

Gaston was sitting down to a large banquet in his dining hall, which was heavily decorated with the various animals he'd killed during his many hunting excursions. The chair at the head of the table, at which he was seated, of course, was adorned with elk antlers and draped with animal skins and furs. His cleft chin was jutting out a bit farther than usual, which was a manifestation of his extreme good spirits—that is, until the odd sisters clamored in, disturbing his banquet for one.

"Look here, foul witches! I won't have you popping in and out of my home unannounced!"

"Sorry to disturb your meal, Gaston, but we have news that you might find interesting."

Gaston slammed his knife into his wooden dining table. "First you send that foul slinking creature to watch over me, and now this! Showing up whenever you desire, to make requests of me, no doubt!"

Ruby twitched her head to the right, about to speak, but it was Martha who defended Pflanze. "She's not here to spy on you, Gaston. She's here to help you."

Gaston's laugh rivaled the witches' own; it filled the hall and reverberated in the witches' ears. "Help me? Help me? Why, I am the strongest, most attractive man in the village!"

The sisters stared blankly at him, wondering if he, or anyone else, really believed that.

"Yes, help you, Gaston. We've found Belle, and she's on her way to her father now."

Gaston fixed his gaze on the witches for the first time since they'd arrived. They had finally gotten his full attention. Their dresses were deep red, the exact shade of their lips, which were painted to look like a baby doll's. Their raven hair was fashioned in shoulder-length ringlets around their pale faces and

adorned with large red plumes. They were painfully thin and looked ludicrous in all their finery,
like skeletal beings brought back from the dead to
attend a fancy dress ball.

"You've found Belle?"

"Oh yes, we've found your dearest love!" Ruby
sang. "She won't be able to resist you!"

Gaston looked at himself in the reflection of his
shiny knife and said, "Well, who can?"

Lucinda grinned, trying not to let Gaston detect
her repulsion. "We have arranged some assurances,
on the slightest chance *she* can." Gaston raised one
brow in curiosity, but Martha continued before he
could comment. "We would like you to meet a
friend of ours," she said with an evil smile cracking her white face, her makeup causing her to
look even more freakishly beautiful. "A very dear
friend who we think would be more than happy
to help you." Gaston had to wonder what sort of
people the witches kept company with. "His name
is Monsieur D'Arque. He runs the sanitarium,"
Lucinda answered, as if she heard his very thoughts.

Gaston wasn't surprised that the sisters were friendly with the rapscallion who ran the sanitarium.

Martha elaborated. "Maurice, Belle's father, has been raving about a beast, has he not? Perhaps the sanitarium is just the place for him." Ruby twittered in delight when she added, "Though I'm sure there would be no need for him to be institutionalized if Belle were to marry you. I'm sure between the two of you Maurice would be well taken care of."

Gaston grasped their meaning instantly, and he was thunderstruck by the brilliance of the idea. He would of course take the credit for the idea entirely.

"Hmmmm. Poor old Maurice *has* been raving like a lunatic. Why, just the other night he was gibbering incoherently about Belle being captured by a beast."

"See? You would be doing them both a favor if you married Belle. Someone needs to take care of the poor fellow."

Chapter XXIV

Belle's Betrayal

D'Arque was more than happy to comply with Gaston's request to put Maurice into the sanitarium if Belle did not agree to marry him. He knew very well Maurice was just an odd little man who loved only one thing more than his clanking apparatuses, and that was his daughter, Belle.

D'Arque was quite content. His coffers were filled, he had made a new alliance with Gaston, and he was about to partake in some good old-fashioned skullduggery.

He was aware of how intimidating he appeared, illuminated by the torchlight, and he loved nothing more than causing fear. Gaston and his mob were gathered in full force in front of Maurice's home. They were a rowdy bunch collected by Gaston from the tavern at closing time. There was nothing quite as menacing as a bunch of hooligans after a long night of drinking with gold in their pockets and hate in their hearts—all of which, in this case, was supplied by Gaston. There was little doubt Belle would agree to marry the braggart, and why not marry him? She couldn't possibly do better. Who else in town would have her with all her strange ways?

Belle answered the door, her eyes filled with fear. "May I help you?" she asked.

"I've come to collect your father," said D'Arque. His withered skull-like face looked horrid in the torchlight.

"My father?" she asked, confused.

"Don't worry, mademoiselle, we'll take good care of him." Belle was seized with fear. She understood when she saw D'Arque's wagon in the distance. They were taking her father to the asylum.

"My father is not crazy!"

198

In the Beast's small study, where the witches had found him brooding, they watched through Pflanze's eyes everything that was transpiring.

"Look! Look here! She's going to betray you!" said Ruby, but the Beast wouldn't come to the mirror the witches had brought with them so he could see what Pflanze saw.

"She won't betray me, I know it!" The witches' laughter filled the Beast's head, driving him mad.

"She never loved you! How could she?" "She was your prisoner!" "She only pretended to love you so you would let her go!" "How could she ever love someone as loathsome as you?"

The Beast's anger rose to dangerous heights. His roar caused the chandelier to rattle and the room to shake, frightening even the sisters, but Lucinda persisted. "Look! Here's proof if you don't believe us!" And she showed him the mirror. Belle was standing in front of an angry crowd. Holding the enchanted mirror, she screamed, "Show them the Beast!"

His face appeared in the mirror, ugly, frightening,

and foul, his roar terrifying the mob.

"See! See? She's betrayed you!" Lucinda said as she danced in the Beast's study.

"She never loved you!" screamed Ruby, joining Lucinda in her absurd dance.

"She's always loved Gaston!" chimed in Martha, prancing about like a deranged peacock with her sisters as they taunted the Beast.

"They're to be married in the morning after he kills you!" they all sang as they danced in a circle. "It was their plan all along, you see!" They cackled as their dance grew even more repugnant.

The Beast was finally defeated. Completely diminished and heartbroken, he could barely bring himself to meet their gazes when he asked the sisters to leave. "Please leave. You've gotten what you wanted. I have suffered for hurting your sister. Now, please, I want to be alone."

Lucinda's laugh was more sinister than he'd ever heard it before. "Oh, and you shall be alone! Alone forever, forever a beast!" And the sisters were gone before the sound of their laughter left his drafty study. He was alone and he knew he had brought all this on himself.

Only one thing comforted him: he had finally learned what it was to love. And the feeling was deeper and more meaningful than anything he'd felt before. He felt like he was dying. To die, one must have first been alive. And the Beast could finally say that by finding love, he had lived.

Chapter XXV

The Witches' Party

The tall green house with black shutters and a witches'-cap roof was silhouetted a little too perfectly against a deep blue twilight, like a paper cutout of a dollhouse. Nothing about the witches ever seemed quite real, not even their house. Inside, the witches danced while watching the Beast's demise in the many enchanted mirrors they had placed around their main parlor. They drank honey wine, splashing it on their deep purple dresses, which blossomed about them as they spun in circles, laughing in the face of their own frenzied insanity. They would stop their bacchanalian antics only to mock the Beast and praise themselves for having seen the curse through.

"He's given up!" raved Ruby. "He wants to die!"

Lucinda scoffed. "He's heartbroken, Sisters. He'd rather die than live without that stupid girl!" All three sisters laughed. "Now he knows what it is to be heartbroken!"

The sisters were even more excited to see Gaston's mob arrive. "They're attacking the castle!" Gaston's mob would have laid waste to the castle if it weren't for the servants.

"Bloody fools!" screamed Lucinda. "They're trying to defend the fiend!"

Martha spat at the outrageous spectacle between the mob and the servants. "Sister! Don't spit on our treasures!" scolded Ruby, and then she saw a most welcome sight. "Look! Gaston! He's there! They're fighting on the roof!" The sisters stamped their feet, flailing wildly in a manic dance while chanting "Kill the Beast!" over and over. They said it until their voices were raw as they watched the bloody encounter between the old friends, who now were cursed so that they did not remember each other.

The Beast didn't even try to fight back. Gaston was going to kill him, and it seemed the Beast welcomed it, as the sisters had hoped he would.

"Kill him, kill him, kill the Beast!" they yelled, as if Gaston could hear their words, but something changed, something wasn't right. The Beast saw something the sisters could not. Whatever it was gave him the will to fight.

"What is it?" they screamed as they scurried from mirror to mirror, trying to surmise what could possibly have inspired the Beast to fight, and then they saw.

Belle.

That horrible girl, Belle!

"We should have killed her when we had the chance!" Ruby cried.

"We tried!" Lucinda, Ruby, and Martha watched as the Beast overpowered Gaston. He had him by the throat, dangling him over the side of the castle.

"Quick, get the scrying bowl!" Lucinda scrambled in the pantry for the oils and herbs they needed for the scrying bowl while Ruby filled the silver bowl with water, and Martha got the egg from the icebox. The egg floated in the water like a malevolent eye while Ruby tossed in the oils and herbs.

"Make the Beast remember when they were young." Martha and Ruby looked at Lucinda, mouths open.

"What?" Lucinda was panic-stricken.

"That didn't rhyme, Lucinda!"

Lucinda rolled her eyes, vexed. "I don't have time to think of a rhyme! Just say it!" Ruby and Martha looked at each other but didn't repeat the phrase. "What?" Lucinda asked again.

"It's not as fun if it doesn't rhyme."

Lucinda checked the mirrors. The Beast still had Gaston by the neck and was about to drop him. "Sisters, say it with me now if you want to save Gaston!"

Ruby and Martha relented. "Fine! Make the Beast remember when they were young." Their voices were flat and unenthusiastic.

"Say it again!" screamed Lucinda. "Say it louder!"

"Make the Beast remember when they were young!" the sisters screeched.

"Remember when you were boys and he saved your life! Just for a moment, *remember each other*," Lucinda cried. Then, looking at her sisters, she added, "Don't look at me like that! I dare you to do better!"

Ruby was transfixed by something in the mirror nearest her. "Look, it worked, he's letting him go!"

The Beast was bringing Gaston back onto the roof by the scruff of his neck. "Get out!" he growled, tossing Gaston aside. The sisters knew Gaston wouldn't leave. They counted on it.

"Beast!" It was Belle. She was reaching her hand out to him as he climbed up the turret to kiss her.

"No!" wailed the sisters. *"No!"*

But before Lucinda could recite another incantation, her sisters screamed in glee at the sight of Gaston plunging a large knife into the Beast's side. Their delight transmuted into fear, however, when they saw Gaston lose his footing and fall from the castle tower to his death below.

207

It didn't matter. Gaston didn't matter anymore—not to the witches. He had given them what they wanted; the Beast was dying. He was dying in his lover's arms, heartbroken.

"Let's get Circe! She has to see this!"

Chapter XXVI

The Enchantress

Lucinda crept into Circe's room, gazing at her sleeping little sister. She looked so peaceful and beautiful sleeping there. As she unfastened the necklace, Lucinda knew in her heart that Circe would be thankful for what her older sisters had done for her.

Circe opened her eyes, then blinked, trying to see which of her sisters was looking down at her with such a buggy expression on her face.

"Lucinda." She smiled up at her.

"Circe, we have something to show you. Something very important. Come with me."

Lucinda led her befogged sister to the other room. How it must have looked to Circe, who hadn't been privy to the evening's events. The room was lit by an extravagant number of candles, all of them white and reflecting beautifully in the many enchanted mirrors placed around the space. In the largest mirror she saw the Beast.

"What's this?" she asked as she rushed over to the mirror and placed her hand on its lovely silver frame. "Is he dead?"

All three of her sisters were standing there, hands clasped, like eager little girls waiting for praise. Circe looked down at the scrying bowl, then back to her sisters. She felt ill, hollow, and inhuman.

"You did this?" She thought she was going to be sick. They said nothing. "You killed him?" she cried.

"No! It was Gaston. He killed him!"

Circe couldn't breathe. "With your assistance, I see!" she said as she threw the scrying bowl across the room.

"We thought you would be happy, Circe! We did it for you!"

Circe stared at her sisters in shock. "How could

you think I would want this? Look at the girl! She's heartbroken!"

She was looking at Belle in the enchanted mirror.

"I love you," Belle said to the Beast as tears streaked down her face.

Circe was also crying. Her heart was filled with dread and regret. "I never wanted this to happen!" she continued. "Look! She loves him! This isn't fair. I'm bringing him back! I'm giving him a chance to break the curse."

The odd sisters started to scream in protest as they advanced on their little sister, but Circe's fury sent them flying back until they were pinned to the wall.

"Not another word, do you understand? You say one more word and I will give your voices to the sea witch!"

Lucinda, Ruby, and Martha knew their little sister's powers were far greater than their own, but they had always been able to manage her because she was the youngest. It looked now as though that time was past, however. They were too frightened to speak; like broken dolls, they looked inanimate and frozen in their bizarre poses as Circe continued to rail at them. "I'm bringing him back! I'm bringing him back to life, do you understand? If he loves her, too, then the curse will be broken. And you will never seek to reverse it!"

Her sisters hung there, pinned, unable or unwilling to move, not saying a word.

"Never meddle with the Prince or Belle again! If you do, I will make good on my promise! I will give your voices to Ursula and you will never be able to use your foul magic again!" The odd sisters just stared at her, wide-eyed, saying nothing, as they had been commanded.

Chapter XXVII

Happily Ever After

Circe put her hand on the face of the mirror where she saw Belle crying over the Beast's dead body. The poor thing thought she had just lost the love of her life. "Not if I can help it," said Circe as she cast her magic. Rose and silver lights showered down around them, lifting the Beast's body into the air. His body twisted and entangled with the glittering lights until he was no longer the Beast but the man Circe had once known so many years before. The Prince. His face was no longer marred with anger, vanity, and cruelty. She could see his soul had truly changed.

With her magic, Circe encircled the lovers in

light that soared upward into the sky and cascaded down again, raining beautiful sparks, transforming the castle and everyone within it to their original forms.

"Lumiere! Cogsworth! Oh! Mrs. Potts! Look at us!" cried the Prince, seeing his fondest friends for the first time in many years.

Circe smiled as she saw how delighted her magic had made the Prince and Belle. They were happy, and they were in love, and they were surrounded by all their friends and family—including Belle's father, who looked more than a little confused suddenly to be at a fancy ball when only moments before he'd been in that appalling sanitarium. But he wasn't going to worry about that just then. He was happy to see his darling Belle again.

It turned out exactly as Circe had hoped. The Prince had finally learned what it was to love—to truly love and to have that love returned.

She smiled again, taking one last look at the Prince and Belle dancing in the great hall before wiping their image from the enchanted mirror, leaving them to live and love happily ever after.

THE END